Bad Luck Girl

Also by Sarah Zettel

Dust Girl

Golden Girl

THE AMERICAN FAIRY TRILOGY

~ BOOK THREE ~

Bad Luck Girl

SARAH ZETTEL

RANDOM HOUSE 🏠 NEW YORK

Text copyright © 2014 by Sarah Zettel
Jacket art copyright © 2014 by Juliana Kolesova

Visit us on the Web! randomhouse.com/teens

Educators and librarians, for a variety of teaching tools,
visit us at RHTeachersLibrarians.com

Library of Congress Cataloging-in-Publication Data
Zettel, Sarah.
Bad luck girl / Sarah Zettel. — First edition.
pages cm. — (The American fairy trilogy ; book three)
Summary: "After rescuing her parents from the Seelie king at Hearst Castle, Callie is caught up in the war between the fairies of the Midnight Throne and the Sunlit Kingdoms." —Provided by publisher.
ISBN 978-0-375-86940-2 (trade) — ISBN 978-0-375-96940-9 (lib. bdg.) — ISBN 978-0-375-98320-7 (ebook)
[1. Fairies—Fiction. 2. Magic—Fiction. 3. Racially mixed people—Fiction. 4. Chicago (Ill.)—History—20th century—Fiction.] I. Title.
PZ7.Z448Bad 2014 [Fic]—dc23 2013013855

Printed in the United States of America

10 9 8 7 6 5 4 3 2 1

First Edition

To Chicago itself.

"And there in that great iron city, that impersonal, mechanical city, amid the steam, the smoke, the snowy winds, the blistering suns; there in that self-conscious city, that city so deadly dramatic and stimulating, we caught whispers of the meanings that life could have. . . ."
—Richard Wright, from his introduction to *Black Metropolis,*
by St. Clair Drake and Horace R. Cayton (1993 ed.)

Contents

Bad Luck Girl

1

This Mornin', Feelin' Bad

June 14, 1935

Once upon a time, a girl from the Dust Bowl traveled across the country to rescue her parents (with some help from her best friend, Jack) from the evil fairy king who'd locked them in his enchanted castle. Now, normally that'd be the whole story, and there'd be the happy ending and all afterward. But that wasn't the way things turned out.

My name, by the way, is Callie LeRoux. My father vanished before I was born, so Mama raised me alone out in Slow Run, Kansas. I didn't know that all that time she was keeping secrets from me. Like how my father was a prince of the Unseelie fairies, which made me a fairy princess, or half of one anyway. What's more, I'd somehow gotten myself born with a special power that allows me to open and close the gates between the fairy world and the human world. This power is so darn special that the fairies—both the midnight

Unseelies and the shining Seelies—had fixed up a whole prophecy about it.

See her now, daughter of three worlds. See her now, three roads to choose. Where she goes, where she stays, where she stands, there shall the gates be closed.

The fairies had been waiting just about forever for the girl with these gate powers to turn up. Now that I had, they all wanted to get their hands on me, or at least keep the other side from getting their hands on me. My own grandparents tried to trick me into promising to stay with them forever, and, incidentally, into helping kill my best friend, Jack. The Seelie king shoved one of his own daughters—a half-fairy girl named Ivy Bright—into doing the dirty work of killing me. But it turned out Ivy's luck was even worse than mine, because I killed her instead. Then I shut the fairy gate on the dragon that was somehow both the Seelie king and the palace on the hill at one and the same time.

It had been a really long day.

I honestly don't remember how we got onto the streetcar out of Culver City, or much about the ride, except that I spent it huddled on the bench with my parents as we rattled into downtown Los Angeles. Papa sat with his arm around Mama's shoulders. I pressed against her other side, and she clutched my hand hard enough to hurt, but I didn't care. I couldn't shake the feeling that if she let go, one of us would vanish. Jack slouched in the seat in front of us, all alone. I knew I should say something to let him know I didn't care about him any less now that I had my parents back, but I couldn't make myself talk. I was banged up. My clothes were torn about to shreds and a map of red cuts crisscrossed the backs of my hands.

I was too tired to hold my extra fairy senses closed, so I felt the look the conductor gave us crawling across my skin as we climbed off the streetcar at the corner of Fifth Street. He was good and glad to be leaving us behind. I tried to be glad too, but in my gut, it still felt like the end of the world. Every time I breathed in, I smelled gun smoke and copper, and I kept hearing the shot that killed Ivy Bright. With that going off inside my skull, nothing else felt entirely real, not even being back with Mama. Not even finally meeting my papa, Daniel LeRoux.

The streetcar rattled away and I stood staring at the hard blue California morning, trying to kick my brain into some kind of action. Papa lifted his arm from around Mama's shoulders. He walked three slow, tottery steps down the sidewalk. Then he took one deep breath, swung both arms over his head, and whooped out loud to the rising sun.

"We did it! You hear? We did it!"

Papa whipped around and grabbed both of Mama's hands. He swung her in a tight circle until she shrieked, half startled, half jubilant. "You were magnificent, Margaret. Magnificent!"

"My God, Daniel." Mama ran her palms across his face and brow. "My God. Is it real? Are we really free?"

Papa laughed and he kissed her, hard and strong. She

broke away and laughed, and he kissed her again. Kissed her so long, in fact, that I squirmed and looked at Jack. He was grinning. I looked back at my parents, and sure enough, they were still kissing.

When Papa did let Mama go, he turned to Jack and pumped his hand hard enough to rattle Jack's teeth. "And you, sir! Jack of Chicago, isn't it? Jack, hero of the day! And you!" Now he faced me with a smile as bright and warm as the sun in July. "My brave, beautiful daughter." He swept off his battered fedora and bowed deep. "It is an honor and privilege to meet you at last, Calliope."

I had no idea at all how to answer him. I wanted to grin, and to shout too, but I couldn't make myself do it. My head was spinning too hard. It was Mama who spoke up first.

"Daniel," she said to Papa. "It's a little early to be celebrating in public. Someone will remark on us."

My mother, Margaret LeRoux, was a tiny woman. I was only a hairsbreadth shorter than she was, and I hadn't even turned fifteen yet. She was a delicate thing too, with white skin, worn hands, and bones like a bird's. Her blue eyes were so big and so pretty, Bette Davis would have paid a year's salary for the loan of them. But there was steel under those fragile looks, and it never did to forget that.

My father settled his fedora back on his head and tugged the brim down low. Papa looked to be a Negro man, tall and slim with clear mahogany-colored skin. But if you got a look at his eyes, you saw that wasn't all he was. His eyes were utterly strange and beautiful at the same time, twin swirls of deep blue, black, and silver, like thunderheads at midnight with the full moon shimmering behind them.

My eyes held that storm-blue color, and when I got mad, they had that same light behind them. From Mama I'd gotten a pointy kind of face that the old ladies back in Slow Run called "dainty," and skin that stayed close to white if I stayed out of the sun. In fact, as long as I kept my coarse hair braided up, I could pass for being as white as Mama or Jack.

"You're right, of course, Margaret," said Papa. "We are not out of the woods yet. Come around here, why don't you? Let's get you all fixed up."

Papa led us around back of the brick streetcar shelter into the shadows, where we'd be screened from the traffic rattling past. With a sharp glance around to make sure the sidewalk itself was still empty, Papa straightened up and pushed his hat back on his head. I could see the shining swirl of his fairy eyes clearly now. I expected him to make a wish, or ask one of us to. Wishes and feelings are a big help to shaping fairy magic. But Papa didn't seem to need any such help. He just looked at each of us, hard. I could feel his gaze sink through my skin and rummage around underneath. Jack actually staggered and Mama laid a hand on his shoulder to steady him. Then Papa pursed his lips and whistled three bright, trilling notes. A dry, sharp-edged wind swirled around us. All at once, I was scrubbed and clean, like I'd just gotten out of the bath. My ruined mission-store clothes were replaced by a blue dress with a drop waist and a pleated skirt and white sash. A cloche hat settled over my head. I stared at the backs of my own hands, now all healed up, and at the nails buffed to a fine gloss. Mama was wearing blue as well—a short-sleeved flowered dress, and white gloves and a sun hat with a blue flower in the band. She had on silk stockings and white patent-leather pumps and a purse to match. It seemed my father was the kind who thought about details. He was all cleaned and pressed too, with a crease in his gray trousers and a snappy tilt to his fedora.

So this was what full-blood fairy magic could do, easy as, well, whistling. If it had been me, I could have made folks just *think* we looked respectable. Papa could make it happen for real, and he wasn't even breathing hard.

"Hey, this is swell." Jack brushed the cuffs of his new shirt and grinned. "I think I'm gonna like traveling fairy class." Jack Holland was tall enough to be taken for a grown man when he wanted to be. He had too many freckles on his face, and when he didn't have his hair slicked down hard, it was a mass of brown curls that stuck out every which way from under whatever hat he happened to be wearing. Just now, that hat was a straw boater Papa had given him to go with the white flannel trousers, blue striped button-down shirt, and blue tie. He looked like he had just come home from some fancy college. I had to look away fast before my cheeks started heating up.

"Unfortunately, it won't last." Papa frowned at the line of light behind the mountains that would turn into full morning before too much longer. "This world can be very hard on such tricks, but it should hold us until sundown."

"So, what do we do now?" Jack looked at me when he said it, but it was Mama who answered.

"We need to get something to eat," she announced. "You children must be starved."

"That's as good a place to start as any," agreed Papa.

So, we picked a direction and started walking. After about a block and a half, we spotted a diner. We must have looked respectable enough because the waitress hustled right over when we took a seat in the red vinyl booth. I wondered if Papa was pulling the magic wool over her eyes so she didn't notice we each had a different skin color, but then, Los Angeles was one of those places where it sometimes didn't matter so much.

Either way, I was awfully glad to see the burgers and French fries she brought us. We all made short work of our meal, including the thick slices of apple pie with ice cream afterward. It felt good to be full and, for just the minute, safe.

It didn't last long. When the bill came, Papa pulled out a money clip, laid down some bills on the table, and hustled us back out onto the sidewalk. We all went quietly, and quickly. Fairy money has this nasty tendency to vanish on short notice, so it's not good to hang around anyplace you have to use it.

I wasn't the only one thinking that. Mama slid her arm through Papa's as we strolled up the street, all of us trying to look like we had somewhere to go.

"What now, Daniel? We can't stay here with no real money. And they . . . they might find us."

"They can't be after us yet," said Jack. "Callie trapped the king on the other side of the gate when she shut it. That'll hold 'em off for a little while, won't it?"

"He might have gotten out," I said. "That dragon was awful strong." I tried not to remember how strong, and how big, but that didn't work very well.

"Either way, your mother's right. It will be safer to get out of town," Papa muttered.

"Can we go home?" suggested Mama hopefully. "You told me the Imperial's protected. . . ."

Papa shook his head. "Not anymore. It will be watched."

"What about trying for New York?" asked Jack. "You lived there a while back, didn't you, Mr. LeRoux? Anybody there who might be willing to help you out?"

"There might be at that. Not a bad idea, boy."

"Jack," he said firmly. "Jack Holland."

Papa cocked his head, looking at Jack in a new way, with just the barest hint of gold glittering out from under his hat brim. "My apologies. Jack."

"New York," murmured Mama. "So far."

"Not for Callie," said Jack. "She can open us a gate and walk us right into Times Square."

Right then I wasn't so sure I could keep on standing up. The reminder that the Seelies were still out there had set my knees shaking and my full stomach churning. I sucked in as big a breath as I could hold and tried with all my might to shove the fear aside. My family needed me now. *I* needed me now.

"I can open the gate," I said. "But steering on the other side, that's harder." Truth be told, I wasn't sure I could find New York on the other side of a fairy gate, let alone get everybody through to someplace I'd only ever seen in the movies.

Papa chuckled. "I think the old man might be able to help you there, Callie."

I wanted to smile back, but my mouth wasn't so sure. There'd been too many times when my magic had gone wrong for me to be easy about the idea of trying to work it now. But the only other choice was to hang around here and wait for whichever of the Seelies were left to come find us, which was no kind of choice at all.

"So, what do we do?" asked Jack.

"Take hands," answered Papa for me.

Jack took my hand, and Mama took his. Then Mama took Papa's so we were all in a line, with me at one end and my father at the other. "Go ahead, Callie." Papa nodded. "I'll be right there with you."

The last time I'd done this, the person who'd been with me was Papa's brother, my uncle Shake. Shake had tried to steer me straight into the Unseelie country so his friends there could make use of me. I didn't for a minute think my father would do anything like that, of course, but something inside me shivered just the same.

Jack squeezed my hand and I squeezed his. Some of my confidence came creeping back for a second look. Jack I could trust. There was nothing we couldn't handle together, from dust storms to fire-breathing dragons. I faced the street and dug down into the place where my magic waited.

When I opened up to magic, I opened up to feeling, layers upon layers of feeling. First, I felt the city—the jostling and chattering of a million living souls with their wishes and their dreams laid over the slow droning vibrations of machinery and the foundation of stone and earth. Then I felt my father. I'd known him less than a day, but he filled a space in my mind I'd never realized was empty. Fear, confidence, love, amazement, and mischief all through him like heat lightning in summer.

In that same place, I heard his voice, clear and calm. *It's all right, Callie. Open the gate. Take us through.*

And just like that, I believed. It would be all right. I could do this, easy as whistling. I made myself see past motion and emotion, down to the warp and weft of the world. It was soft and fluid and tough to get hold of, except for one spot. One spot was solid with clear edges, like a closed door. Life and time just flowed around it. I could shape my personal magic into a key, put the key into the lock of that door, and turn, until the way opened in front of me. I tightened my hand around Jack's and stepped through.

2

Went Downtown, Hat in Hand

There's the human world, there's the fairy world, and then there's betwixt and between. Betwixt and between is a place that's no place in particular. It's got no shape of its own, except it's all the shapes of the surrounding worlds piled on top of each other. It's got no time except forever, and no light, except all the sunlight, starlight, and fairy light leaking through from one side to the other.

At least, that was what it was like last time I walked out there.

This time somebody'd turned those lights out. The whole world had gone gray. I froze on the threshold of the gate I'd opened. While I stared, something grabbed hold of the part of my blood and brain where my magic waited. It turned me, like I was a compass needle, toward the Unseelie borders, toward the home I'd never really seen. It tried to tell me this was the right way to go, whether I wanted to or not.

"What's happening?" asked a voice from far away. I thought it was Papa, but I wasn't sure.

I had no chance to find my words. A low, terrible river boiled out from the direction of the Unseelie world. It rolled through the shifting twilight that had taken over betwixt and between, making the air ripple with a rough and gritty darkness, like the wind that brought the dusters to Kansas. But this was more than wind or thunder. This was alive. In fact, it was a whole lot of alive. A thousand thousand separate beings boiled past me in that dark. All of them grappled and fought to move faster. They climbed over each other, straining to reach their destination. And as I stood there, openmouthed, I felt their hunger, fear, and anger rush over me. They must have felt something too, because they all turned, and they all looked at me.

The shock of recognition from those thousands of minds staggered me, and I toppled over. My hand slipped from Jack's, and I was falling into nothing. Jack's hand snatched at mine, but he screamed and his fingers spasmed.

"Trap!" I heard him holler. "It's a trap!"

Betwixt and between trembled around me. I twisted my mind and my body, struggling to hang on, to find a foothold, anything. But the pull, the pressure, and the craziness were too strong. Someone was grabbing at me. My fingers were slipping. My ankles were being pulled apart. I clamped my hand around Jack's curling fingers and felt him wish me out of there. But it wasn't just him.

"I wish it open!" shouted Mama. "Daniel, I wish it open!"

Their wishes were faint and shaky and far away, but I grabbed at the straws of power they loaned me, jammed them into that tiny space I could sense around Jack's wrist, and shoved hard.

The pressure snapped. Jack hollered. I shrieked and shot out of the darkness, tumbling down onto the pavement. Next thing I knew, Mama had her arms around me to pull me to my feet.

"Look at me, Callie. Look at me." Her hands cupped my face. I made myself pull my eyelids open. Everything was blurry for a second, but it cleared up quick and I could see Mama's frantic eyes staring into mine.

"Are you all right?" Mama's rough fingers poked at my skull and my arms, feeling for breaks. "Do you hurt anywhere?"

Truth was, every bit of me hurt, but I shook my head anyway. "Jack?"

"Yeah." Jack was slumped against a streetlamp, cradling his wrist. His face had turned a really bad shade of white. "That sure was a surprise," he croaked.

"Here." Papa took Jack's arm. Jack winced and hissed a curse through his teeth. I felt Papa's magic wrap around Jack. Jack winced again, but his face flushed from dead white to red, and I felt his pain dissolve as easy as sugar melting in the rain.

"Thanks." Jack flexed his fingers as Papa lifted his hands away.

"What happened, Callie?" demanded Mama.

"I don't know. It was like . . . I can't describe it."

Papa came up beside her. The shine from his fairy eyes had dimmed down almost to twilight. He'd lifted his face, turning this way and that like he was trying to catch some scent or sound that had already passed. There was a closed-up drugstore behind us, with posters for Pepsodent and milk of magnesia hanging in its plate-glass window. Papa breathed on the glass and rubbed it with his sleeve.

"Think about what you saw, Callie," he said urgently. "This is important."

I swallowed, and as much as I didn't want to, I made myself remember the storm of bad feeling, the rolling darkness, the churning lives. Papa stared into the glass, and I thought I saw something ugly that shifted vague and dim in the reflection. Whatever he saw, it seemed to draw the strength out of his straight back. Papa leaned against the window, pressing his palm hard against the glass.

"I was afraid of this." Papa's fingers curled up, scraping at the glass, looking for something to hold on to. Mama moved up next to him, resting her hand on his shoulder. His free hand stole around her waist.

"What is it, Mr. LeRoux?" asked Jack.

"The war," Papa said as he wiped his hand hard across that magic reflection. He did not let go of Mama. "It's started."

"But it can't!" The words burst out of me, like if I said it strong enough, I could make it true. "It's too soon. It'd take time to get the armies ready and, and stuff. Wouldn't it?"

"They've been ready for years," said Papa. "The Seelie king was just waiting for an excuse."

"Ivy." The smell of gunpowder and copper came right back when I said it, and I heard the explosion of the gunshot all over again. "When I killed Ivy, he declared war."

Papa nodded. "The blood of his daughter has been shed. He has the right to exact a blood price in return. My parents have been building up the defenses of the Midnight Throne for years, waiting for the attack." He looked back at the window, a sour mix of disappointment and anger bubbling around him. "I am sorry, Margaret," he whispered to Mama. "I had hoped we'd have at least a small moment. . . ."

"The king can go ahead and start a whole war because one girl got shot?" said Jack. "And it's legal? That's nuts!"

Papa suddenly went all stiff and formal. He plainly did not care for Jack's assessment of the situation. "The whole human world went to war when one man was shot. What was his name? Archduke Ferdinand, I believe."

Jack dug his hands into the pockets of his new white flannel trousers. "Well, that was different."

"Was it?"

"This is no time to argue politics." Mama gave Papa's shoulder one firm squeeze that seemed to straighten them both up again. "We need to work out what to do."

I tried to quiet the shivers that ran up my spine. We

couldn't stay here. If the Seelies were already on the attack, they'd be after me. Us. I was the one who'd killed Ivy. It was an accident, but that didn't seem to matter. She was still dead and I still did it. They wanted the gate powers I worked. They wanted the prophecy on their side, and they weren't going to care a whole lot about what I wanted. "I can try again. . . . Maybe if I open a different gate, we can get around it."

"No," said Mama flatly. "I know you've been through a lot, Callie, but we are not walking into a war zone. We need to find another way."

"Train?" said Jack.

"No," said Mama again. "Not that either."

"What's the matter?" I felt something smoldering behind my eyes. Where'd she get the idea she was in charge all of a sudden? She didn't know anything about my magic or the gates, or everything we'd already been through. "If we can't walk through betwixt and between, the train is easiest."

"It's the iron," Papa said lightly. "In the train and the rails."

Iron's poison to fairies. It didn't bother me so much because I am half human, but I'd seen the kind of things it could do to full-blood fairies like Papa, and they were not good. Guilt smacked hard against me. How could I have forgotten?

"It's going to be a little uncomfortable for me, but I'll be fine." Papa made his voice bright and easy and patted Mama's hand for emphasis. "We need to get a move on. With the war started, the court's allies in this world will be out, searching for power to feed the armies, and looking for Callie especially." His voice went grim. "With her power over the gates, she's a living weapon worth all the armies either side could raise."

Right then a siren wailed in the distance and we all jumped. Then we looked at each other and saw how pale we'd gone. Without any more argument, Jack and I moved up close to my parents and we started walking.

As usual, Jack knew which way to go. It was like he'd been planning how to hightail it out of Los Angeles since the day we got here. Maybe he had. He'd hoboed around a lot, both before and after taking up with me. Another streetcar carried us up Central, taking us to the Southern Pacific Railroad's Los Angeles station. From there we could catch a train east, maybe even all the way to New York. With the way things had gone so far, though, I wasn't figuring we'd have that much luck, or any at all.

We looked more respectable this time, and the car was starting to fill up with people on their way to work, so we didn't stand out so much. We got out near Fifth Avenue with a small crowd of men with hard hats and lunch pails. These streets weren't like any of the Los Angeles I'd seen so far. I'd gotten used to thinking the whole city was white, clean, and brand-spanking-new. In this neighborhood, though, sooty brick alleys sliced apart rows of mismatched buildings, and sagging black power lines stitched them loosely back together. Raggedy hoboes rolled up in their coats and tried to catch a little sleep in the fading shadows. Chinese men eyed us from the doorways of battered shops and shuttered restaurants, some dressed in shirts and trousers, some in long coats with round caps on their heads. They looked hard and sad, and moved around at their work to the clang and clash rising up from the train tracks behind the jumbled buildings.

It was easy to see what saddened those men. One wall of the street maze had been demolished. Instead of city streets there was a flat expanse of pale dirt with cranes and bulldozers standing guard. It looked like somebody had dropped a piece of Kansas in the middle of Los Angeles, and then fenced it in with barbed wire and wooden slats. The hot, hard California wind stirred up miniature dust devils in the tire tracks. The Chinese men eyed it uneasily, like they were waiting for the day the dirt would stretch out and flatten the last few buildings blocking its view of the tracks.

We paired up as we started up the sidewalk. Papa walked ahead, his arm in Mama's, and I walked beside Jack. We were all on edge and trying not to show it, but it was hard. Even Papa looked too stiff as we walked the gray line of cement street that cut between the old Chinatown and the new construction site. The railway station, a square granite building with tall windows and wide steps, was up ahead, across a broad, busy intersection. People were heading in and coming out, and everything about it was normal and everyday under the bright morning sun. At the same time, I couldn't help feeling like I was in one of those dreams where I was in a long hallway, and no matter how fast I ran, the end kept getting farther and farther away.

Cut it out, I told myself. *There's nothing wrong. It's a normal day, full of normal people. Wherever the Seelies are, they're not here. Look around. It's just us.*

It was good advice, even if it came from myself. I did look around. I saw the men heading into work. I saw the broken Chinatown with its people talking with each other or carrying boxes in and out of the stores. Even though it felt like it was taking a million years, we were getting closer to the street corner and to the intersection. It was a matter of taking one step at a time. We just had to get across those streets with their noisy rivers of traffic. We just had to get to the train station. Just one more step, and one more, and one more.

I was all but chanting as we walked. Papa looked over his shoulder once, and I bit my lip. Could he feel me being afraid? I dragged my emotions deeper inside and put some space between me and Jack. And kept walking. *No matter what,* I told myself, *we will keep walking.*

We passed a broken-down shop—if it wasn't a restaurant—with a neon sign that was a bunch of Chinese characters. It was the last building of the broken Chinatown. On the far side was a lot that would have been vacant except somebody had cobbled together a sad little cluster of shacks from scraps of cardboard, lumber, canvas, and tin.

Jack and I had seen a lot of these places since we'd left Kansas. We'd even stopped overnight in a couple. They were called Hoovervilles, after President Hoover, who oversaw the stock-market crash that brought the Depression down on the country. Some of them were not okay. They were hobo jungles full of hard, dangerous men looking for a drink or trouble, whichever came by first. But mostly these shanties were built by people who'd lost their homes. They'd been put out, shut out, tractored out, starved out, and now they were here, huddling together, trying to stay alive long enough for things to get better. Probably some of the Hooverville men would be hanging around that construction site's gate, hoping for a day's work. The rest would either be out on the bum or curled up in their shacks sleeping off whatever they'd found to ease their way through the night before. If there were families living there, we'd see the kids running around, kicking a can or some such.

At least, we should have. This set of tin-and-scrap shacks, though, was less like the Hoovervilles I'd seen before and more like a miniature ghost town. There weren't any kids, or anybody else. The crooked doorways waited blank and empty. One black crow perched on a roof and looked out at the morning with its shining eyes. Nobody was hanging around by the fence to ask about a job. The only people at the gates of the construction site were the men with their hard hats and lunch pails.

"Where're the people?" Jack asked softly. "In the Hooverville?" He'd noticed it too. There were men hunkered down in the broken alleys and pale shadows of Chinatown, but nobody around those empty houses. Where had they all gone?

Cold worry touched the back of my neck. I didn't like it, and I could tell by how Jack's face had gone all tight that he didn't like it either. Had the cops cleared the place out? That made no sense. If the people had been run off, the Hooverville would've been torn down to keep them from coming back. This was a deserted place where there should have been people. Instead, there was only that fat crow, looking very satisfied with itself. That crow, and a smell like burning rubber.

No, whispered a voice in my head, and I pulled up short. Because that voice was not mine. Jack shot me another worried look. But his look was nowhere near as worried as the way Papa was staring at that crow.

Not them, said the voice in my head that wasn't mine. For a wild second, I thought it was the crow talking about us. *Not here. Not yet.*

But it wasn't the crow I was hearing or Jack. I was hearing my father thinking.

"What is it?" I caught Papa's sleeve. "What's happening?"

That startled him. I felt a shift around the edges of my mind, like a very small door closing, and I knew I was right. This was one of the things that could happen when Unseelies got together, and probably Seelies too. Our minds and magics would try to cozy up close to each other, and it took work to keep them apart, just like it took work to keep out the wishes and feelings of the humans around us. I hated this bit about being part fairy. The last person who got in my head without permission was my uncle Shake. But he had wanted me either under his thumb or under the ground, so he had encouraged the situation. I hadn't really thought I'd have to watch out for this around my father. His thoughts must have leaked out by accident, or maybe I leaked in because he was so worried he couldn't completely close his magic self. That was not a comfortable idea. What if my thoughts sprang their own leak? I wanted to get to know Papa, but I had plenty of secrets I wanted to keep to myself, thank you very much.

"Don't stop." Papa moved one extra inch closer to Mama's side and lengthened his stride, forcing me and Jack to pick up our pace. "Keep moving."

"Why? What is it?" Jack asked.

"Come along, Jack," said Mama. "You too, Callie. We don't want to miss the train." But she didn't know what time the train left any more than we did. She was just afraid. I could feel the fear beating against the inside of her mind. If we didn't get away, if we didn't make it into the safety of the railway station, we could be caught by the Seelies. She could be dragged away again to be locked in another magic prison. But she would not show her fear. She would not look around and let any of us see the terror in her eyes. She would be strong.

I swallowed hard and tried not to know what Mama wanted so badly to keep private.

Papa didn't bother to answer Jack. He just took a better hold of Mama's arm and kept right on walking. Something sizzled, and that burning-rubber smell I'd noticed before got stronger. One of the Chinese men came out of the last shop on the edge of the Hooverville and cussed something in his own language. He lifted his battered broom and beat at the switched-off neon sign over his doorway. I swear I saw a spark jump from the sign's twisted symbol to the black wire sagging overhead. It sizzled again and slid along the power line. Now I smelled smoke.

"Papa?" I said. My father ignored me. I tried again, but silently this time. *Papa?*

Not here. Not now, said his thoughts, but I couldn't tell if he was actually answering or if I was just eavesdropping some more.

"But what . . . ?" Jack was saying.

"Trouble," said Papa evenly. "That's all you need to know."

We had to stop at the curb and wait for a clear spot in the roaring traffic. Even though this was the intersection of two four-lane streets, nobody had bothered to put up a street-light on the corner. There was just a little cement island in the middle. All the cars seemed to be taking advantage of this fact to rattle past at top speed. Jack eased himself back behind the rest of us. His worry spiked. I could feel it pricking at my mind, even sharper than Mama's. He was getting ready for whatever new, bad thing was set to catch up with us.

I clamped my teeth down on my temper. Papa had no business treating us like we were know-nothing kids. If something was up, we had a right to hear about it. Then we could stop being scared and start being ready. He didn't know what we'd been through already any more than Mama did. Less even. He'd left us and gotten caught and started this whole mess tumbling across our lives.

Callie, I do know you've been through a lot. Papa's voice was back in my head, this time on purpose, I could tell. I could also feel him forcing himself to be patient. *But in this city, we are behind enemy lines. We've got your mother and Jack to think about, and the only way we can keep them safe is to get out of here as fast as possible.*

He was right, but I didn't want him to be, especially not while he was brushing Jack off and ordering me around like a little kid. Papa slid his arm around Mama's waist, letting her know he was close. If I could feel her fear, he definitely could, and I was sorry for my anger. Guilt was another feeling I didn't need. But I still wasn't going to let them, *him*, keep us in the dark.

Right then my parents weren't paying attention to either me or Jack. They were watching the cars honking and swerving and pushing between each other. They were waiting for their chance to get us across that river of moving metal. But on the other side, the iron and steel in the cars might smother

up my magic senses enough to keep me from learning anything on my own about what had Papa so scared. Jack craned
his neck, like he was trying to see a break in the traffic, but
he nudged my arm with his elbow. I was sure he'd been
thinking the same thing. I nodded once. Then I sneaked my
fairy senses open and turned them back on that empty
Hooverville.

For a couple of seconds, I didn't feel anything. The worn-
down men and the Chinese shopkeepers going about their
business were ignoring us. The workers sauntering through
the gate around that big, dusty construction site had their
minds on their work, or the contents of their lunch boxes, or
their wives and families. Normal things. Human things.

But there was something else too, something that dragged
itself over my senses like a storm cloud over the sun. It was
hunger. It rose up like it was coming straight from the earth.
It cramped up my stomach and dried up all other thoughts.
Behind us, someone who was invisible even to my fairy eyes
was starving to death.

A break in the traffic opened, a heartbeat pause in the
noise for two of the four lanes. Papa was leading Mama
across, and Jack was following, and I had to go too. But I
caught Jack's sleeve. We reached the island in the middle of
the intersection. We were halfway, with traffic in front and
traffic behind, and waiting ahead the solid, square lines
of the train station, our goal, the place we absolutely had to
get to.

Jack looked into my eyes, and he saw immediately there

was a whole lot wrong. He knew, and I knew, that we should keep going, like my parents wanted us to. Like we had every reason to do. Whatever was behind us, it was Seelie.

But the Seelies didn't build that Hooverville. That was a home for humans, and something had happened to those humans.

Jack swallowed and reached up to his hat brim, like he meant to scratch his head. Instead, he nudged his new straw boater, just a touch. Just enough so that hot California wind and the smoggy traffic breeze caught the brim and whipped it backward off his head.

Jack cussed and turned and ran, chasing after his new straw hat, like anyone would do. The cars screeched and honked and skidded to a halt, sometimes just inches from his flailing fingers. On the far side of the street, Jack, who never, ever missed a step in his life, stumbled hard on the curb. He fell on his knees, right in front of the Hooverville.

"Jack!" I yanked myself out of my father's grip and dodged into the snarled-up traffic, running after my best friend, like anyone would do.

3

Ol' Willow Tree, Weep for Me

Both my parents were shouting behind us, but I ignored them. The cars were honking and revving their engines and fighting to get going again.

I knelt beside Jack like I was about to help him get to his feet.

"What do you see?" he whispered, putting out a hand like he was signaling me to back off.

I eased my magic senses open again and lifted my eyes to the Hooverville. I saw the shacks and the crow and the empty doorways. I felt the hunger. It was hot and desperate and it filled the air, but I still couldn't see where it came from. Now that I was closer, though, I could feel something else underneath that hunger. This new something stole across my senses like a lullaby. It was a wish. There was a wish being granted, right in the middle of the hunger that sloshed through the deserted Hooverville. It was a wish for peace, a wish for rest.

It was sweet and happy, and so completely wrong it made my skin crawl. It crept close to the ground, like fog, like dust. But like the hunger, it seemed to come out of nowhere.

"Callie!" Mama was shouting from the intersection island. The blaring, roaring traffic noise made her sound faint and far away. "Callie, get back here! Now!"

But I wasn't getting back there until I knew what was going on right here. It was dangerous for me to go slinging my own magic around even this little bit, but there was one other trick I could try. Before I left Kansas, I'd gotten three wishes of my own granted. The first of them let me see clearly through dust. That might not sound like much, but when you have to walk through some of the biggest storms of blow dirt in the history of the country, or across a chunk of California desert, being able to see through all that dust gets to be surprisingly useful. I might be able to make use of it now.

There were pockmarks in the cement sidewalk, and they were filled with dust from the construction site. I scrabbled with my fingertips in the nearest little hole and came up with a pinch of dust. As Jack and I both climbed slowly, deliberately to our feet, Jack waved back to my parents to let them know everything was fine, and we'd be along directly. I held up that pinch of dust so the wind caught it and blew it straight into my eyes.

The dust stung. I sneezed and blinked hard. I looked again at the empty, hungry Hooverville with its soft, creeping lullaby from nowhere. This time I saw clearly.

A tree stood in the middle of the Hooverville. I couldn't

see it with my regular daytime eyes, but my magic eyes, my dust eyes, saw its stout trunk and smooth silver bark. The empty shacks drooped down from the tree's spreading branches like overripe apples until they touched the ground.

I was right. The Seelies hadn't built this Hooverville. They'd grown it. And those shacks growing from that tree's branches weren't really empty. A human figure huddled in most every one. Some had their mouths open, with sloppy, dreaming grins on their faces. The lullaby, the wish for peace and rest, came from that tree. It was lulling those people into sleep and keeping them there, forever and for good. Through some of the doorways I could see bones.

Jack put his hand on my shoulder. "Show me."

I swallowed, and I did it, putting enough of my magic into Jack's veins so he could see what I saw. Each one of those fake shacks was a mouth, and the tree was starving for its human flies. A wave of greed, hot and crazy-making, rose up from the ground, joining the hunger, overwhelming the lullaby.

Another sizzle sounded. There was a fire on the wires overhead, sparking blue and white at the junction box near the poles. It stank of burning rubber and hot electricity. The tree swayed and dragged its shanty cages closer to its smooth, shiny trunk. The ragged men inside just grinned wider.

Jack shuddered hard. "We gotta get them out of there."

But hands grabbed me by the shoulders and spun me around. Mama shook me, her face tight with fear and flushed from the heat and her anger. "Callie! You get away from there! You heard your father! You mind him!" Papa, though, wasn't looking down at me. He was looking at the Hooverville. He knew what was wrong. He could see the people dying in there, and he wasn't going to do one thing about it.

Anger hit me hard and knocked all the sense out of me. I knew Mama was scared, and I knew Papa had a world of very good reasons to want us to clear out. I knew what they'd both been through. But in that moment, I just plain didn't care. Nobody treated me like a baby, not even them. I was not going to leave a magic trap behind to take people who'd done nothing worse than try to find a place to sleep.

I looked right at both my parents and deliberately stepped across the line from sidewalk pavement to vacant-lot dirt, my magic wide open and spoiling for a fight.

As soon as the sole of my shoe touched the ground, greed poured down over me. The tree drank down the lives of all its hostages, but it was starved for more. Much more. A whole world's worth of more. If it got enough, it would be allowed to live. If it got enough, it might finally be free.

While I was still trying to get a handle on all that, a voice shouted out of the clear blue sky: "Get out of here, dum-dum!"

My head jerked up, and I saw fire on the power line. But not normal fire. It was silver, white, and blue, and clutched a sparking wire in its hand.

Hand?

"I said get out of here!" The silver fire critter had no real face, just a pair of pale, almost-human eyes in the middle of its blue-white glow. He—she—it flickered and buzzed as it slithered down the pole, brandishing the power line at the tree, or maybe at us.

I staggered back and bumped into Jack. We lurched together. Something caught my ankle and yanked. All at once, I was flat on my face in the dust between the shacks. I coughed, and for a second I saw the tree's twisted, greedy face peering out from under its waving branches. Its roots bunched up under my arms and my shoulders, and where I touched the warm, soft bark, I stuck.

For a moment, it was like I was plunged into dark water. Lungs and heart turned to stone. I didn't know which way was up. I could barely remember how to move.

I'm sorry, gasped the prison tree inside my head, and it meant it.

Jack reached down for me immediately.

"No!" I shouted, but I couldn't twist away. His fingers closed around my arm, and I cried out, not because it hurt, but because I felt the paralysis run through me, straight into Jack. I felt it yank him down into the cold of the tree's enchantment, right beside me.

Jack didn't go quiet like I had. He cussed and pulled, but only succeeded in throwing himself off balance. He wobbled and dropped to one knee, and stuck there. Mama screamed and dove forward, but Papa caught her around the waist and hauled her back.

Two more, two more. A voice shivered out of the bark beneath my belly, slow and low and gleeful. I recognized the greed and good cheer. This was the tree too.

I'm sorry, it said again, and it still meant it. *I'm so sorry.*

"What are you?" I couldn't move my body, but I still had hold of my magic. I pulled my fairy senses open wider, searching for edges to the prison tree's power. There had to be some spot I could grab hold of and bend with a wish or a willing. But there was nothing except the greed and desperation as sharp as the Santa Ana winds. "What do you want?"

Don't want, sobbed the tree. *The Seelie king needs you all. Drink you up, drink you deep, and I'm sorry. I'm so sorry, but the king must have you all.*

The Seelie king. It was a trap. It was all a trap. It wasn't meant for us, but I'd dragged us in all the same. I tried to yank my magic closed, but it was way too late. The river between me and the tree was flowing freely, like blood from an open wound. Magic ran out of me, and in its place, the tree's sweet lullaby flooded in.

I felt heavy. Jack's hand on my arm was deadweight, pressing me down. I knew he was trying to wish. I felt that too. Jack was frantically wishing me strength, but that wish couldn't make it upstream against the tree's magic. I scrabbled around weakly, trying to form a wish of my own, for freedom, for help, for anything. But it was all gone.

Jack was down on both knees now, his mouth open and his eyelids drooping. His strength, his will to fight was draining right out of him. It drained into the sap that ran through the tree's veins. Because my magic was being held open, I knew what was happening. The tree would store up the strength it stole until the servants of the Seelie king came by. They'd drain off that sap filled with human strength, human life, and haul it away to feed those the king deemed worthy.

The tree was laughing, unless that sound in my head was it crying.

The silver fire critter cussed with words I wouldn't have thought a magic being had any business knowing. "Stop, Stripling!"

"It's no good, no good, Edison," the prison tree cried. "Get away!"

A small square of roots was spreading out around Jack and me. I blinked. The roots sprouted twigs. Those twigs broadened into milled lumber and cardboard. The tree, Stripling, was growing another shack around us to swallow us whole.

The fire critter, Edison, cussed again and jammed that live power line into the dirt.

A massive, numbing blow ran through the ground, the tree, me, and Jack, freezing us solid, standing our hair on end. The tree screamed. Jack flew backward and plowed into Papa, so they both fell together in a heap. The fake shacks rocked and shuddered, and I smelled ozone and burning. My heart was banging out of control and fire crawled across my skin, but I was still stuck fast.

"Let her go!" Mama charged into the Hooverville, brandishing a saw in both hands.

She must have run to the construction site. She must have charged right past all those working men and snatched up a saw and run back. Because for better or worse, that was the kind of thing my mama did.

"And it's another one!" Edison fell back in astonishment, dragging the power line with it. "Who are you people?"

Mama brought that saw down against the nearest branch, digging the teeth hard into the slick silver bark. The tree screamed again.

"Stop!" cried Edison.

Mama, though, wasn't paying any attention at all. "Let. Her. Go!" The saw scraped and wobbled as she hauled it back and forth, trying to dig the teeth into the living bark. Edison charged at Mama, waving the power line. Papa cussed and whistled. The wind blew hard, and the line's sparks guttered, and then died. He whistled again, and the critter's fire sputtered, and it crumbled to the dirt.

The tree screamed and screamed again. Something hot and wet dripped against my skin, like blood. "No! Stop! Stop!" Edison staggered to its feet, its fire, its whole body flickering.

The tree let out another shriek as the pain of Papa's magic and Mama's saw blade dug in together. This time Stripling's hold loosened. I felt the glamour that hid it from human view shiver and then break. I yanked myself backward and toppled against the too-warm wall of the nearest shack. The hoboes who had been hunkered down in the alley shook themselves out of their coats and climbed to their feet, gaping at the chaos that hadn't been there a second ago.

"HEY!" Jack bellowed at the top of his lungs. "SOME HELP HERE!"

I could hear swearing and pleading from inside the shack behind me. An arm thrust out of the doorway, waving frantically, looking for something to grab. Jack caught hold of that ragged arm and pulled. A man—hairy, filthy, and skeleton-thin—tumbled out.

This was a sight the hoboes understood. They barreled across the alley. Papa scooped me up off the ground and carried me back to the sidewalk. The men ran straight past us and dove inside the prison shacks. They yelled and cussed and kicked, but they made it back out, carrying prisoners to lay on the sidewalk.

Papa shot the tree a look of pure, hot poison. Then he turned toward the cracked-open Chinatown and shouted a string of high-pitched, lilting words that I didn't understand at all.

A few Chinese men hurried into the street. Papa shouted some more and pointed toward the tree. Next thing I knew, those Chinese men were all hollering and pointing at the prison tree. I had no idea what they were saying to each other, but they were saying it fast and loud, and it got results. Maybe a dozen men and boys came running out of the shops, and they brought cleavers and hatchets with them. Jack grabbed Mama and pushed her out of the way. The hoboes cussed and called the new crowd a bunch of names, but they got themselves out of the way too.

The armed Chinese men surrounded the tree, screaming in their own language so loud it drowned out any cries coming from the tree as they laid into it with their cleavers and their knives.

"No, Papa, stop it!" My voice was hoarse. "It didn't mean it. It was trapped. It . . ."

But Papa wasn't listening. He just gave me one hard shove so I stumbled against Mama, and she dragged me backward to a clear patch of sidewalk.

"How dare you disobey your father like that?" Mama grabbed hold of my shoulders and shook me again. "What were you thinking? You could have been killed! We all could have been killed!"

"What was I supposed to do?" Shame and anger flushed my cheeks, and I struck her hands away. "They were dying!"

By now the men from the construction site across the way had noticed something was up, and they were running through the fence, shouting and waving their arms. The Chinese ignored them and kept hacking at the tree. It had stopped screaming. The greed was gone. So was the desperation. Inky blackness ran down the silver trunk, like dirty water or dirty blood. It sank into the dusty ground of that vacant lot and disappeared.

"Let's go, let's go!" Papa grabbed up Jack and dragged him out of the crowd of hoboes, Chinese men, and builders.

"You didn't have to do that!" I wanted to scream as I

stumbled to keep up with him and Mama, but it hurt too much. "It wasn't the tree's . . ."

In answer my father reached out and turned my hands over to show me my own palms, the skin all torn up and bloody and covered in what could only be tooth marks. More red stains blossomed around the sides of my new dress. Jack looked down at his hands and saw they were just as torn, just as bloody. More blood spread out on the knees of his white flannels. The only thing I couldn't figure out was why it didn't hurt.

"It will," said Papa as if I'd spoken out loud. I was leaking thoughts again. I tried to pull the edges of my mind properly closed, but I was drained of magic and blood, and it was real slow going.

Papa dragged me and Mama across the street, dodging traffic and rubberneckers all the way over to the train station. Jack followed close behind. Blue-uniformed cops pushed past us out of the station doors, billy clubs out and whistles shrilling.

By that time, my skin had decided something was wrong after all. Pain throbbed in my arms and belly. Papa didn't say a word. He just took my wrists, and his magic flowed across my skin like cool water. It stung for a second, but when I turned my palms up again, the skin was whole. He looked at me with his swirling, shining gaze, but the light wasn't as bright as it had been, and I saw there were dark rings under his eyes and his face was drawn tight. My father was wearing out. He'd been using a lot of magic, fast, and he was still weak from his imprisonment, not to mention the fight with the Seelie king, and he'd just had to rescue us again.

I bit my lip and turned away.

Papa sighed and moved off to heal Jack and clean him up, same as he'd done to me. My mother had put on the look that meant a lecture was coming. But I wasn't going to hear it. I knew I was wrong. I knew it was my fault Jack was hurt, but I couldn't make myself say anything about it. It didn't make any sense, but there it was anyhow. I turned away from all of them and marched to the granite station wall. I folded my arms stubbornly, and bent my knees until I slid down the wall and crouched in the shade. I would be double-darned if I was going to apologize for what I'd done. I was trying to save lives. And I wasn't a baby. I knew what was what. I took my own chances. And Papa hadn't needed to sic those men on that tree, whatever it was. Why couldn't he hear it? Why couldn't he have *tried* to help?

Something sizzled overhead, and then it hissed, "You!"

My gaze jerked up to the swaying power lines. Edison looked down at me with its almost human eyes. It had dimmed its white blaze, so it was barely more than a heat mirage rippling in the bright daylight. It swung down from the line, stretching its arms out like rubber bands until it dangled almost level with my eyes.

"You killed her," it breathed, if that's a word you can use with something that flickers and burns.

"Wha . . ." For one wild second I thought it was talking about Ivy Bright.

"You killed Stripling." Its words spat and scattered like sparks. "You stood there and let her get hacked to death!"

I winced, and batted at the sparks as they fell. "It wasn't me," I tried to say. "I—"

"Oh, save it!" The creature swung toward me. Edison might have dimmed down, but its heat still prickled against my skin. I tried to press backward, but there was nowhere to go. "You listen to me, Bad Luck Girl." It stretched its glowing mouth out into a thin, mean grin. "Oh, yeah, I figured out who you are. Didn't take me long neither. You'd better be real careful from here on in. 'Cause I'm putting the word out on you, and you can bet your last nickel the Halfers are all gonna know which side you're on."

"What . . ." But the creature flashed back up to the power line. It balanced on the curve of black wire for a second, blazing bright, and then it was gone.

4

The Rock Island Line,
She's a Mighty Good Road

I hurried back to my parents, mumbling apologies and ignoring Jack's frantic looks. I stuck to them like glue the whole time we were navigating the Central Station, even though I could barely look at Mama. Every time I did, I saw her face drawn up tight with hurt and anger, and how she kept holding tight to Papa's hand.

Getting on the train was less of a problem than I'd been afraid of. Jack—helped out by the fat wallet Papa's magic had given him—bought us tickets for a drawing room compartment on the Golden State Limited to Chicago, with a change to the 20th Century Limited to get us through to New York City. The sleeping-car porter was an old man with bent shoulders, sparse gray hair, and rich black skin. He showed the four of us to the drawing room without so much as remarking on the fact that we had not one piece of luggage between us, or even seeming to notice about us being different colors, which made me a lot more nervous than it should have.

I'd never been in a Pullman car before, never mind in one of the private compartments. You could have lived for a month in there and not felt cramped. There was a dining nook by the window with two benches and a gateleg table that folded out from the wall. A curving cupboard overhead held the spare berth. There was a clothes closet, and two chairs, and a daybed made up so tight you could have bounced a quarter on its blue blanket. There was even a carpet on the floor, and cream and green paper on the walls. A separate door opened onto a washroom about the size of a postage stamp.

If it wasn't for what it was doing to Papa, I would have had the ride of my life.

As soon as I got on board, the iron blocked up my magic senses, so everything was kind of dim around the edges and my head felt stuffy, like I had a bad cold. But where I was a little uncomfortable, Papa was sick as a dog, and maybe even sicker. When we first climbed up the steps behind the porter, Papa was as debonair as ever. But by the time we reached our compartment, perspiration dripped from his forehead and he leaned on Mama's arm so he wouldn't stagger too bad. As soon as the porter left us alone, Mama propped Papa up in the daybed with the pillows behind him and all the blankets over him because he couldn't stop shivering.

All that day, while the train rattled through the mountains and down into the desert on the other side, Papa lay in the daybed, and got worse. Jack shut the transom windows to keep out the draft and smoke, and got an extra blanket from the porter. As it came onto evening, we rang for tea and toast. Papa tried hard to take a sip, but in the end he just pushed the cup away. First Mama, then Jack, offered to try wishing for him, but he smiled and shook his head.

"It's just the one night," declared Papa hoarsely. "We'll be in Chicago tomorrow." And then we'd have to get on another train to get out to New York. Mama forced a smile, and squeezed his hand. She looked to me, and I tried to pull out some magic for him, I swear I did, but I could only reach a tiny, shapeless trickle. I was as cut off as Papa was. The difference was, being so cut off was killing him. Maybe it wouldn't have been so bad if he hadn't already been so tired out when he got on board, but he had been and it was.

I suddenly couldn't stand being in there anymore.

"I'm gonna go find Jack," I said to Mama. Jack had gone into the main compartment about a half hour ago, on some errand he hadn't bothered to explain, and he wasn't back yet. I didn't wait for anybody to answer; I just went straight out the door. I especially didn't look back. I didn't want to see another of Mama's hurt, puzzled looks. Or worse, see that she wasn't looking at me at all, just at Papa.

Our drawing room was at one end of the sleeping car. After us came the section with the open berths, and after them were the bedrooms, which were smaller than the draw-

ing rooms, just big enough for a couple of bunk-type beds.
Past that there was the lounge section with its swivel seats
and pairs of sofas facing one another. Some other travelers
played cards across the fold-down tables, or read the paper.
Cigarette smoke turned the air hazy. Mothers and nurses
shushed children and tried to make them pay attention to
their books and crayons. A prim woman bent over her
needlework.

I didn't have to look hard for Jack. He was coming up
the central aisle toward me. I opened my mouth, but he
hooked his hand around my elbow and steered me into the
little space by the public washroom.

"I was talking to the conductor," Jack whispered.
"Tomorrow morning, we're coming up through Texas and
Arkansas."

Those were segregation states. I swallowed. If anybody
saw the color of Papa's skin, they'd make him move into
the stripped-down Colored car, where he wouldn't have a
bed, or blankets, or water, or a fan for the heat. Just bare
benches and open windows. He might even have to wait for
another train if this one didn't have a Colored car, and sure
as sure, they wouldn't let Mama go along to take care of him.
I had a feeling Mama wasn't going to stand for being separated from her husband, especially while he was so sick. But
if we kicked up a fuss, we wouldn't be allowed on any train
at all. We could even be arrested, or worse, especially if
Mama forgot herself and pointed out they were married. If
there was one thing I knew about Jim Crow territory, it was

that they did not like seeing a white woman anywhere near a black man.

"And that's not the only problem," I muttered. This was the first time Jack and I had been alone since we got on the train, and with Papa getting so sick so fast, I hadn't wanted to give Mama anything else to worry about. So I hadn't told her about the fire critter, or its threats.

But I told Jack right then, and his face tightened up. "Yeah, okay. That does not sound good." He let out a long sigh. "But we'll just have to cross that bridge when we come to it."

We stood quiet for a long time, trying not to fall over as the train swayed around a bend in the track. The door at the end of the car opened, and the old porter came out, balancing a tray with a decanter and two glasses on his fingers. He bowed and smiled as he presented the tray to a pair of men playing cards. One of them took the bottle and glasses, and dropped a nickel down.

I swallowed. "I'm gonna see what I can do for Papa," I told Jack. "You go warn Mama we'll have to stay in the room for the rest of the ride."

Jack nodded and headed back to the drawing room. The porter, in the meantime, had tucked his tray under his arm and was starting back up the aisle.

"'Scuse me, Mr. Porter . . . ," I began as he drew even with me.

He turned, beaming brightly and ducking his head so he

wouldn't be much taller than me. "Now, missy, you just call me George. What is it I can do for you?"

I bit my lip. It took a minute's hard struggle, but I was able to crack open my magic a little. Enough to sense this man's name wasn't George. That was just what the company told the porters to say. His name was Lincoln Jones. With that to hold on to, I could work an illusion on him, for a little while at least. Especially if I could sit down soon, because my knees were already shaking from the effort of keeping my magic open. I didn't want to have to fool him, because Mr. Jones was just doing his job, and I was pretty sure he was a good man, but Papa had to be able to stay with us, and never mind what Jim Crow had to say about it.

But as I stood there trying to shape the illusion in my head and in my power, Lincoln Jones laughed at me. "Don't you worry, missy," he said. "I see how your father's so sick. No one will disturb you until you get where you're going. That's a promise."

"I . . . Thank you."

"Oh, don't thank me. Word's come down the line about you."

"What? How . . . ?" My insides bunched up tight. But of all the things I could see about Mr. Jones, I didn't see the least tiny bit of fairy light in his kind brown eyes.

"Word's from Daddy Joe hisself." Mr. Jones winked. "The porters were to ease your way if you ever came on the rails. Some of us old-timers heard and we've made sure those as need to know do know." His eyes narrowed and his head tilted. It was a small change, but for that single moment, that Pullman porter called George was gone, and I was seeing the real Lincoln Jones. He was careful and he was smart, and he knew every inch of the risk he was taking. "You and yours play it cool until we get into Chicago, and we'll all be fine," he whispered. "Get me?"

I nodded and Mr. Jones broke out the great big porter's grin again. "Well then, missy, you get back to your mama, and tell her not to worry none. I'll be taking care of you personal." He gave me another bow and a smile, mostly, I think, so nobody watching would think he'd said anything out of turn. Then Mr. Jones started up the aisle, walking as smoothly as if that rattling train was standing still.

I collapsed back against the window. I'd met Daddy Joe on another train—a long black train that runs between this world and the next. Daddy Joe was the porter in charge there. He wasn't a fairy, though. I wasn't exactly sure what he was. Like the Indian spirit Coyote—who I also met—Daddy Joe was a mystery of his own kind. He was plenty powerful, though, and I guess he looked after his own.

I looked at Mr. Jones's bent back and I wondered how close he was to being taken up on Daddy Joe's train. But unlike the prison tree in Hooverville, there really wasn't anything I could do about that, except for maybe one thing.

"Thank you," I breathed. "If ever I can return the favor, I will."

* * *

Mr. Jones was as good as his word. He was the only one who knocked on our compartment door during that trip. If he had the conductor with him, he announced it, so Jack could be at the door to hand over the tickets to be inspected and punched. Mr. Jones brought us dinner, and came back at nine o'clock to set up the second bed and open the upper berth so we could all try to get some shut-eye. He even rustled up some pajamas and bathrobes for us, and took away our clothes to be cleaned and pressed for morning.

Mama insisted I take the second bed, saying she'd sit up with Papa. I climbed under the covers and pulled the starched sheets up to my chin while Jack swung himself into the upper berth. I didn't figure I'd sleep with so much rolling around in my head and the noise of the rails under the floor. But I was wrong. The past few days had been too long, and though it wasn't anywhere near as bad as for Papa, I had the iron dragging on me too. When I shut my eyes, I didn't so much fall asleep as fly straight toward it.

I don't know how long it was before the dream caught up with me. It wasn't any kind of normal dream, where you're inside a picture show that sort of makes sense. I don't even know if *dream* is the right word for what happened. It started with me slowly understanding that something was going on, even though I was still firmly in sleep's pitch-black and dead quiet. I couldn't seem to get my eyes to open or my arms to move. I thought for a minute I was back through the fairy gate, and fear woke up along with the rest of my brain.

Yesssss . . . , said a soft, beautiful voice. *There she is. Yesssss . . . I see her now.*

Away wherever my real body'd gotten itself to, I'm pretty sure my heart stopped and my mouth went dry. I knew that voice. I'd heard it before, coming out of nowhere, just like this.

"Shake," my dream mouth said. "Uncle Shake."

I felt a jolt of recognition, and more than a little fear. But just for a minute. *Well, well, little niece.* I could hear the smile Uncle Shake forced into his voice. *You have been a busy girl.*

"Where are you?" I tried to turn around, but since there was nothing but a world's worth of solid black all around me, I couldn't tell whether I actually managed it.

Nowhere you know, my uncle's voice answered. *Where are* you?

I tried hard to think about the boarding house where I'd stayed in Los Angeles, about Ivy Bright's bungalow, about anything except the train I was riding on. The last thing we needed was Uncle Shake coming around to add to our troubles. The Seelies and their friends were giving us more than enough to do.

Unfortunately, what popped up easiest in my mind was my father lying in his bed, sweating and restless from the fever the iron laid across him. Maybe I couldn't see a single thing about my uncle, but he had a front-row seat to what I was thinking.

I heard Shake's tongue click. *Does my brother really look that bad, or are you having nightmares?*

"Show yourself!" I shouted back. I did not like his voice coming out of nowhere and everywhere. I did not like being blind as well as frozen and the rising fear was making it hard to think straight. "Show me your face, Lorcan deMinuit!"

The power of my uncle's real name rang through that nightmare dark, and all at once, I did see him.

The first time I met my uncle, he was a handsome man with medium-brown skin, a pencil-thin mustache, and fairy eyes like amber and starlight all mixed together. He'd stood at his royal father's side and his smile was full of confidence and cleverness. The second time I met him, he was nothing but a broken-down hobo who'd been kicked out by his parents, my grandparents. They'd left him with a scar that had ruined one of those eyes, turning it milk white and near blind under a sagging eyelid. I'd never found out how it happened, but it sure looked like somebody'd cut him deep.

Wherever he was now, he'd changed again. Uncle Lorcan sat in a chair carved of ebony, his crooked hands lying lightly on its arms. He wore a black silk shirt and gray silk trousers trimmed with silver, and boots cuffed and traced with more silver. He looked like a Russian dancer I'd seen once when my human grandparents took me to a vaudeville show, only more sparkly. I guessed these were his fairy prince clothes. He wore a mask too. It was shining, obsidian black, molded across his eyes like a second skin. Silver ribbons tied it to his head, and more silver made patterns across the front, like vines, or maybe veins. Where the eyeholes should have been, there were mirrors, round and shining. Anyone who met Shake's gaze would see their own eyes staring back at them. I shivered. That mask reminded me too much of being in the Seelie king's palace. There'd been a whole party's worth of fairies there, all of them in jeweled masks, all of them laughing at me.

My uncle wasn't alone. A crowd of what had to be fairies surrounded his ebony chair. They were tall and beautiful, but more like trees than humans, with long white fingers and blank white eyes and glimmering white robes. There were other, smaller people clustered around their knees, people like pale sticks, and people like marble stones, all of them beautiful and terrible in their own ways. Every last one of them was armed. They carried spears or swords, or long-handled axes. A silver shield rested at my uncle's feet, marked by a golden mask. All the pale people around him had that golden mask on them somewhere too, on a shield or embedded in a spear shaft, or sunk straight into their white skin.

Now that Shake could see me, his friends could all see me as well, and they did not like what they saw. There was somebody else too. Behind the rest of the crowd I could feel the burn of a fire made from nothing but hate.

So, my little niece thinks she knows how to use true names now. My uncle's sneer was as smooth and sharp as any knife blade and all those pale, pretty creatures laughed at it. *That's good, that's good. You keep thinking, Callie LeRoux. Think very hard about this war you've made possible, and how soon you're all going to die for it.*

It was too much. I couldn't stand it anymore. "You get out of here, Lorcan deMinuit!" I shouted. "And stay out!"

I put everything I had into the command. But it went nowhere. It just swung back around and I felt the blow of my own power knock me back, all the way out of my own dream. Behind me in the dark, my uncle and his friends all laughed, and kept on laughing.

5

I've Got Double Trouble

My eyes snapped open. It was still dark, but nothing like as dark as my dream had been. The shadows of the drawing room compartment rocked with the steady rhythm of the train's wheels against the tracks. After a few hard, panicky blinks, I could make out Mama sitting on the bed, holding Papa's hand like she hadn't moved since we'd shut off the lights. Jack's snores drifted down from the upper berth. Of course he was sound asleep. There was nothing on God's green earth that could keep Jack Holland awake when he'd decided to get his forty winks.

I lay still for a while, waiting for my heart to slow its galloping and for my fingers to decide to let go of the bedsheets. Papa coughed hard. Mama held a glass of water for him to drink and then patted his forehead with a handkerchief. All her attention was on him. She didn't even notice me waking up after my nightmare. I bit my lip hard against the anger. I wouldn't give in. I couldn't.

"I'm sorry," I whispered. I didn't want to be mad at her. I didn't want Papa to be so sick, or her to be so worried, especially not with my uncle's voice ringing in my head, saying I should think hard about how soon we were going to die.

I'd thought when I found my parents, everything would be all right. Well, I had found them, but if I counted up the number of seconds when things had actually been all right since then, I might have had all of a minute and a half.

Of course I didn't really believe anything like she might love me less now that she had Papa back. He was sick. Of course she had to pay attention to him now. Thinking she should have taken my side just a little back in Los Angeles was small and mean. After all, I was supposed to be on Papa's side. That was where a good daughter would be, wouldn't it? I turned that thought over. Some kind of charity or sympathy should have come up, but none did. What came up was the idea that that was my fairy Papa over there, and if neither one of us was going to sleep, I might as well try to get some answers out of him.

I kicked back the covers and swung my legs over the edge of the bed. The movement finally got Mama to turn around.

"What's the matter, Callie?" she said, and I couldn't help hearing the fear underneath the words.

"I can't sleep." Which was mostly true. I'd scared myself

good and awake. "I'll sit up with Papa a bit. You should get some rest."

"Oh, no. I'm fine," Mama lied right back.

"We get into Chicago tomorrow. We're all going to need to be ready to help Papa change trains." I felt bad playing on her worries like that, but it was the one thing I could be sure would get through to her. Papa lifted his head and coughed again, and I saw by the shine of his eyes that he knew exactly what I was doing. I was getting Mama out of the way.

"Well. I suppose," Mama said slowly, like you do when you're pretty sure you've just agreed to a bad idea. "For a few minutes."

She slid under the covers of the bed I'd just left, adjusting her borrowed nightgown. I took her spot on the edge of Papa's bed and sat there, staring at my hands. I felt Papa watching me, but I didn't look at him. Not until Mama's soft breathing slowed and deepened, and I knew she was as sound asleep as Jack.

"So, Callie." Papa's fairy eyes glimmered silver, gold, and midnight blue in the darkness. I didn't answer, just squirmed in my seat. I thought I'd known what I was going to say, but right then it hit me how this was the first chance I'd ever had to talk with my father, and suddenly I had no idea what to do with myself.

"Me either," Papa croaked in answer to my thoughts, and tried to give me a grin. I almost managed one back. Silence fell again and I spent the pause pulling my leaky thoughts closed. I didn't want him to find out what was going on inside me until I was ready, if I ever was. I knew I should just go on and tell him about Uncle Lorcan, but what good would it do? It wasn't like either one of us had enough magic to do anything about it, and an extra worry wasn't going to help him when he was so weak.

Say something! I shouted at myself. *Anything. You can't just sit here!*

But it was Papa who spoke next. "You've been through a lot, Callie." His voice had turned ragged and raspy, nothing like the clear laughing voice he'd had before we got on the train. "I can see it in you."

"You can?"

"It would take more than a bit of iron to completely separate me from you, especially now that we've met and learned each other's names."

"Oh. I guess . . . I guess I've got a lot to learn about being a fairy." So that was the source of the leak: the names. It would be. Fairies were flat-out crazy over people's names and what they could do.

"And I've got a lot to learn about being a human . . . and more, I think, about being a father." Another smile flickered in his dimming eyes. "I do intend to be the best father I can. I'm only sorry I've made such a bad beginning of it."

"It's not your fault," I whispered to my hands.

"Well, that's nice of you to say, anyhow." Silence fell again, and it was heavy, but not cold. Something was different this time, a little bit, around the edges. This silence held a feeling like a memory returning. It was the feeling of having my father close by, and I wasn't even trying to reach out to him. He was right. We weren't ever going to be truly separate again. I squirmed. I'd been lonely for so long it should have been a beautiful idea, but I just couldn't be sure how well I really liked it. Especially not with Uncle Lorcan waiting back in my nightmares like he was.

"How about you tell me about your journey?" Papa sagged farther down onto the pillows. "I haven't heard the whole story yet."

Mama rolled over, murmuring uneasily in her sleep. I swallowed. I told her I'd look after Papa. I should at least try. "Um, shouldn't you be trying to sleep?"

Papa's smile was as weak as the light from his shining eyes. "No. To tell you the truth, I think sleep would be very bad for me right now."

I understood what he wasn't saying and fear skittered through me. He knew that, of course, but neither of us mentioned it. Instead, I started talking. I told him about the dust storm that took Mama away from Slow Run, and about the monsters that had come for me afterward, about meeting the Indian spirit Baya, about meeting Jack, and the half-fairy woman Shimmy, who did the best she could for us, and finally, about meeting Uncle Shake and all he'd tried to do to me.

Nothing could have gotten me ready for my father's anger. It swept through me, raw, red, and hotter than any fire. His eyes flared red and gold with it until all the storm-cloud blue burned away. He reared up hard on those pillows, and Mama whimpered in her sleep and even Jack's snores hitched.

"Stop, Papa," I gasped, dragged halfway to my feet by a need to run, or hit something. "Please, you'll wake them up. . . ."

After a moment's struggle, the anger pulled back, and I dropped back onto the bed. Another coughing fit reached up and shook Papa hard. I grabbed the water glass and held it for him so he could sip. He waved me back.

"I'll be all right. I'll be . . . By my blood and bone, Callie, I never, ever thought he'd try murder."

"He wants the throne," I said. "He says he's got friends who can help him get it." I thought about all the pale fairies I'd seen around him. I should have been thinking about something else, something important. An idea was scratching at the back of my head, but I couldn't tell what it was.

"He has nothing. Not while you breathe," Papa muttered.

"I told him I'd abdicate, like you did. But he wasn't interested. It's probably got something to do with the prophecy. Everything else does." This time the anger I felt was my very own. "Why's there a prophecy at all? Why's it got the Seelies in such a lather? And my . . . our . . . family? They're so high and mighty, why would any of them even *care* what I do?"

"They may be so high and mighty now, Callie," said Papa seriously. "But your power could lay them all low in very short order. You must see that."

"No, I don't. How can that be?"

Papa stared at me in disbelief for a long time. "I forget," he breathed at last. "There's so much you can do, I forget how little you actually know. Callie, we of the fairy kind don't just like humans, we need them. We are dependent on them." He coughed again, and that one cough touched off a whole storm of others. He pressed his arm against his mouth, trying to muffle the sound, and screwed his eyes shut. I knew how bad that kind of coughing hurt. I remembered it from when I had the dust pneumonia. Was that what was ailing Papa? Was the iron somehow filling up his fairy lungs? I opened my mouth to ask if he wanted some more water or if I should rub his back. But Papa held up his hand and managed a couple of deep breaths.

"Why're you . . . How could we be dependent on humans?" I asked. Fairies were the ones with magic and illusions and all the other powers. Fairies could make human beings do anything they wanted, even dance themselves to death. How could creatures like that be dependent on humans?

"We can't heal," said Papa.

"What?"

"We can't heal," he repeated. "Unlike humans, we can't renew or heal ourselves from the inside. We need to use magic to heal, or change, or grow. And when we use up what we have inside us, we must replenish ourselves from the outside, with the magic or the life essence of other beings."

"Like human beings?" I thought about how many times

I'd used Jack's wishes to shape my magic. I'd needed his help more than once to be able to do anything at all. I hadn't stopped to think that taking his wishes might be hurting him.

"Wishes, creativity, imagination, will, and feeling," Papa said softly. "All of this is the essence of what mortal beings are. It is the power of this world manifest in them. If we can reach it, our kind can convert any or all of it into our magic, in much the way one of those new dams Mr. Roosevelt is building can convert the motion of water into electricity. You've felt this, I'm sure." He didn't exactly look toward Jack in his upper berth, but I knew he was thinking about him. I sure was.

I clenched my fists. The cabin rocked around us, and the noise of the tracks clacking under the wheels sounded very loud as I tried to get my mind around what Papa said about what he was, about what we were, and I did not like any of the ideas that came running up to meet me just then.

When I was little, before the dusters started, there was a pond down by the school. Everybody knew there were leeches in it. Casey Wilkes had gone wading on a dare and come out with his legs covered with squishy brown sluggy-things. I remembered the blood running in red ribbons down his shins. I'd actually been glad when that pond dried up, because it meant all those nasty things died. I could sort of stand being bad luck, and being a fairy princess had some advantages sometimes, but what if I was also some kind of gigantic Callie-shaped leech?

"No," said Papa, and I jumped and cussed silently. I'd

been leaking thoughts again. But Papa just waved his hand. "You were thinking it loud enough that they probably heard you in the caboose. One wish taken at a time, a little feeling, a little music or good cheer won't hurt your friend." He waved his hand again, this time sort of toward Jack. "Or anyone else. Especially if it's freely given, and only once in a while. It's when you keep drawing it down that they wither and they die, whether they are human or fairy kind."

"But you're saying if I start closing gates, so the fairies can't get to human beings, I'll be, what? Starving the fairy country out?"

Papa swallowed some more air. "Succinctly put. There are many gates, large and small, but close even a few and the Seelie or the Unseelie would begin to lose touch with the essence of life and magic they need to survive and to flourish. They'd set to fighting over what access remained, which would use up their magic more quickly, which would starve them faster. Oh, yes, Callie," said Papa as the blood drained slowly from my cheeks. "You could kill them all if you decided to. And they know it."

I had no way to answer this. It was too big. I didn't want to understand it. I didn't want to be the person who held that much power inside her. So I shied away from it. "What's the third world?"

"I'm sorry?"

"It was something Mr. Robeson said, about the other part of the prophecy. *See her now, daughter of three worlds. See her now, three roads to choose. . . .* Well, there's the human world, and the fairy world, and everybody's trying to get me to choose between them. But I ain't seen a third world yet. Where's that?"

Papa was quiet for a while and I swear I could feel him fighting to think. But in the end he just shook his head. "I don't know. I never did pay much attention to the prophecy when I was still with my family. I never thought to see it fulfilled, so it didn't seem important. Another mistake, I suppose."

That felt like an honest answer, but it wasn't the one I wanted. "How do we find out, then? Because it's a little important."

"A little," Papa agreed, and coughed again. "I think perhaps that's our first order of business, after getting to New York in one piece, of course. And when we do get there, we can't have any more scenes like back with that prison tree, do you understand, Callie? Not until we've found help, and a protected place to stay."

I didn't want him to be right, and I sure didn't mean to make any kind of promise like that. Not even to my father. I made sure to keep that thought to myself, though, and quickly changed the subject.

"What was that tree?"

"Sorry?" Papa coughed again.

"When we went past the Hooverville, in Los Angeles. You saw something was wrong right away, but you wouldn't tell me what it was. You said, 'Not them.'"

"Oh." He was trying to decide how much of the truth to

tell me. I could feel it, and I wasn't going to put up with it. And he could feel that. And he smiled. "They are the Undone."

"The what?"

"Not all offspring of the magic and the mortal are, well, babies, like you were, or Ivy, or this Shimmy. Sometimes magic works on the world itself, or on . . . lesser creatures. The result is an in-between creature, one very much subject to manipulation by both worlds. They're weaker than we are, and malformed. They've got no place in either world, no proper role in the web of being, or even any real business existing at all. That makes them . . . more easily swayed, I guess you could say, very ready to be used by anyone stronger."

I thought about the determination in Edison's eyes as he whispered his promises to me, and I realized I was not sure about that last bit at all. I strained to hush that idea, but it turned out I needn't have bothered.

Papa wheezed a few times and sagged farther down against the pillows. "I'm sorry," he croaked. "I'm afraid I have to rest for a while."

He struggled for a minute and I realized he was trying to lie down. I helped get the pillows out from behind him and held his shoulders so he could lie back slowly. He felt light and bony under my hands, like there were no muscles left under his skin.

"Never thought," Papa breathed.

"Sorry?"

"Never thought to have a daughter, especially not one so brave. Or so like her mother." He breathed in and out hard, three or four times. "I do love her, Callie." His eyelids fluttered. "Not as a fairy, loving her life like a glutton loves a good steak. As barren as it may be, I do have a heart, or I did. I gave it to her."

He didn't say anything after that. His shining eyes drifted shut. I sat there a long time, staring at him. Papa coughed and twisted like he was trying to turn over but couldn't quite. My stomach knotted up. I didn't know what to feel. I wanted to love my father. I wanted it so bad it was like a hunger inside me. But I couldn't tell if I really did love him, or if he was worth loving. He said he wanted to be a good father, and I believed that. But at the same time, he'd been ready to leave people to die back under the prison tree, and he had Mama so snarled up, she'd been ready to smack me because I wouldn't do what he said. He'd gotten us into trouble, but he'd gotten us out too. His courage in riding the train was genuine, because this trip was just plain killing him. It wasn't being slow about its work either. If Papa was this sick already, how was he going to last all the way to New York City?

I wished hard I'd never thought of that, but nothing happened.

6

To My Sweet Home Chicago

"LaSalle Street Station!" called the conductor outside our compartment door. "Final stop, LaSalle Street Station! All change at LaSalle!"

I have never in my life been so glad to hear anything as I was to hear those words.

I didn't sleep the rest of the night. When morning finally came, Jack took Mama to the dining car, so she could get a little fresh air and stretch her legs. I went myself after that, but I couldn't eat anything, and I hotfooted it back to the compartment after about five minutes. Papa didn't even try to sit up. I don't know for sure what Mama and Jack saw when they were with him, but to me it looked like he was fading away. Once, he slid his hand across the blankets to touch Mama's, and I was sure I saw her pale fingers right through his dark ones.

The Golden State Limited pulled into the station with a

long whoosh of steam and a squeal of brakes. Jack, as usual, scrambled out ahead of the rest of us. While Mama and I were trying to figure out if Papa was even going to be able to stand, Jack slipped back in through the door.

"It's all set," Jack said. "Mrs. LeRoux, the porter will come knock when the rest of the passengers have cleared out and help you with Mr. LeRoux. Callie can come on ahead with me to scope out the station." The look Jack gave me then hushed my questions. "We'll meet you both on the platform."

The platform was a stretch of concrete in a long shed made of iron girders and frosted glass. The smell of diesel and hot metal filled the air and the platform itself was filled to the brim with passengers and porters trying to sort out who needed to be where. I glanced around, half afraid to open my magic senses, but more afraid not to. But when I did, all I felt was the tumult of the human beings surrounding us. I tried to stretch my awareness out, but I kept running into the blocking iron—in the trains, in the support beams and girders that held up the shed around us and framed the glass panels in its roof. This place wouldn't give Papa much of a break.

Jack pulled me away from the train, toward a big marble archway I guessed led to the main station. With his usual instinct for navigating a crowd, he found what seemed to be the single empty spot near the wall.

Jack faced me. "Callie, there's something I need you to do."

"What?" Jack seemed anxious, which was not normal for him. I wondered for a second if it had something to do with being in Chicago. Jack had been born here, but he'd run away from his bootlegging family years before he'd met me. I could imagine all kinds of reasons he might not be so glad to be back.

Turns out I was wrong again. "I want you to fix my eyes so I can see fairies, like you can," said Jack.

My first reaction was to tell him to keep his voice down. Then I realized nobody in the crowd could hear us. With the clash of voices, steam whistles, and train brakes, we could have planned a bank job without anybody hearing a word.

"Oh, Jack, I don't know." Everything Papa said about fairies sucking the life out of human beings came flooding back. "What if I get it wrong? I could make you go blind, or worse."

"Then we'll just wish me back the way I was," Jack said breezily.

Somehow I didn't think it'd be that simple, but I didn't say so. Not that Jack gave me time to.

"Come on, Callie, you gotta. The Seelies have been one step ahead of us the whole way. They're waiting for us around here somewhere, and they'll be in New York too. If we can both see the magic it'll be that much harder for them to sneak up on us."

I really hated to admit it, but he had a point. I wasn't going to be able to watch all directions at once and if the Seelies weren't here now, they would be soon. Heck, it might even be the Unseelies. Uncle Shake knew where I was, and who I was with. It wasn't going to take a whole lot of work for him to figure out where I was going.

"Okay." I tried to summon my nerve. Then I tried to figure out how I could do what Jack asked. "You'd better . . . you'd better bend down."

Jack brought his face level with mine. He smelled like coffee and Pepsodent. I laid my hands over his eyes. Touching him did not help me think straight. Instead, the warmth of his skin under my palms brought on butterflies in all kinds of new places. Especially when his breath touched my cheek. I needed to get past this. One thing I did know about magic was that if you didn't concentrate while you worked, you could really mess up. The idea of hurting Jack stuck straight into my heart, and twisted. That sure didn't help the whole thinking-straight situation any.

"Should I wish?" Jack asked. "Or sing something? *Close your eyes.*" He started warbling a tune we'd heard on the radio coming in. *"When you open them, dear, I'll be here by your side. Close your eyes. . . ."*

I giggled, more than a tiny bit nervously, and he chuckled. Jack's voice resonated through my fingers and that shared laughter was just what I needed.

Magic is warm when it's working, and comfortable. It also has this nasty tendency to stop me from thinking clearly and make me believe I can take on the world with one hand tied behind my back. But right then my worries were more than enough to keep my head clear. I caught the feel of Jack's laughter up and swirled it around and shaped it into light. Then I let that light flow into Jack's clever eyes.

See clear, I wished for him. *See true. No magic can fool your eyes now, Jack Holland, Jacob Hollander, and not ever again.*

I closed off the magic, bit my lip, and lowered my hands slowly. Jack's eyes hadn't changed, except maybe they were a tiny bit brighter, and maybe a tiny bit bluer. Or maybe that was just because we were standing so close together. I wasn't even touching him anymore and I could still feel how warm he was.

"Well?" I asked. "Did it work?"

Jack squinted around over my head. "Hard to tell. Nothing looks different." He flashed a grin. "That's probably a good thing."

"How about me? Do I look any different?" I was part magic, after all.

Jack tilted his head a little sideways, considering this, and my cheeks started to burn.

"No," he said softly. "You look just like you should, Callie." He raised one hand and ran his fingertips down my braid, where it lay against my shoulder.

Those butterflies changed into woodpeckers, and they all started drumming against my heart. I might not have looked different, but he did, as if he was seeing something new, and he liked it. I would have given everything I had to stand there forever and have Jack look at me just like that. But as much as I wanted that, part of me was shouting I wasn't ready. Why'd this have to happen now, anyway? We were on the run and we were going to stay that way for who knew how long. Plus, my parents were going to be out here any second now.

It was right then, in fact, that I saw Mama step off the Golden State Limited. Mr. Jones, the porter, all but handed Papa down the steps to her. Papa sagged hard against Mama and she half supported, half dragged him away from the train.

"We gotta get over and help." I was saying the words, but they seemed to be coming from a long ways away.

"Yeah." Jack lifted his hand away from my braid, and curled his fingers under before he stuffed his hand back in his pocket. "Yeah, you're right."

Jack followed me to my parents, keeping close the whole way.

The grand hall of LaSalle Street Station was the biggest place I'd ever been and still been indoors. Its glass skylight opened about fifteen stories overhead, bringing sunlight down into a great hall decked out in creamy beige marble and gold trim. Rows of wooden benches stretched down the center, like pews in the God Almighty grandest church ever. On the one side of the hall were shops where you could buy magazines, tobacco, candy—anything you'd need for your trip, really. There were sandwich shops too, where people stood elbow to elbow around little tables to eat their lunch, drink their coffee, and fill the air with a swirling fog of cigarette smoke.

On the other side, would-be passengers lined up at about a dozen different windows where men in peaked hats and blue coats could sell a person tickets to anywhere from Milwaukee to Timbuktu. Voices on the loudspeakers announced trains. At least, I thought they did. There were so many other voices echoing through that huge marble hall, I couldn't understand a word any of them said.

Jack and I walked ahead of my parents, clearing a way through the shifting crowd as best we could. Mama struggled to keep Papa upright and keep pace, the whole time staring around that overflowing railway hall like a lost kid. I found myself wondering if she'd ever even been out of Slow Run in her life, and then wondering why I'd never thought to ask before.

"See anything?" Jack bawled in my ear.

"Nothing," I bawled back. "You?"

Before Jack could answer, the doors to the street flapped open and a flock of boys in knickerbockers and flat caps charged straight through, newspapers under their arms and held high over their heads.

"Extra! Extra!" they shouted. "Special edition! Ivy Bright vanishes! Get it while it's hot!" The boys spread out through the crowd, ragged brown sparrows among the ghost-gray businessmen and ladybird travelers, who all handed over their nickels and dimes to grab up that special edition: BRIGHTEST LITTLE STAR VANISHES FROM MGM STUDIOS! POLICE BAFFLED! EXTRA! READ ALL ABOUT IT!"

My stomach twisted up and the memory hit so hard and

sudden I was almost sick. Ivy Bright was gone. She'd been the most famous girl in the country, right after Shirley Temple. Of course the papers would have the story. But she wasn't gone where the police would ever find her. My hands shook, and my knees were getting in on the act too.

Jack, of course, saw the tight, sick look that scrunched up my face. "It'll be okay, Callie." He moved even closer, as if the newsboys' shouts were a storm wind he could shield me from.

"Yeah. Yeah, sure." I didn't believe him. Just the same, I knew I had to pull my head out of those bad memories. But it was slow going, and I was getting stuck on dumb little details. "How come they're saying she's vanished? They've got to know . . ." That she was dead. That she was shot. I remembered the weight of the pistol in my hand, the noise and the kick in my arm and my shoulder as it fired.

Jack cut me off before my babble could really get going. "There's a whole department at the movie studio with the job of putting out the news the way they want it. Probably saying she disappeared off the back lot is better than saying how she was found up at the Hearst mansion. He wouldn't want the police sniffing around there. Especially with . . . everything." Mr. Hearst had made some kind of deal with the Seelie king. I didn't understand it, but I did know that the king sometimes lived in Mr. Hearst's house. Sometimes, the king lived under his skin.

"Look, let's sit down." Jack was pointing at the nearest bench.

I nodded. I told myself I couldn't worry about what the papers were saying, or what anybody thought happened. There were more than enough things to worry about right here at hand. This didn't help a whole lot, but it got my head far enough back in the present that I could help Mama ease Papa onto the bench. After a couple of hard breaths, he managed to sit himself up straight. He patted Mama's hand and gave her a smile as he remembered to adjust his fedora to hide his eyes. Mama smiled back, tired and glad, her deep blue eyes bright despite their bags and dark rings. I looked around quick to see if anyone was taking special notice of our mixed bag of a family, but nobody did, not that I could see anyhow. An ache made up of equal parts hope and worry took up residence low in my throat.

"Callie, honey," said Mama. "I'm going to use the powder room. You wait here."

"No, Mama, I'll come with you." There was no way I was letting her out of my sight, not with who-knew-what-kind of fairies out there looking for us. Besides, it'd get me away from all the shouting newsies for at least a couple minutes. "Jack can stay with Papa."

Mama looked like she wanted to protest, but instead, she pulled her manners and deportment over her and marched into the crowd. I followed, trying not to listen to the newsboys, or see the headlines on the papers people were holding up in front of their faces. I didn't have much luck, but I did try.

The powder room was as full as any other part of the

station, with women going in and out of the stalls or standing in front of the sinks to wash their hands and fix their lipstick. Mama shut herself into a stall while I waited for a turn at the sink. When I got there, I filled my cupped hands with cold water, slapped my face down into it, and stayed there until I needed to breathe again. When I finally lifted my face, the mirror showed my reflection with water running down my hollow cheeks where my face had pulled itself tight around my bones.

It'll be all right, I told my reflection. *Just gotta give it time. Just gotta hold it together until we get to New York.*

But why was what happened to Ivy coming back now? I tried to tell myself it was just the news. It was nothing personal, like my bad luck hard at work again. But I didn't believe that. I felt wrong, like there were eyes watching me out of the dark. I grit my teeth and shook the water off my hands, looking for a towel.

Calliope.

Movement in the mirror caught my eye and I whipped myself back around.

Hear me, Calliope. You must hear me.

Under the reflection of that marble room with the women putting on their red lipstick and adjusting their hats, there was another reflection. It was a room all decked out in jewels and silks, rich as a pirate's cave. But there was something wrong with it, like it had been broken and put back together badly. I squinted. Then I stared, because in the middle of that shattered room, there was a ghost. A woman, as broken as the room around her. She looked as if she was made of obsidian and diamonds, and I knew her.

Granddaughter, you must hear me.

The shattered image of my grandmother, the queen of the Midnight Throne, crouched in the middle of that broken room. Why hadn't I thought about this? If we could see in to them through the reflections, they could see out to us. She'd done it before.

Grandmother stretched out her hand, trying to reach right through the glass. I jumped back.

Callie! Her voice rang in my head. *Granddaughter, run! Your father . . . Help us. . . .* The reflection shuddered and it twisted. *He's here. He's come back.*

"Mama!" I shouted. The women at the sinks turned to stare, but I didn't bother about them.

Mama came out of the stall, questions plain on her face. I didn't bother about those either. I grabbed her hand and dragged her out of there. "They found us."

7

Hellhound on My Trail

Mama caught my elbow up in hers, linking us tight together as we burst out of the powder room. Despite her high-heeled shoes, she broke into a run, and after a couple hobbling steps, I caught her stride. We barged through that train-station crowd, right up to the bench where Jack and Papa were sitting. Jack was white as a ghost, but Papa was on his feet, filled with a desperate energy. It was all but crackling out of the ends of his fingers.

"Something's happening," said Papa to me. "Something's gone wrong."

I nodded and Jack cussed hard. "I'll go find out what platform the train's leaving from." He put on his hardened hobo-kid face as fast as Mama pulled on her manners and shouldered his way toward the ticket windows.

"Where are you?" I moved close to my parents, trying to

see in every direction at once. "Come on, I know you're here."

But it seemed like everybody was holding a paper in front of them. Either that or they had their hats pulled down. I couldn't get a good look at anybody, and I couldn't feel anything clearly because I was buried by my own fear.

"Uh-oh," breathed Papa. I whipped around and saw what he was looking at. Jack had made it up to a ticket window. He was waving his hands at a man in a blue coat and black cap. In response, the man shook his head.

I slid my elbow out of Mama's grip and pushed her toward Papa. I didn't wait to hear what either of them had to say about it. I just ducked into the stream of people and threaded my way toward Jack.

"Sorry, sonny, but there's nothing I can do." The uniformed man was handing our tickets to Jack when I got there. He was a white man with a blotchy red face and a brass badge that read PAULSON.

"Is something wrong?" I asked, trying to sound all worried and little-girlish. It didn't take much pretending.

"Oh, there you are, sis." Jack's voice strained at the edges, and he rubbed the corner of one eye. My mouth went dry. "Seems there's a misunderstanding about the tickets."

Mr. Paulson pushed his cap back and sighed. I eased my magic open another notch. Enchantment lay like a bandage over the ticket man's eyes. Jack met my gaze and nodded. He saw it too.

"Like I was telling this young man, these ain't for the

Limited." Mr. Paulson handed Jack the tickets, long strips of paper that we'd already had punched four or five different times as we crossed the state lines. His wrinkly forehead was shiny with sweat and I could feel him wishing for a drink from the bottle back in his desk. "These are for the Union Pacific. I'm sorry, sonny, you're a"—he consulted his pocket watch—"half hour late on this."

Anger can clear your brain faster than any other feeling. Someone didn't want us to make that train. Someone wanted to trap us here. I yanked the tickets out of Mr. Paulson's hands.

"Oh, Jack! Silly! You've got the wrong ones!" I dug into my handbag. Inside myself, I pictured that bandage lifting off Mr. Paulson's eyes. I thought hard toward him that the sooner he saw what I needed him to see, the sooner he'd get that drink he wanted. Then I handed him back those same tickets he'd gotten from Jack.

Mr. Paulson looked at them again, but this time he was all smiles. "Ah, there now. These are the Limited tickets. Trust a little lady to have it all organized." He beamed at me. "Platform twenty-six, but you'd better hurry now. Train's leaving in"—he looked at his watch again—"twenty minutes."

"Thank you!" I grabbed Jack's arm. "Let's go."

Jack made a beeline through the crush toward the benches, with me all but pushing him from behind. I wanted to hurry. Heck, I wanted to break the record on the forty-yard dash, but a new train must have just got in or something, because all of a sudden that huge hall was overflowing with people. Our "excuse me's" tumbled over each other as we tried to find a way between the men in their summer suits, the ladies in their skirts and hats, and all the little kids being dragged this way and that by impatient parents. Their voices filled my head and their feelings pulled at my concentration.

A sharp bark cut through the crowd's noise, and the backs and shoulders in front of me shifted and parted. A thin, old woman wearing a white suit and a diamond pin in her hat staggered forward, struggling to keep hold of the red leashes for six—maybe even eight—poodles, all white, all different sizes from a fluffy toy to one about as big as a woolly sheep. With my magic open, my gaze dragged itself toward them and warning bells sounded loud inside me. That lady with her poodles was the fairy kind, and those dogs were pulling her straight for my parents.

I didn't really think about what to do next. I let go of Jack and ducked straight into the path of that mess of curly-backed dogs. They pulled up short, yipping and barking. The biggest of them jumped up, straining against its rhinestone-studded collar with its heavy paws waving in the air. One claw caught on the corner of my sash and tore a long strip down the center.

"Oh, Mimi, no!" The old woman threw up her hands in astonishment, and, incidentally, dropped all the leashes. All Mimi's curly-backed kin decided she had the right idea. They surrounded me, jumping up, jostling, and pawing, and all barking at the top of their poodle lungs. They smelled like old meat and every last one of them had yellow eyes with pupils shaped like black diamonds.

"Oh, dear! Oh, dear!" The old lady flapped her gloved hands. "You bad, bad dogs!"

I grabbed the heavy, furry paws leaning against my chest and shoved them down. The world had gone strangely silent around me. The old lady was working her magic, hiding me and those filthy, stinking poodles from the regular people. But Jack could see us, and Papa. And so, it turned out, could Mama. Because the next thing I knew, Mama was wading in behind me. She didn't have a saw this time, but she was right there just the same, beating on the backs of those mangy poodles with nothing but her handbag.

"Get back! Get back! Get off!" Mama seized the nearest dog's collar and hauled with all the strength in her country woman's arms. The nearest dog turned and snapped at her hems, and Mama swatted it across the drooly muzzle with her purse. Amazement and a strange sense of pride swelled in me. The dog actually looked affronted, but not as affronted as the Seelie woman.

"You dare!" The old woman lifted her face, and showed us all how her eyes were as yellow as her dogs'. "My king is coming for you! I've already sent him word. He will hollow out your soul, and leave your husk to feed to my darlings."

"Will he?" interrupted a low voice. Papa had moved to stand beside Mama. He was sweating with the effort it took to stay upright, but his voice was steady and hard as stone. "Will he indeed?"

The old woman cringed like she was a dog herself as the force of Papa's presence and magic rolled over her. Clearly, he'd gotten a lot of his strength back. But not quite enough.

"Fetch!" the woman shouted. All the dogs howled. Their red leashes lashed out like whips to wrap around Papa's arms. He shouted again and I felt his magic, but there wasn't any focus to it. The old woman threw back her head and howled as her dogs dragged my father down. I screamed and tried to dodge forward, but Mimi, the lead poodle, got in my way. While I gaped at her, she swelled up until she was the size of a bear and her teeth grew as long as my pointer finger. Her drool swelled up too and fell in great splashy blotches all over that marble floor.

"Jack!" I shouted.

"I wish you were gone!" Jack shouted back. "Wish you were all in the pound!"

He meant it too. It was a good, hard wish, easy to grab hold of. But Mimi leapt forward, jaws open wide enough to take my head off, and all I could think about was getting out of the way. She landed and skittered on the marble, and turned, and lunged at me again. I dodged sideways, banging up against Jack.

"Get them out of here!" I shoved him toward my parents to emphasize the point. Mama was grabbing up the leashes that tangled Papa, and together they were struggling and shouting for help that wasn't going to come.

"Hey, you!" I shouted to Mimi and her pack. "Come on! Come and get it!"

Mimi barked something that might have been a command, and two of the other poodles unwound their leashes from Papa. Together, they plunged toward me.

I ran. The magic bubble of silence and invisibility shattered and voices rolled back down like thunder. People shouted, cursed, and screamed as I ducked and shoved my way between them with those evil, diamond-eyed poodles right behind me. Jack hollered something, but I didn't dare look back. The dogs moved like snakes and howled like banshees, and people were scrambling to get out of their way, and mine. But those dogs were small enough to dodge the crowd even faster than I could, ducking between legs and leaping over luggage carts. Even Mimi had shrunk again so she could slide through the crowd like a hot knife through butter. I couldn't get away. Teeth caught my skirt, and I lunged forward, tearing cloth and kicking hard at the little critter that tried to take a chunk out of my ankle.

But there was one person—a kid with a battered cap and patched dungarees—who wasn't trying to get out of my way. This kid waved his arm at me. I tried to ignore him, but he ducked forward and grabbed me. In fact, he about yanked me off my feet. The poodles hurtled past and by the time they noticed I wasn't up front anymore, they were slipping and skidding on the marble, trying to turn around. A police whistle cut the air, and a man in a blue uniform coat came charging up from somewhere, night stick out. The boy who'd grabbed me took off in the opposite direction and I ran with him toward the train platforms.

Out of the way! I tried to form the thought into a wish and drive it in front of us. I charged under the archway that separated the great hall from the train platforms. *Out of the way!* The crowd opened out a little, which was the idea, but it turned out not to be a very good one, because it meant the dogs were able to crowd closer to each other, and us.

"Climb!" the boy hollered. He jumped out of my field of vision. I stared all around me like a fool until I saw him clinging to one of the iron pillars that held up the roof.

"Climb, you idiot!" The boy caught hold of my wrist and yanked me toward him. I grabbed the pillar more in self-defense than because I knew what I was doing.

I climbed. We didn't have a lot of trees in Kansas, but I'd shinnied up plenty of barn poles. The iron pillar with its big rivets was practically a ladder by comparison. Fast as I was, though, the boy ahead of me was loads faster. He swarmed up the pillar, all the way to the girders that crisscrossed the space under the shed's glass-paneled roof.

Below us, Mimi barked and whined in frustration. I scrabbled for my magic. The iron that was keeping her back from us was blocking my powers. I could barely even feel the dogs. I had to get them to come closer. All of them.

I made myself focus on Mimi. She was hungry, starved. If she got me she'd be fed, she'd be full, and she'd be a good dog. "Get in here, girl. You can risk it. You're strong. Big dog, good dog, good girl, Mimi. I'm right here. Everything you want is right here."

It was enough. Mimi pulled back and bayed. Like, well,

like magic, the others were there, the big ones and the little ones. Their fangs flashed as they barked and growled. They stood on their hind legs, clawing at the beam, even though they were yipping in pain at the same time. I almost felt sorry for them. Almost.

Gone. I shaped the wish with every ounce of mad in me and shoved it straight down. *Gone to the pound. Gone. Gone!*

The dogs flickered. They howled, and were back solid and strong. The boy lashed out with some cusses I bet Jack didn't even know and wound his long fingers around my arm. I felt his magic winding around mine too. I didn't stop to wonder about it. I just reached out and grabbed hold of it. I felt my papa fighting away in the distance, and I took that too. I felt Jack wishing he knew where I was. I felt the driving winds of emotion in the crowd of travelers and railroad crew, and the sharp hunger and greed of the fairy hounds, and I hauled on as much of it as I could, despite the iron, and despite my fear. And I wished again.

The dogs flickered, and they faded and they were gone.

My arms and my mind both went limp. I would have fallen if the boy hadn't caught me. I stared at him, trying to remember what I was doing up here and what he was doing with me.

He had a sharp face—sharp nose, sharp chin, sharp grin, and pointy little ears. His body managed to be snaky and plump at the same time, but his arms and legs were too long and skinny for the rest of him. His hair was long, dark, and greasy. So were his fingers, where they curled all the way around my upper arm. So were his toes, which I could see because he wasn't wearing any shoes on his filthy feet. His dungarees were made of dozens of patches of colored cloth. Instead of a belt, he had a rope tied around his waist. A burlap bag dangled at his hip.

He giggled. "Engine, engine number nine . . ."

Fear started up again. This boy wasn't just magic, he was completely off his rocker.

"Going down Chicago line . . ." The boy laughed as he pulled that bag off his rope belt.

I tried to scoot away from him on that girder. My tongue had gone all thick in my mouth, but I got it moving anyway. "Who're you?"

The boy shoved his battered cap back from his sloping brow and looked up at me with a pair of glittery black eyes. "And if the train should jump the track, Callie LeRoux, get in the sack."

And I did.

8

Where'd You Come From?

It may be that sometime I'll have a more uncomfortable ride, but it ain't happened yet. My knees were jammed up against my mouth and my arms were all tangled. No matter how I pushed and twisted against the prickly burlap, I couldn't get a decent grip on anything. There was some hard stuff in there too. It banged against me and dug its corners into my sides. It was pitch-black as well, and getting hotter and stuffier by the second.

I made myself take a deep, dusty, burlapy breath. And another. I wasn't hurting all that much, I told myself. I had all my limbs and the other important bits as near as I could tell. I had my magic. I could feel it simmering under my anger. If somebody thought they could steal me like a broody hen out of the coop, they had another think coming.

I reached out with my magic. The first thing I understood was that there was a whole lot in here besides me.

Anything you might pick out of a city's leavings, in fact: cooing pigeons, broken axles, and gears. There was something that could have been a shovel, along with old bottles and rags. Something squeaked and I decided I didn't need to do a whole inventory just now. I could look past it all to where the shifting softness of the magic waited underneath all us flotsam. Cramped, uncomfortable, and mad as a hornet I might be, but I could still run my magic along that layer, and find the one place that was firm and had edges. I could shape the key of my power to turn, and to open it up.

I didn't forget what happened last time, but I did tell myself there couldn't possibly be a repeat. That had been in Seelie territory. This boy wasn't a Seelie. His eyes had been beady and nasty, but they were human, or nearly so. My bet was he was another one like Edison and Stripling, the ones Papa called the Undone. That he might be working for one of the courts like Stripling had been was something I'd deal with when I had to. I grit teeth and nerve, and reached my little finger through my tiny new gate.

It grabbed hold of me instantly, like tar, like teeth.

Here!

Panic bubbled up, seeping around thought and sense. I snatched my finger back, tearing my nail in a bright flash of pain. My magic worked faster than I could think and slapped that little gate shut, and I huddled in my burlap jail, trying to catch my breath.

I should have known. I should have known from the

first. But there was so much going on I hadn't wanted to put it together. Who would know when I was working my gates but the one who'd taught me how to open them? The one who was still lurking in the back of my nightmares. Uncle Shake was watching me. He was waiting for me to use the one power that made me stronger than the ordinary Unseelies.

I clutched my hand to my chest, pulled my elbows and knees in close, and tried to think. And tried again. It wasn't fair. The bad just kept coming. It came from every direction and it didn't stop, and now it was piling on top of itself. The Seelie king wanted me alive and my uncle wanted me dead and this kid and his sack wanted . . . I didn't even know what.

"Gonna have to get in line, whatever it is," I muttered, and I wasn't sure I was laughing or crying.

Callie? The voice filtered through my mind, soft and scratchy, like a radio that wasn't quite tuned to the right station. Another wave of panic rolled over me before I realized this time it wasn't my uncle's voice.

Papa? I thought back.

Where are you, Callie? I can barely hear you.

I stirred against the burlap and the bumping trash, trying to sit up straighter even though I knew it was foolish. *Are you okay?*

Yes, and your mother.

Relief turned my insides wobbly. *What about Jack?*

He said he knew where he could get us a car. I bet he did, and I hoped my parents were both sensible enough not to ask for the details. The list of skills Jack had picked up on the road included hot-wiring engines. I also hoped Papa couldn't hear my thoughts well enough to hear that part.

If Papa did hear, he didn't care. *Where are you, Callie?*

It took a minute before I could think of any kind of way to answer him, and even then it wasn't much. *I'm caught. There was this boy—he's magic, or partway magic, and he's got me in some kind of bag.*

There were no words in my head for a long moment. Instead, there was a wash of anger, bright and dangerous. *Can you open a gate?*

I tried. Papa, Uncle Shake's on the other side. He's . . .

A beam of daylight slammed against my eyes and I screwed them shut with a shout.

"Keep quiet down there, youz!" came the boy's voice from overhead.

And just like that, Papa was gone. I was alone in the dark with the rest of the trash. I curled in tighter and clutched my hurt hand to my belly. All I could think was that boy, whoever he was, better hope he could run good and fast when I got out of here.

I don't know how long that rough, itchy, angry ride lasted, but eventually the bumping stopped, and something hard hit me in the bottom and back, like I'd been dropped. I cussed and after a bit managed to get up onto my knees. I heard traffic noises, roaring close by. But they echoed strangely, almost like we were back indoors. The sack around me lurched and I toppled onto my side and squeaked. I couldn't help it. The bag and I were being dragged along. I came up against something pointed and cussed again. I was going to be a mass of bruises when I got out of here. Something else I'd be taking up with this beady-eyed boy. I could hear voices out there somewhere. The noise of my own angry breathing was loud in my ears and it muffled their words. I held my breath and swallowed, and did it again, until I quieted down, and strained my ears to listen.

"Well, well. Dan Ryan," said a voice that rushed and creaked at the same time. "You actually came back. Will wonders never cease?"

I shuffled forward on my knees, bringing my face up to the closest fold in the burlap I could find. I knotted my fingers in the material to try to find someplace I could poke or tear to make a hole to see.

"Course I came back, Cedar," sneered the beady-eyed boy, who I guessed was Dan Ryan. "What'd you think I was gonna do? Skip town?"

"How should I know?" That Cedar was out of my sight, but they had rushing, whispery voices and their s's were twice as long as normal. "You wass gone long enough."

"Never mind that." Whoever was talking now sounded like he had a mouthful of broken china. "What happened? Did you see her?"

"See her? Claremont, I did better 'n *see*."

I tried to brace myself. It was no good. The burlap wrappings flew apart. Dim light and exhaust-filled wind engulfed me, and I tumbled tail over teacup onto cement. My head spun hard, and when I could see again, I wanted to crawl back into that pitch-black sack.

The people that surrounded me were all magic; they had to be. But they couldn't be fairies. Fairies didn't ever show you their real faces unless they had to, and any face they did show you was as beautiful as it was fake. The half-dozen faces that looked down on me as I blinked and tried to push myself to my knees were real. I could see their eyes clearly, and no matter what the shape of the face, no matter what their bodies seemed to be made of, those eyes were human shapes and shades. But the people were all . . . awkward. Not ugly, exactly, but they all looked like they'd been meant to be something else. One person looked like someone had tried to build a kid out of broken bottle shards. That one might have been Claremont. Another was coal black and all hard angles like the girder I'd climbed with Dan Ryan to get away from the Seelie dogs. Another was thin and tall and branching, like a spindly city tree that had been wrapped in checked gingham. It made me think of the prison tree back in Los Angeles and my skin curdled tight around my bones.

Edison had said he'd put the word out. He'd said the others of his kind would hear it, and if these were his kind and they had heard, they'd heard I'd helped kill one of their own.

Goose bumps stood up good and strong all up and down my arms. I got to my feet, because I couldn't think of anything else to do. I couldn't make any more sense out of the place we were than I could out of the people surrounding me. It was a cavern of cement—cement ceiling, cement pillars with a curving cement wall close at their backs. There was a rumbling overhead that made me think we must be under a bridge, but there was a road alongside as well. Trucks rattled past in both directions, belching out smoke and the daylight that looked too far away, so I guessed it was some kind of tunnel. An idea about running for the street to flag down a truck came and went. They were moving too fast, and I had no idea what kind of glamour I was under here. So instead, I faced my kidnappers. Being stared at by that whole crowd of half-finished magic folks was scaring the daylights out of me, but I didn't intend to let them see that. Especially because while I turned around to get a good look at them, they were shrinking back, clanking, whispering, and whistling in surprise.

The boy who brought me here, Dan Ryan, did not shrink back with the rest of his pals. He grinned all over his too-long face and his little piggy eyes glittered. I leveled my best glower at him. *You and me ain't done,* I tried to tell him. If he understood, or cared, he gave no sign. That was okay. He'd learn to care later.

"I'm gonna make a guess you know who I am," I said, planting my hands on my hips. "Now, who in the heck are you all?"

They ignored me.

"You brought her here?" shrieked the bottle-shard girl I figured was Claremont. "Have you gone screwy? You'll have the courts down on us in no time!"

"That's the idea." Dan Ryan grinned all over his ratty face. "The courts are both offering bounties on her. Now's our chance to finally cut a deal!"

"You can't be serious!" The tree man shook with anger, or with fear. "We can't deal with the courts!"

Dan Ryan cocked his head at the tree. Strings of greasy, dark hair slanted across his sloped-back forehead. "Can't we, Cedar? Not even to get our own back?"

"You people got something you want from me, you talk to me!" I shouted.

"You shut up," snapped the tree called Cedar. The words hit me so hard I knew there had to be magic behind them. "Ain't nobody talking to you."

"How come you're all standing around like those babies on the council?" said Dan Ryan to the others. "What'd we form up for anyway? We said we was gonna do a raid—well, now we don't have to. We can just do a deal."

The little gang was murmuring in that way that lets you know people are thinking about what they just heard. Maybe even agreeing with it. Goose bumps puckered the skin over my spine and I started looking around for a way out. Nothing good was showing itself. I was hemmed in between a cement wall and a stream of rushing, rattling traffic, and these magic people who thought I could be auctioned off like a prize pony.

"We got together to *plan,* you dope!" The girder boy's voice creaked sharp and painful enough to make me wince. "So we could figure out what . . ."

But Dan Ryan wasn't having any of it. "We don't need to plan no more neither! That's what they do. Plan, plan, plan. Talk, talk, talk! They don't *do* nothin'! Ain't that what we all said?" Nobody answered him. "Well, I done it! We got the Bad Luck Girl now! The courts will give anything to get their pretty, grubby hands on her! We can drive a bargain that'll make 'em squeal and they'll never even think of touching a Halfer again!"

Halfers. That was the word Edison had used. Not *Undone,* as Papa had called them. *Halfers* made them sound like they were half fairy, like Ivy Bright was, and Shimmy, and me. But the three of us were half human and they were . . . they were half everything but. Half glass, half tree, or ragbag, or railroad bridge. Half anything and everything and half magic all shook together and coming up alive.

"What'd you pay?" whispered someone. The voice was light and high, so something in my head labeled the owner as a girl.

"What?" snapped Dan Ryan. His greasy hair on his head bristled like he was raising his hackles. The Halfers shifted, and one of them stepped forward. "She" was rumpled and wobbly, and looked like she was made out of paper strips, newspaper scraps, pieces of brown bags, and white butcher paper all bundled up together. She even rattled like paper as she moved forward.

"Touhy!" Dan Ryan's whole long face wrinkled up as if he smelled something bad and he glowered at the rest of the Halfers. "Which of you clowns told her about this?"

"Nobody told me," answered paper Touhy before any of the others were done glancing around. "I followed you. It wasn't that hard. The whole 'ville's known for weeks you're up to something, Dan Ryan."

"Yeah? So? What're you gonna do about it?"

While I stared, the crumpled surface of Touhy's skin shifted and rattled. Edges and patches folded together and opened back up again. Now, instead of just a crazy paper quilt around her eyes, there was a newspaper photo of a plump-cheeked girl, and that girl was talking.

"Word down the line was the Bad Luck Girl was traveling with her family. You must have stole her from them." Touhy folded and unfolded herself again, and now she had a black mask over her big green eyes. "What did you leave in return?"

I opened my mouth and shut it again. I wanted to say I wasn't for sale, but I got the feeling this paper girl—Touhy— might be trying to help, so maybe it was better to keep quiet. If nothing else, she was buying me time. Jack and my folks were on the way. I knew that down in my bones. I had to hang on until they got there, or until I could find my own fast exit.

"If you stole her without making payment, you can't bargain her to the courts." Another three trucks barreled past practically bumper to bumper on the roadway. The harsh breeze doubled Touhy over, but she snapped back up straight. "If the courts find out you're bartering stolen goods, they'll use it as an excuse to cheat any deal you make."

"*If* they find out." Dan Ryan snarled at Touhy and swiped the air with hooked fingers. If that boy was half anything, it was half rat, and I suddenly wanted to find me the world's biggest tomcat. "Who's gonna tell 'em, huh, Touhy?"

"You big dope!" Touhy twisted herself toward the others. She was thin as paper too. From this angle I could barely see her. "Her father is high court! You think he'd wait to squeal on the likes of us? You have to pay for what you take, or it's theft, and the rules can be broken!"

"Well, I didn't take her," announced Dan Ryan. "She followed me!"

"Is this true?" The girder boy creaked hard as he turned suspicious brown eyes toward me.

I licked my lips, trying to pull together the exact right words. Words were important to fairies, even half fairies. Dan Ryan, with his twitchy snout and raised hackles, was waiting for one little mistake. If I didn't get this exactly right, he'd jump all over me and he might just bring the rest of his gang along. "I followed him to get away from the dogs that were chasing me. But I didn't volunteer to get into his sack, and I sure didn't want to leave my family." *Or Jack,* I added silently.

"There!" Touhy's soft voice crackled angrily. "She *was* stolen. If Dan Ryan can't pay a fair price for taking her, he's got to give her back!"

"That's if she belongs to the people she was traveling with." Claremont tapped her glass chin with her glass finger, making a bright clinking noise. "If the Bad Luck Girl belongs to anyone, it's to the Unseelie court, and they owe us for all they've taken." She smiled, showing rows of teeth like a broken rainbow. "We can claim payment."

A snide chuckle drifted up from the gang and my anger reared back.

"I don't belong to the Unseelies!"

"Whaddaya mean?" said Dan Ryan. "You're the heir to the Midnight Throne!"

"That doesn't mean I belong to them. That means *they* belong to *me.*"

This earned me a long, startled laugh. Paper Touhy nodded once. She didn't want to, but she approved. Dan Ryan, however, most definitely did not, but I wasn't going to give him a chance to get any more digs in.

"You got no right to rule anything about me," I told them all. "You got no right to do anything but let me go."

"Why should we?" The tree, Cedar, swayed forward, bending its branches down, like it meant to claw at me. I hate to admit it, but I took a half step back. "You already killed one of us. What's to stop you going after the rest?"

So Edison hadn't been exaggerating. Word had gone out, and it had gotten here first. "That was an accident," I croaked, trying to pull back my eyes, which were about ready to pop out of my head. "I didn't know. . . ."

"You high court hotshots never do," Dan Ryan sneered.

The Halfers snickered and elbowed one another. "You think you can do whatever you want to us. The Undone, you say. We don't count for nothin' to you."

"I just wanted to help," I tried. "If I'd known the tree was . . ."

"Stripling." Cedar's mouth was a ragged hole in the tree bark and its eyes were barely knotholes. If it stood still, I wouldn't have seen anything but the tree. I could hardly believe I was holding a conversation with it. I almost wanted to laugh, but I saw its hooked branches and how it loomed over me. I thought about that other tree and its prison shacks and that urge to laugh died away. "Her name was Stripling. You will show some respect."

"Stripling," I agreed. "If I'd known Stripling was in trouble too, I would have done what I could." The problem was, I had known. And I hadn't done anything like enough.

"Too late for that." Cedar stretched its arms, its branches, toward me. I smelled damp, rotting wood over the exhaust that filled the tunnel. "You owe us for the death of one of our own, and we mean to collect."

"Stripling wasn't part of our 'ville," said Touhy firmly. "We can't claim the blood price."

I thought for a second about edging toward Touhy, but she looked at me with murder in her bright green eyes, and I stayed put. She might be defending me, but she was not interested in being friends.

"What is the matter with you, Touhy?" roared Dan Ryan. "The courts and their mob are raiding every camp they can find. We can't wait anymore! We've got something to bargain with, and we need to use it!"

"Touhy's right," said girder boy. He unfolded himself until he was almost as tall as Cedar. "If Bad Luck was taken from her family, the act needs to be paid for. That's the law."

"She's mine!" shouted Dan Ryan. "I found her, and if you're all too yellow to do what we gotta, I'll keep her!" He shook open his burlap sack and I grabbed at my magic. There was no way I was going back in there.

The Halfers screamed and for one wild second I wondered if I was just that scary before I heard an engine gunning and the squeal of tires.

"Leave her alone!" thundered a new voice.

A black Ford sedan swerved off the road with Papa on the running board on one side and Mama hanging out the window on the other and Jack hunched behind the wheel.

I'd been found.

9

If You See Me Comin'

Jack swerved that Ford sedan out from between the trucks, over the low curb, and straight through the heart of the gang. Halfers jumped and scrambled every which way and Jack slammed on the brakes so the car spun out in a mad squeal of tires one bare inch away from the wall. Dan Ryan shrieked high and sharp, squealing out the word of his nonsense chant of a spell like an angry pig. Or an angry rat.

". . . train should jump the track, Callie LeRoux, get in the sack!" His magic swung at me, with the full force of his anger behind it. But this time I was ready.

"You first, Dan Ryan!" I grabbed that order up, twisted it right around, and threw it back at him.

Dan Ryan hollered, and he was gone. The burlap bag was on the ground, with something kicking around inside it. Claremont's scream was like a whole brewery's worth of bottles falling downstairs, and she lunged for me. Girder boy yanked what could have been a plumber's wrench out of his pocket and was raising it up to take a swing at my head. I snatched the burlap sack with all my strength, swung it around, and let it fly. Girder screeched and ducked.

Papa jumped off the running board and spread his arms wide.

"Back off!"

Papa's magic hit the Halfers like a storm wind, slamming them all against the tunnel wall, except Girder. He was struggling to get the sack open. I took off running. Mama had the sedan's door open. I scrambled in over her lap and plopped down in the space between her and Jack. Jack didn't even wait for her to get the door shut. He just gunned the engine and slammed the gears into reverse. Papa charged alongside and jumped onto the running board, just as the car leapt backward. Jack shoved the pedals down, crashed the gears together, and we were headed forward, jouncing down over the curb and into the street. Horns blared and truckers shouted and Jack ignored them all. He just kept his foot pressed hard on the accelerator. The sedan shot out of the tunnel and up a ramp into daylight.

"What were those things?" cried Mama as she fought to get the door closed.

"Nothing!" shouted Papa from his perch on the running board. "Detritus. Callie, did they hurt you?"

"No, I'm fine. But, Papa, they said they were—"

"Jack!" Papa cut me off. "Where are we going?"

"Away from them!" Jack wrenched the wheel around.

The sedan took the corner hard. I slammed against Mama, and the only reason Papa stayed on that running board was a burst of magic. The car dropped down again and bounced. Mama grabbed my shoulders with one hand and the door handle with the other and I didn't even try to pull away.

Jack was driving us straight into traffic. Cars and vans and pedestrians swerved and dodged. A police whistle shrilled as we went past, and I swear I heard a cheer. Jack wrenched the wheel around again. The sedan plunged into an alleyway. He gunned it hard to cut across the path of a big black van. Mama screamed and I ducked reflexively, and then we were through, bumping down into another street. Jack turned right and geared down. All at once, we were rolling gently along like the calmest Sunday driver you ever met.

A streetlight turned red, and Jack stopped.

"Do you want to get in, Mr. LeRoux?" he asked.

"Yeah," breathed Papa. I noticed his knuckles had turned white where he hung on to the door. "I think I'd better."

It took him long enough to climb into the sedan's back-seat that the traffic behind us was starting to honk. Jack ignored them until Papa tapped the seat to say he was ready, and then Jack drove on at the same stately pace.

"Where do we go now?" asked Mama. "The train left hours ago."

"And the station's watched," added Papa. He was looking at his palms. They were blistered. My own hands tightened up in sympathy.

"This is Chicago." Jack shrugged. "We can get a hotel someplace. You can protect us, can't you, Mr. LeRoux? Callie said you put a protection on the Imperial, back in Kansas."

"It's not that easy. I can set a protection around a place, yes, but it's got to be a home, not just a hotel."

"What? Why?"

"Because otherwise it won't work, that's why!" Papa shouted, and I jumped. "This blasted and bedamned world of yours! It's got boundaries, it's got *time*. It plays Cain with what magic can do! It—"

"Daniel!" said Mama coldly and Papa stopped. I felt him trying to wrestle his temper back into place. "We're going to need *somewhere* to stay while we work out what to do next," Mama went on. "Have we got any *useful* ideas?"

"Jack?" I said softly. I knew what had to happen. I also knew how bad Jack was trying to come up with a different answer. I was having a hard time believing any place could be safe again. We had the courts at war on the other side of the gates, and the Halfers (the Undone, whoever they were) after us on this side. But we had to at least try to get out of sight. "Jack, we're in a stolen car and you've only got"—I tapped the gauge—"half a tank of gas, and no real money. And those guys, the Halfers, they saw this car. We try to get out of the city like this, they'll be after us in a heartbeat."

Jack stopped at another streetlight. He clenched the steering wheel. I watched his face. He was struggling with something at least as tough as Papa's sudden burst of temper or my fear of being caught again. When the light changed, he eased us forward. His eyes flickered to the street signs, to the street in front of us, and back again. Not once did he look over at me. "All right. I guess I'm gonna have to take you home."

Chicago's a pretty flat place. I don't quite know why it seemed like we were going down as we drove, and down deep at that. At first, we made our way between skyscrapers and stores with signs like Walgreens, O'Malley's Gentleman's Tailoring, and Paddy's Saloon. White men and women in stout but stylish clothes walked the streets. Slowly, the buildings got lower and older and crowded closer together. The signs changed to things like Polanski's Quality Butchers, Petrovski's Fresh Fish, and Gutman's Pawnbrokers. The women weren't so stylish here. They wore dark skirts with their hair tied up in colored scarfs. Another few blocks and I couldn't read the signs at all because they were written in swoopy, squared-off script. The men wore black coats and black hats with round crowns here, and most of the women were in black dresses and had dark wigs on their heads. There weren't any street signs that I could see. But Jack, as usual, knew where he was going.

He turned up a narrow side street that was more mud than cobblestone. Raggedy kids in short pants who had been playing stickball scrambled out of the way, and then ganged up behind to chase after us and cheer, because we were in what was easily the fanciest car on that block. The buildings here were mostly wood: squared-off, three-story clapboard places with peaked roofs, dark windows, and faded curtains. They were crowded so close together you could have sat in your kitchen and still snatched a doughnut off the dining room table in the house next door. Smokestacks made a distant, forbidding fence for one side of the neighborhood. There was a smell too, and it was everywhere. I'd never been in a barnyard or outhouse that smelled as bad as that smudged-over, crowded-up, worn-down street.

The roadster splashed through a long set of potholes as Jack drove right up to the street's dead end. Beyond it was the kind of muddy, open space I'd hesitate to call a field. Heaps of ashes and clinker had been dumped there, making a set of gray and black dunes that stretched to the river. Crows and seagulls traded insults across the ash heaps. More raggedy kids climbed over the piles, calling to each other in raucous games of king of the hill. Jack parked, and I climbed out of the car, stunned. I'd known he came up poor, but I never imagined he came from someplace that made my dust-bowl home seem rich.

Jack wasn't looking at me. He was walking over to the last of the narrow buildings on the right-hand side of the street. The porch steps creaked as he climbed up to the front door. The screen door squeaked even louder when he pulled it open, and we all followed Jack inside.

The outside stench was replaced by smells of old fish and cabbage. A narrow staircase ran up along the left-hand wall. A dark and dingy hallway ran along the right. As we crowded inside, its one door opened so a hatchet-faced woman in a sack of a dress could peer out at us.

"Well, Jacob Hollander." Her words were thick and hard. "You've come home, have you? And brought some friends."

"Looks that way, Mrs. Burnstein," said Jack. He didn't look back at her either, just started climbing the stairs and we all followed. Papa touched his hat to the woman. She slammed the door shut.

Jack stopped at the second floor. There was another dark door, with a worn spot on the varnish that made the silhouette for the number seven. A radio on the other side blared hot jazz. There was a thing hanging on the threshold that looked like two little tubes tied together with blue thread. Jack looked at it and a muscle in his cheek jumped. He touched it, and my magic told me something sparked way down inside him. Then Jack shouldered the door open.

The room on the other side was a match for the hallway: narrow, dim, and dingy. Somebody'd tried to make it respectable once. There were lace curtains on the windows, but they were as worn as the carpet on the floor. There was a sort of sitting room with a sagging sofa and a pair of threadbare chairs drawn up to the radiator like it was a fireplace. A dusty upright piano stood in one corner. The blasting radio sat on top of it. A Murphy bed had been unfolded from the wall and it was covered with a mess of tangled sheets and newspapers. There was a tiny, dirty kitchen with a sink and a cookstove. A table and six mismatched chairs created the dining room. Two of those chairs were occupied by hard-eyed men who twisted around as Jack led us inside. One man jumped to his feet, his hand digging into the pocket of his corduroy jacket. Jack froze in place, and the man stared, and then he smiled.

"Well, well. Hello there, Jacob." The man was tall like Jack was, with Jack's kind of popped-out blue eyes and curly brown hair. But where Jack was skinny, this man was filled out thick with muscle and fat. He brought his empty hand out of his pocket and I saw how the knuckles were a mess of scars. He used that scarred hand to smack the other man on the arm and point at us. "Look, Simon! Jacob's home."

"Well, well. Who'd've thought," the second man said, without bothering to take the cigarette out of his wide mouth. He wore a blue work shirt and dungarees. The bridge of his nose had been mashed flat against his broad face and all in all, he looked like the world's biggest, whitest frog. His hair was starting to thin on top, and he had at least a day's worth of dark stubble on his soft, round chin. He had the Hollander blue eyes too, but his lids seemed to be half closed, making him look like he was sneaking a permanent peek out at the world.

"Hello, Ben," said Jack carefully to the thick-muscled man with the scarred hands. "Hello, Simon." The frog-faced man grinned at him, squinting his eyes down even farther. "Where's Ma?"

Ben's jacket rumpled as he shrugged his broad shoulders. "Dead." The word dropped cold and hard from him. He cracked his scarred knuckles as if for emphasis. "Pop too."

Jack froze like he'd been cornered, except for his Adam's apple, which kept bobbing up and down.

"When?" he croaked finally.

"Last year." Simon puffed hard on his cigarette. It wobbled between his lips and sent a shower of ash sprinkling down on the tabletop. "Doc said it was the diphtheria."

I moved closer beside Jack. Nothing could have stopped me. Mama and Papa closed up behind us, not saying anything, just being a wall at our backs. I wanted to say sorry to Jack. Something. Jack was just finding out his parents were dead and he shouldn't have to face it with nothing but silence. But I didn't want to say anything soft in front of these two.

"So." Ben dropped himself back down in his chair, one leg kicked out in front of him and his blunt, hard fingers brushing the battered tabletop. "What're you doing back here? And what's all this?" His popped-out eyes looked us over as sharp as his brother's half-closed eyes had.

"Friends of mine," answered Jack stonily. "We need a place to stay."

Simon finally took the cigarette out of his wide frog mouth. He fished a battered pack out of his shirt pocket with the other hand, shook a fresh cigarette out of it, lit the new one off the stub of the old one, and slotted that fresh cigarette into place between his lips. There was an old saucer on the table that did double duty as an ashtray, and he ground the other cigarette butt out thoroughly. It was only when he finished with that important business that he peeked up at us again. "Got any money?" he asked.

Ben cuffed Simon's arm again. "Now, Sy, is that any way to talk to your brother?"

"Brother. Right," wheezed Simon. His half-moon eyes narrowed down to slits. "He's such a brother he don't even bother to write his poor old mother to say where he's got to. He runs out on his family, until he needs a place to stay." He hawked and spat on the floor. Mama winced. "So, like I said, you got any money?"

Ben rolled his eyes to the ceiling. "See what I gotta put up with? Better answer him, Jacob."

Jack's eyes shifted sideways to me and Papa. I saw the anger and the shame, and I understood like I never had before why he'd run away. I'd thought it was the bootlegging, and how his sister died. But if these two were his brothers, what could his parents have been like?

Papa stepped up. He fixed his gaze on Ben and Simon and the fairy light behind his eyes flashed. He reached into his pocket and pulled out a wad of bills in a gold money clip. He peeled off a fifty and laid it down on the scarred and greasy table.

"Will that be enough, gentlemen?"

By then I'd seen a lot of nasty things, but nothing quite as nasty as the way Simon looked my father slowly up and slowly down again. It was only when he nodded that Ben's hairy, scarred hand closed over that fairy fifty-dollar bill and dragged it across the table to his pocket.

"You can stay in the back room." Ben jerked his chin toward a door at the rear of the flat. "No one is in residence there at this time."

"Thank you," said Papa evenly. "I'm sure that will be just fine."

The back room wasn't any better than the front. Its one bed had a rusty iron frame, a torn quilt, and a mattress that looked like it had been starved for stuffing since birth. The dresser had a broken leg. A crack ran straight across the middle of its speckled mirror and the bottom drawer was missing. There was an old, stained pot in the corner and a smell I really, truly did not want to think about.

But none of that was as bad as seeing the way Jack's face twisted up as he sat on the edge of that rusted bed. He pressed his elbows against his knees, and his face into his hands. I sat down next to him and wrapped my arm around his shoulders. Jack shuddered, and he shuddered again. He wasn't crying. He didn't dare, I was sure of it. If he started, those two mooks out front who happened to be his brothers would hear. A sudden picture flashed in front of my eyes, of Jack sitting in this room, shuddering just like this, just after his sister died, just before he decided to hit the road. I stared up at my parents. They stood shoulder to shoulder, their fingers twined together, and in Mama's blue human eyes and

Papa's bright fairy eyes I saw the same sympathy, the same wish to make things better. I saw they understood what Jack meant to me and I saw they were glad for it.

I bit my lip hard, because if I didn't, I would have bust out crying myself.

Eventually, Jack stopped shuddering. Even though his eyes had stayed dry, he wiped his face hard against his sleeves. I pulled away and kept my mouth shut. As hard as that was, the grateful glance he gave me made it worth it. He knew I understood, and I knew he was thanking me, and we needed nothing else right then.

"So." Jack took one more deep breath and squared his shoulders toward Papa. "We're home. Now how're we gonna get ourselves out of here?"

Papa pushed back the tattered curtain and eyed the clinker piles, the river, and the towering smokestacks like he was sizing them up for a fight. But when he faced us again, his manner was bright and brisk.

"First things first. I'm sure you are all as hungry as I am." He pulled out his money clip again. "Jack, if you'll oblige us by finding a delicatessen or diner and getting us something? You need to pay before full dark."

"Sure thing." Jack slid a bill in his pocket. Could he feel Papa was holding something back? I could, and I didn't like it. "I just need to go around the corner, and you don't need to worry . . . I mean . . ." He fumbled and nodded toward the door.

"We'll be fine," Mama said firmly, but I saw the "I hope" look on her face. Jack was in too much of a hurry to notice. He slammed out our door, and then the apartment's front door. The sound of his running footsteps vibrated through the walls as he barreled down the stairs.

"What was that about?" I asked Papa. "Why'd you want him out of the way?"

"That was about needing to set the protection for us." The light in Papa's eyes sparked. "Jack does not need to see how that involves his brothers. Callie, will you please come with me?"

Mama frowned at him. "Daniel, are you sure?"

"Callie needs to begin to understand her magic, Margaret. It's been left too long already." He paused. "I think it would be better if you stayed in here."

Mama hesitated, then nodded, and a strange rush of disappointment passed through me. I wanted her to argue, but I had no idea why. I knew how my magic worked, but not well. I wanted to learn more, and if anybody could teach me, it would be Papa. Why would I want Mama to get up in the way of that?

I glanced at Papa to see if he'd picked up on any of that stray thinking. In answer, he just flashed me a smile that was meant to be encouraging, but it didn't quite do the job. We had to settle for me following him like a good daughter.

Out in the other room, Ben and Simon were still sitting at the table. They'd gotten out a battered deck of cards and were playing two-handed pinochle across that greasy surface. As Papa and I stepped out of the back room, their expressions slid from startled to slimy.

"Now, is there something we can do for you, folks? Wouldn't want you to think you were receiving less than our finest hospitality for your fifty." As nasty as the look Simon had given Papa had been, the one he gave me was worse. He looked like he was wondering how I'd taste between his dirty teeth, and if I'd run too fast to be worth the trouble of catching.

Papa didn't seem to see it. "I hope neither of you gentlemen would object to a little music?" He snapped off the radio.

Ben didn't like that. "Depends," he said darkly, "on who's playin'."

"Well, that would be myself." Papa gave them a fine, shining smile and bowed, reminding me a whole lot of Lincoln Jones putting on his porter face. At the same time, though, I felt the magic swirling out of him, making its way across the room, easing into Jack's big brothers.

Simon shrugged. "The boy wants to play, let 'im play. Come on, Benny, your bet."

Papa didn't say one word about being called *boy*. He just lifted the lid on the piano keys and beckoned me over to sit beside him on the bench. He touched the middle C and winced. Even I could tell that piano was really out of tune.

"You'll be taking the bass line," he whispered. "Here,

and here." He showed me where to put my hands and set his fingers to the keys farther up the board.

"I don't know, Papa." I knew I could play. The magic in me could turn out music without me even having to think about it. But the one time I'd actually sat at a piano, things had not gone so good, or any kind of good at all.

"It'll be all right," he murmured. "Just follow my lead."

"But Jack . . ."

"We don't need his permission anymore," said Papa, entirely missing the point he hadn't given me a chance to make. "Those two accepted our payment and laid no conditions on our stay. We are already inside." Papa nodded his head, marking time. "Five, six, seven, eight . . ."

Papa began to play. His music was slow and lazy, light, gentle, and complicated all at once. His graceful hands drew a soft stream of song effortlessly from the old piano and somehow the bad tuning didn't matter. It was still beautiful. It made you think of sunrise, of anticipation.

I don't think I could have kept my hands still if I wanted to. The magic in me caught up that anticipation, that ease, and spun it into music. I touched the deeper keys, and built up a foundation for the tune, a rich bass contrast to support the sweet melody line.

Ben and Simon weren't playing cards anymore. They'd shoved back their chairs to listen. I could feel their attention as clearly as I could feel the keys under my fingers.

Now, daughter. Papa's voice sounded in my head, and it wasn't startling at all. He'd been there since we'd begun to play. It was so natural, I just hadn't noticed. *Here's where we show them we mean business. Five, six, seven . . .*

I knew what I needed to do and I knew I could do it. I changed the rhythm I was keeping. Slowed it down, making the tune deeper and calmer. Papa's hands and magic took that calm up into the brightness of the melody line, spreading it wide, turning the music into sunrise to fill the room, the whole dingy apartment, and Jack's no-good brothers.

You're safe, that tune said. *All safe. This place is ours. We belong here. As long as we are here, you are safe and sound. There can be no danger while we are here.*

Very good, daughter, came Papa's voice. His magic worked on mine, showing me how to make the spell shaping easier, to make each note, each beat of my heart, each idea do what was needed, no more. He showed me how to stretch out and lay claim to what I needed, but quietly, carefully. Insidiously. We needed this place; we needed these two. We'd make them ours and this was how.

These walls and roof will shelter us. We belong here. You will protect us.

That spell sank into Ben and Simon. Ben's scarred hands stopped their restless fiddling with the cards and instead started to drum in time with our lazy, persistent rhythm. Simon's half-moon eyes crinkled around the edges, not like he was smiling, but like he might be thinking about it. I did smile as I played, enjoying the way my fingers added little flourishes to the tune. This was good. Those two greasy mooks had to do what we said now. Our spell wrapped itself around their hearts and tied a pretty bow. There'd be no more dirty looks, no more snide little insults. We owned this place now. It was ours.

Now, the big finish, Papa told me.

The tune changed again. It became slower yet brighter, stronger than it had been yet until we brought our hands down together in a final rich, ringing chord. As the music faded, the magic dissolved into the flat, becoming part of the boards, the bricks, the window glass, the warp and weft of the ragged carpet, and the blood and bone of the Hollander brothers.

My father lifted his hands from the keys and turned himself around to face the Hollanders.

"Thank you, gentlemen," he said. "I hope that did not offend anyone's sensibilities."

"Uh, nah, nah." Benny shook himself. "You play anytime you want, ol' man. That'll be fine by us."

"And I trust there will be no problem with us staying as long as we wish?"

Simon pulled his cigarette out of his mouth and frowned at it, trying to figure out why it had gone dead. "Sure, sure, whatever you want."

"And you will say nothing to anyone about us," Papa went on, his voice velvet soft, and just as dark. "Or any other matter we do not choose to have discussed."

"Yeah, yeah, just like you say." Ben had already scooted his chair back around to face the table. "Come on, Sy, whose bet?"

They went right back to the cards. I got the feeling I could have danced the tango on the piano bench and they wouldn't have looked up, unless and until Papa told them to.

Papa smiled. I had to look away. That smile made him look way too much like Shake. It didn't sit well with the shine I felt in my own eyes, and a shiver skittered between my shoulder blades.

The door downstairs opened and footsteps pounded up the stairs. A second later the knob rattled and Jack burst into the room, a half-dozen paper sacks clutched in his fists.

"Ah, our hero yet again." Papa slapped his knees and got to his feet. "Thank you, Jack. I'm sure Callie's about perishing, aren't you, Callie?"

"Yeah. Thanks, Jack."

But Jack wasn't looking at me. He was looking at his brothers. Simon puffed his cigarette. Ben tossed a card down. Neither of them so much as turned his head to see him standing there. It was like they had blinders on. But Jack didn't have any kind of blinders. He saw plain as day, thanks to the wish I'd granted him, and Jack's understanding that we'd enchanted his brothers slid knife-sharp across my skin. Then I felt something else. Jack was afraid. Jack Holland was really, truly, badly afraid of me.

I hauled my magic senses shut before I had to feel that for one second longer. I followed Papa and Jack into the back room like nothing had happened. But it had, and I was never getting away from that look in Jack's eyes again.

10

Man's Got a Heart

We didn't sit down to dinner right away. First, Papa fixed up our room. As quick as being on the train had robbed him of his strength, being out in the open air had brought it back. Cinderella's fairy godmother would have blushed to see the kinds of changes my father was able to work. By the time he'd finished walking round it, the grimy back room had turned into a tidy hotel room, with a plush carpet on the floor. There were three beds so spick-and-span they could have been just made up by Mr. Jones, the porter, plus a plump sofa long enough for even Jack to stretch out on. There were clean clothes in the closet and in the dresser. Four chairs clustered around a table with a vase of flowers and a lace doily. The window was not only cleaned, but dressed with fresh, ruffled curtains. Best of all, the old-cabbage smell was gone, replaced by the scent of wash soap and lavender.

"It's just for tonight, right?" Jack turned in place and stared at the now-comfortable room. He didn't sound anywhere near as excited as he had when he first got his set of new clothes for traveling fairy class. "It'll be gone in the morning?"

"Not this time," answered Papa cheerfully. "Now that we've laid the protection down, we belong fully in this place and what we do here can be permanent."

I didn't quite like the slow way Jack mouthed the word *permanent,* as he pulled up a chair with the rest of us and took the sandwich Mama handed him. Or the way he sat quiet through the rest of the meal. Or even the way he offered to take all the wrappers and empty paper cartons out to the trash. But most of all, I didn't like the way he didn't come back.

Papa had declared we were to all spend the evening resting, and Mama agreed. He'd managed to conjure a couple of books from somewhere, and now my parents sat together on the sofa, reading over each other's shoulders, just being close. I should have been glad to see it. And if Jack had been there, I think I would have.

I excused myself, saying I needed to go to the bathroom. There was just one for the entire building, and it was down the dingy hallway next to the door that let out onto the porch. Each of the three floors had its own back porch. Maybe it was supposed to be someplace you could get fresh air and sun, but it would fail pretty miserably at both, because all three porches were stacked right on top of each other like pancakes. So here in the middle, there wouldn't be any sun getting through, and there wasn't any fresh air in this part of the city anyhow.

Jack was sitting on the porch railing with his elbow hooked around the post. He did it so easily, I knew he'd sat like this for hours, probably with a book in his hands, like he did now. The torn screen door squeaked when I pushed on it, but Jack didn't turn around. He just stayed bent over his notebook, slowly turning the pages. The only light was the dim lamplight filtering through the curtains, and the lights of the barges slogging their way up the river, so I wasn't sure he could actually read anything. Maybe he just wanted to touch the pages, to remember that he had things to write about, that he'd been somewhere else and there was still somewhere else to go. Or maybe he wanted an excuse not to look at me.

I walked across the warped boards to stand beside him. I knew he heard me, but he didn't look up. I swung my legs over the rail so I was sitting on it like I would a fence rail back home. I looked down into the dark alley for a little while. Then I looked up. The smoke and clouds had cleared just enough overhead to show the bleary face of the moon. Cars roared and honked. Somebody down in the street shouted and somebody else cussed. The train Jack called the El rattled in the distance, flashing silver light up over the tenement roofs. A hot breeze blew hard. The tar paper rattled on the roof above us and the old building creaked uneasily in answer.

It was a long time before Jack closed his notebook. He

still didn't look at me. He stared over the ash piles toward the river. "I never should have brought you here," he said.

"There wasn't anyplace else to go."

Jack's jaw had hardened, and right then he looked years older than he should have. In fact, he looked a lot like Ben.

"You did something to them," he said flatly. "You did something to Ben and Simon, and you didn't tell me."

"We didn't have a choice, Jack, and besides . . ."

"Besides nothing! Your old man just went and magicked them and you didn't do anything to stop it! You didn't even bother to tell me!" His voice was tight and hard as his jaw. It would have been a shout, but Jack knew how thin the walls were, and that there were people on the other side listening. So he kept the words low, but they were deadly sharp all the same.

"You didn't need me to tell you. You saw it for yourself."

"Yeah, I did, and maybe you should remember that. Or are you going to take back that wish so I won't find out anything else I'm not supposed to?"

His words slapped me hard enough to knock any answer right out of me. The one thing I'd been able to count on for this whole long disaster of an adventure was Jack, and now he'd stopped trusting me. Over one stupid thing.

Worse than that, though, was how my magic stirred under my skin, like it was woken up by my anger. *You can make him understand,* it told me. *It would be easy. You know how.* I wouldn't have to worry about anybody else knowing I'd done it either, not even Papa or Mama. Jack wouldn't even know himself.

I told my magic to put a sock in it, but that took a lot longer than it should have.

"I'm sorry, Jack. I should have done something, you're right. But Papa was afraid they might decide to kick us out after all, or ask for more money." I'd felt that. I was sure of it when we were working the spell. That was why we did it. It was part of the protection. Wasn't it?

"Oh, yeah?" Jack's voice dropped even lower. "And what's he gonna decide to do if *I* don't behave right?"

"You don't . . . you don't think I'd ever let anything happen to you, do you?"

"No, *you* wouldn't."

He meant Papa might. "You can't really think that," I said, but what I really meant was I didn't want to think that. I didn't want to remember the soft, satisfied tone in Papa's voice after we'd worked the protection spell and the Hollander Brothers had started agreeing with whatever he said. He'd never do anything like that to Jack. I wouldn't let him. Ever.

Jack shrugged and opened his notebook again, turning over another page. He pulled out his pencil and started writing slowly, carefully, and very thoroughly, not paying any attention to me. We sat there, with the traffic noises filling the world around us. A dog barked somewhere and I winced. It reminded me too much of Mimi, and all at once my thoughts were off and running, like they didn't want to be here, where Jack was so angry. Where was the pack now? I had no idea where I'd sent them, or even how far. Were they out there someplace, trying to pick up our scent for the Seelie king? Where was the king? That old woman said she'd sent him word. Was Papa's protection enough to hide us from him? What about when we had to leave? And what about Uncle Shake, with his pale friends and their spears and swords? And then there was my grandmother on the other side of the mirror. She'd said there was someone coming for her, and all I could think was that he might just as soon be coming for us. What would we do then?

And what was I going to do if Jack stopped talking to me for good?

"I don't know what to do," I said, to Jack, to the city, to my own miserable runaway thoughts. "I keep trying and things just keep getting worse. I get away from the Hoppers and the vigilantes, but I kill Shimmy. I find my parents, but I kill Ivy. I want to save those men in the Hooverville, but I kill Stripling. I want us to be safe and I . . ." I couldn't go any further. I didn't know what I'd done. I just knew I couldn't stand how Jack wouldn't even look at me. "They're right. I am bad luck."

Jack's pencil went still on the page. "No. You're not." He said it slowly, like he'd just made up his mind. "None of this is your fault."

"It feels like it. Like I should've known . . ."

"What?" He scooted toward me along the rail until we

were so close our shoulders rubbed together. "You should've known you're a fairy princess? Or that the rest of the fairies would be falling all over themselves to get hold of you because you've got extra-special powers? Or maybe you should have known the Seelie king would be ready to sacrifice his own daughter to get to you?"

"No, I mean . . . I don't know what I mean." I had to hold tight to that railing to keep from wobbling, or leaning any closer to Jack than I already was.

"We'll figure it out," he told me. "We've figured everything else out, haven't we?"

"Yeah, we have."

We were quiet again after that, but it was the comfortable kind of quiet we'd shared before. What we'd said, and what I'd done, it wasn't forgotten, but we could let it be for now.

A strange thought struck me. "Jack, what day is it?"

"Ummm . . . the sixteenth, I think. Why?"

"Nothing." I felt myself blush. Of all the stupid little things to think about now, this had to be the stupidest, and the smallest.

"Nuh-uh. You're not getting away with that." He nudged his shoulder against mine. "What?"

"I . . . It's dumb. It's just, it's my birthday tomorrow."

"Birthday?" The word straightened Jack up.

"What are you so surprised about? I did get born, you know."

"Yeah, I know. Sorry, I just . . . yowza." He scrubbed his

head and looked at me again. "Your birthday? That makes you, what? Fifteen?"

I nodded.

"Gosh. Happy birthday, Callie." Jack smiled, and this time it was one of his genuine hundred-watt smiles. I was so relieved, I could have melted right there, and my cheeks started up with a fresh burning blush.

Fortunately, Jack wasn't looking at me right then. He just shoved his hands in his pockets. "I wish I had something . . ." He stopped. "Wait. Maybe . . ."

He swung himself up so he balanced on the rail, and dug his hands into the rafters overhead. After a minute, he gave a grunt that was both surprised and satisfied. When he jumped down, he had a rusty metal cash box in his hand. He popped the lid and I saw what could only have been a kid's treasure stash—a dime novel with a giant octopus on the cover, a few sticks of petrified chewing gum, a model truck, and a few old coins. He must have been hiding stuff in there since he was little. Jack rummaged through the stash and pulled out a pocket-sized notebook, a lot like the one he carried with him. There was a stub of a silver pencil tucked into the space between the spine and the pages.

"It's not much, but, well . . . happy birthday." Jack handed me the notebook. He was mumbling, and I had the strange feeling if the light were strong enough, I'd be seeing his cheeks turn at least as red as mine. Could that be right? Could I have just made Jack Holland *blush*?

That little question took over my entire brain, and all at once I couldn't do anything but stand and stare. But then my own blush decided to double down, and I decided it'd be safer to be looking at my present instead. I opened it up at random. The page was covered in tight, smeared penciled words.

"The square-jawed lawman leveled his trusty six-shooter at the masked bandit's heart. 'You hand over the little lady's purse or I swear by God I'll . . .'"

"You don't have to read that." Jack riffled the pages. "There's still a bunch of blank pages at the back. You can use it to make lists, or notes, or you know, stuff like that. I'll get you something better later. Promise."

"No!" I snatched the book away from him. "I don't want anything else. This is . . . this is swell, Jack. Thank you. For everything."

He was looking down at me, and I was looking up at him. I was past blushing, and past the butterflies and the wood-peckers, even though he reached out and ran his fingers down my braid, just like he had before. It was a soft and gentle feeling and I liked it. He was making up his mind about something. I didn't want to believe I knew what it was, so I just stood there and felt his fingertips against my braid, and let him think until he was ready to lean just a little closer.

Somewhere the El rattled down its track again, kicking up another hot wind. A scrap of colored paper caught in the gust tumbled across the gap between the buildings and

landed on the porch beside us. The paper rustled, and unfolded, and stood up.

Jack yanked me backward and we both twisted around
to stare.

It was Touhy.

11

What's a Poor Girl to Do?

Jack ducked around me, putting himself right between me and the paper girl. She crinkled and folded, making herself into a wrinkled nest of scraps with a plump-cheeked photo looking out.

"It's okay." I laid my hand on Jack's shoulder as I stepped past him. "At least I think it is. Right . . . Touhy?"

"Touhy?" repeated Jack. "You gotta be kidding me."

"Truce, okay?" Touhy pushed out one hand from her paper nest. Her palm crackled and unfolded to make a white flag on a stick. "I'm just here to talk."

"Right." Jack didn't move. "Like that other bunch of . . . of . . . look, just who *are* all of you?"

"We're the Halfers," she announced proudly, unfolding herself all the way into her scrap-paper silhouette. "I figured your girl would've told you by now."

We both ignored that. "What in the heck's a Halfer?" asked Jack.

"They're like me," I said. "Half fairy."

Touhy laughed and crinkled again and her face came up with a cartoon man falling down and slapping his belly.

"We're nothing like you, toots. You've got yourself a fancy pedigree and parents and a birthday." She leaned heavy on the word, letting us know she'd been listening in for a while. Which got me blushing all over again. I don't know about Jack, because there was no way on earth I was going to look at him right now. All of this just made Touhy crinkle some more. "Halfers . . . we're part this world, part the other, and part who knows what. Some of us was found, some made, some just . . . grew." She spread her arms to show trails of torn billboard ads hanging from her arms and her face changed to a photo of a flower garden with a prize ribbon in the corner. "Your daddy must've told you. Bet he called us Undone and everything."

"You mean there've been . . . people like you in Chicago this whole time, and I never knew?" said Jack incredulously.

"Surprise!" The top of Touhy's head tore off and a shower of confetti spilled out.

"Cut it out, can't you?" snapped Jack. "I'm getting sea-sick!"

Touhy made a harsh tearing sound I suspected was a laugh. Then she crumpled herself down into a ball, and that ball rolled into the corner of the porch. Slowly, she unfolded herself, and when she did, she had a proper girl's shape. Her face and hands were paper-bag brown and she wore a little pink dress that looked like it was made of tissue, with black patent-leather shoes and white stockings, and a white ribbon in wavy brown hair. I had a feeling if I'd seen her in full daylight, I would have noticed there was something funny about the way her skin was as wrinkled as her dress, but there in the dark, she could pass for human about as well as I could pass for white.

"So, what are you doing here?" I asked. "Aren't you going to get in trouble with Dan Ryan and the others?"

She shrugged. "Not as much as you will if they catch up with you now."

"What's that supposed to mean?"

"After your people came charging in like that, you kinda blew any chance you had of making a deal with the council, let alone with Dan Ryan and the others. They're out for blood now."

Jack put his hand under my elbow. "Well, gosh, thanks for the warning." He started to turn us back to the door. "You can go now."

"You ain't heard my offer yet."

"Not interested." He yanked the screen door open.

"You always let him do the talking for you?" Touhy rolled her eyes, and I found I'd just about had it with her.

"You better watch your mouth," I said, but I shook my elbow out of Jack's hand when I did. "You're kind of on your own here." My magic was stirring again. It wanted something to do, and Touhy was making herself into a terrific target. I suppose that should have worried me, but right then I was busy watching Touhy smirk and settle farther back into her corner.

"Holy smokes, you really are high court, aren't you? I'm gonna be sorry I came here."

"You got that right," muttered Jack.

I gave him a shut-up glare, but he didn't look like he was ready to go along with it. "Okay," I said to Touhy. "You got something to say. I'm listening."

All at once, Touhy didn't seem so sure of herself. The wind off the river stirred around us, making her paper shape wobble like she hadn't quite decided what to do next.

"You wanna get out of town, right?" she said finally. "We can help you do that, and make sure you're left alone by the other Halfers once you get where you're going. But you gotta do something for us."

Jack and I moved closer together. "I'm still listening," I told her.

"I don't know how much you heard before, but the courts have been sending in people to raid our camps. They've been taking Halfers away, back into the fairy worlds."

"What for?" asked Jack.

She gave that crackling little shrug again. "Considering there's one of their wars on, our people are either going to be soldiers, or lunch."

"Lunch?" repeated Jack.

Touhy tipped her head toward me. She was going to make me answer that. Because I was high court. "Papa says fairies, full-blood fairies anyway, can feed off the magic of their own kind," I told Jack. "They can use the feelings from humans too."

I watched Jack turn that over in his head a few times. "So that's what that tree in Los Angeles was doing? It was draining feeling out of those men?"

"To feed itself, and the Seelie king. Yeah."

"When the courts get hungry, they take our people to the fairy lands." The bitterness in Touhy's voice was hard enough to cut diamond. "Once we're there, they can put the whammy on us, and make us obey their orders, or hold us still long enough that they can suck the living right out of us."

Jack was looking at me. I didn't like it. I was sure he was thinking about all the times he'd sent me the magic of his wishes and his feelings. He was thinking about my papa, and how he held on so tight to Mama when he was sick. He was thinking about his brothers too. Shame crawled out from its hiding place under my skin and covered me over.

"Why do they have to take you back there to do it?" I asked.

"Because this is our world, same as it is yours," said Touhy. "While we're here we've got a chance to fight back. Back there . . . it's all their world and their magic."

They're weaker than we are, Papa had said. *More easily swayed . . . very ready to be used by anyone stronger.* I figured I better not bring that up right now.

"Dan Ryan figured since they're so hot on catching you, we could strike a bargain," Touhy went on. "Trade you to get our own people back. And don't you go holding it against him too much," she added quickly. "His father's one of the ones they took."

Those words hit me hard. I couldn't even move for a long time. I didn't want to feel bad for that greasy rat-kid with his burlap sack, but how could I stand there and not feel for someone else who'd had a parent taken away?

Jack put his hand on my shoulder.

"I'm sorry," I whispered, wishing the words would get from here to Dan Ryan.

"So, will you help us?" said Touhy.

I hadn't been planning on it, after being kidnapped and everything. But now . . . now I had to think again. "What do you want?"

Touhy unfolded further, stretching herself out until she was tall enough to look me in the eye. "Open a gate for us. Give us our own way into the fairy worlds so we can rescue our people."

My fingers curled in on themselves. "I don't know if I can."

"Oh, don't gimme that! We all heard the prophecy too, you know. You can punch a hole through anything! *And* you already went and bulldozed the Seelie Castle out in California."

"You know about that?" interrupted Jack.

"Are you *kidding*? Everybody knows about that."

"Who's everybody?" My head was starting to spin. I was used to being one of a kind. The couple of times I'd found another half fairy, they'd been as much on their own as I was. But now . . . now it was turning out there were whole camps full of them. "Just how many Halfers are there?"

"Enough to make your life miserable if we decide to," Touhy shot back.

Touhy might be made of paper, but she was no weakling. I had no idea where Papa was getting his information from, but it was starting to look a little out-of-date.

Something in her bluster sounded a little off-kilter, though. I took a deep breath and held it, and made myself think about how I'd heard the other Halfers arguing in that tunnel. "What about this council Dan Ryan was talking about? Do they know you're here doing a deal with me?" Touhy didn't answer and I knew I'd hit it. She was here on her own, so any threats she made were her own as well. "How about Dan Ryan?" I added. "Does he know you're here?"

"I told you, he's just mad." But her nerve was flagging. She rustled and crackled and shrank back down to her little-girl size. "He's really all right. And he's strong. We'll need him if we're going to make any kind of raid work."

"Because of that bag of his?"

"That, and because he's so plain nasty, nothing can keep hold of him."

I snorted. There was a good chance Touhy was telling the truth about what was happening to the Halfers. It sure sounded like something the Seelie king would do. If he could send his own daughter to be shot, he wouldn't even bat a borrowed eyelash at sucking the living out of some stranger.

And if that was true, well, maybe it didn't matter what Dan Ryan had done to me personally (although we were still going to have a talk about that). Nobody deserved to have their folks dragged off by the fairies.

What was worse, though, was I could picture my grandparents doing the exact same thing if they needed to.

"You do owe us, you know," said Touhy. "They may not be ready to do a smash-and-grab on the high courts, but the 'ville council is all set to rule on Stripling's death, and I don't think they're gonna let you off."

Jack frowned. "For somebody who wants a deal, you're sure making a whole lot of threats."

"I'm just telling it like it is. Bad Luck here's gotten too big to hide." The front of Touhy's pink dress bunched up and smoothed out to become a sandwich board with newspaper headlines: STILL NO LEADS IN IVY BRIGHT CASE—HOOVER CALLS FOR JOINT INVESTIGATION.

I winced. "That's not fair."

"Doesn't matter. It's still true." Touhy closed her pink dress over the headlines again. "You got whole worlds after you. No matter how you pull down the shades in there, somebody's gonna find you. You need help."

Even Jack didn't have an answer to that one. "It's not like we're asking you to come with us," said Touhy. "Just open the gate. We'll do the rest."

I didn't know what to do. I wasn't even sure how to think about this. She'd been ready to help me when I was in trouble with her people. Kind of, anyway. But it was pretty plain she didn't like me or trust me much. Same went for the rest of that Halfer gang, beginning and ending with Dan Ryan.

"So what if she does it?" asked Jack suddenly.

"We get you out of Chicago," Touhy answered. "All of you. Safe and sound."

"Would you promise?" I asked.

"Swear to it," said Touhy. Promises were serious business among magic folks. They are really hard for us to break. Some of us can't do it, even when we want to. That's why there's the whole big deal around words and rules and agreements. They could make up those bindings and borderlines for magic that Papa was getting so upset over.

"Callie?" Jack was asking.

There were a thousand and one reasons to say yes. Not the least of them was that Jack wanted me to. Unfortunately, there were just that many reasons to say no, plus one extra.

"Papa won't like it." I still could see how his face screwed up tight with disgust as he spat out the words *nothing* and *detritus* to describe the Halfers. What did he know about them that made him hate them so much?

"He wouldn't have to know."

A minute ago Jack had been so angry about me keeping secrets from him. Now I was supposed to go set up a huge one to keep from Papa? Why would he ask that of me? But I knew why. Jack was thinking about getting us away from his brothers, before Papa took it into his head to work any more magic on them. I couldn't say anything about that in front of Touhy, though. She already knew too much about our business for anybody's good.

But how could I say yes when I couldn't open any kind of gate at all? My uncle was waiting on the other side for me. If I couldn't get past him to save myself, how was I going to smuggle a whole boatload of Halfers past him?

The old, tired anger that I'd been carrying since I walked out of Kansas leaned hard against me. I didn't want any of these gate powers. I didn't care about fairies or Halfers or anything in between. I wanted to be left alone with my family and with Jack. I'd give anything for it. Anything and everything.

My thoughts skipped a groove, and played over again. I'd give anything and everything to be left alone. I'd cut any kind of deal, sign any kind of paper. But there were so many enemies in this mess, which of them could I cut a deal with? It wasn't like I could sit them down like some kind of magic League of Nations or anything.

My throat clamped shut.

"What is it, Callie?" said Jack.

I turned to him. I felt my heart swelling and my eyes shining. There was a way. We could do it. There was a third road and I finally knew what it was. I grabbed Jack's hand, but before I could say anything, the porch door opened and a shadow fell across us.

"You get away from my daughter."

12

Daddy, What You Doin'?

Papa stood in the doorway, the light shining hard and cold in his eyes. "I said, get away!" For one wild second, I thought he was talking about Jack. But he meant Touhy, and she was already retreating to her corner of the porch.

"It's okay, Papa . . . ," I started.

"It is not okay. What do you want here?" He glided forward. There was a strength and a grace about him I hadn't seen before. "How dare you come to *my* door?"

"No, Mr. LeRoux, it's not like that," began Jack, all calm and casual. "Touhy tried to help Callie when she was with the Halfers and she was just making sure we were okay. Right, Touhy?"

Touhy didn't answer. She let herself drift backward until she was plastered against the porch railing. She didn't take her eyes off Papa, and I couldn't blame her. If this was the first time I'd seen him, I'd've been scared too.

"Get out of here, Undone." Papa said the word like it was something filthy. "And you tell the others to stay away from my family." He lifted his hand, and his palm was shining as bright as his eyes.

For a couple seconds, Touhy didn't move. She wanted to let Papa see she wasn't afraid, even though she was. Her edges were trembling and her green eyes darted this way and that.

"Well," she said to me and Jack finally. "You can't say I didn't try." Then she folded and twisted, sliding between the railings. The sooty breeze blew, and Touhy threw herself on it, tumbling away like the stray bit of paper she was.

Papa planted both hands on the porch railing and watched until Touhy was well out of sight.

"Jack," he said, without turning around, "I'd like a private word with Callie, if you don't mind."

From the way Jack looked at me, I got the idea he'd stay if I asked him to, but that'd probably just make everything worse. So, I jerked my chin toward the door as a signal he should go on inside. Which he did, slowly. Like Touhy, he meant to show Papa he wasn't afraid. Except he was, and his fear tightened up my throat.

Papa didn't turn around. He just waited until we heard the screen door swing shut. I stayed where I was too, my heart drumming louder than all the city traffic.

"I warned you about those creatures, Callie." He spoke so softly that for a second I thought he was talking inside my head.

"Jack was telling the truth," I said to his back. "Touhy did try to help me."

"It doesn't matter. She's still one of them."

"What's so bad about the Halfers?"

Papa swung around, genuine shock plain on his face. "What kind of question is that? You've seen what they are."

"They're magic people. I've met worse."

"They tried to hurt you; that should be enough."

I couldn't believe what I was hearing. It was almost as hard to believe what I was saying. "All kinds of people have tried to hurt me, Papa. I don't hear you talking like this about the Seelies, or your parents, or your brother either, and they all tried to kill me."

"That is entirely different."

"How is it different? You're not making sense."

Papa leaned his weight against his hands, staring down into the darkness that had gathered below the tenements. "Callie, I have said they are dangerous. They don't belong in any world. There's no place for them. That should be enough."

"Well, it ain't." The words were out of my mouth before I had time to think they might be a bad idea. All I wanted was to get him to turn around. If he was going to spout nonsense, he was going to look at me while he did it.

He did turn. Slowly. His face was tight, and the shine from his eyes laid more shadow than light across his face. "Callie, I know you're used to making your own decisions," he said with that hard calm that people use when they want to make you think they sort of agree with you. "This time, though, you just have to accept I know more about these things than you do. You stay away from the Undone. You do not talk to them, and you do not listen to them. If they try to get near you again, you call me." He moved closer, one slow step at a time. I felt as if I were shrinking down, becoming younger and smaller the closer he got.

Time to stop that, right now. No matter who this was in front of me. "But *why*? What's so bad about the Halfers?"

That surprised him. He pulled right back. "We're done talking about this. You need to get inside."

He was almost to the door before I figured out what to say next. "You sound like you don't even know why you're so scared."

He lifted his hand off the screen-door handle. His shoulders slumped, in defeat, I thought. I even thought I might actually get an answer. "I'm not scared, Callie," he said, turning to face me again. "Their power is nothing compared to ours, but they are dangerous, and you will do as you are told."

I felt it then, the pressure of him. Papa was willing me not just to understand, but to believe, and to do as I was told. I bit my lip hard, because in that moment I wanted to. Not because of the magic, but because this was my father. I'd wanted to find him, to have him come home and be my family as bad as I'd ever wanted to find Mama, and for much, much longer. If I turned away from him now, would any of the badness I'd been through be worth it? Would I have killed Ivy Bright for nothing? I didn't think I could stand it if that was true.

I don't know what of all that Papa picked up on. Maybe none of it. Maybe he just saw the look on my face. He sighed and rubbed his eyes. When he looked up again, he didn't look scary anymore. He just looked sad.

"I'm sorry I was cross, Callie. You will understand one day. I hope, anyway." The silence that fell between us wasn't anything like as comfortable as the one between me and Jack. We were both searching after something to say, and neither one of us could find it. "You'd better go in to your mother and get some sleep."

My jaw dropped. "You're scared to death of the Halfers, Uncle Shake's spying on us, Grandma's sending me warnings through mirrors, and there's a war going on over in the fairy world, and you want to send me to bed!"

He bowed his head. "Tomorrow, Callie. When the sun's up again. We'll face it then, I swear, but I need time." His shoulders shook. "I was so long in that prison, Callie. You have no idea how cut off he kept us, how starved I have been." His words curled around me, sinking in through my skin. They brought the hunger with them, the fear, and the loneliness, and the loneliness was worse than anything else. It was like the end of the world. "Then on the train . . . all that life. All that heart," he whispered, and that whisper shook. "I could feel it, but I could touch none of it. I thought I would die. I thought I would run mad, and all that time your mother was beside me. I almost . . . She can never know how close I came . . ." He didn't finish. He didn't have to. I understood, no matter how badly I wished I didn't. Papa lifted his eyes to me, and this time it wasn't the fairy lights that made them glitter. It was tears. "You must let me have tonight, Callie."

"What are you going to do?" I croaked, and tried not to be afraid, but I didn't make it.

"I'm going to keep watch out here for a bit. Tell your mother not to wait up."

I left him there, facing out across the back alley, his long fingers resting lightly on the rail. I felt his magic stirring at my back all the way down the hall. At first, I thought he was extending the protection, but slowly it came to me that he was reaching out much farther than the boundaries of the porch. He was letting his magic touch the houses and the streets. It eased between the nearest boundaries to find the dreams, waking and sleeping, of the people here. He was sipping just a little from each person he touched to ease his magic hunger. He was healing himself from the dreams of a hundred different strangers, so he wouldn't be tempted to draw too much from Mama. Or Jack. Or me.

I let myself back into the dark hallway. I didn't want to think about it. I didn't want to think about anything any- more. Except when I walked into the apartment, there were Jack's brothers sitting at the greasy table, playing cards, a cluster of beer bottles standing guard between them.

I bit my lip again and walked up to them. Ben glanced past me, like he'd already forgotten why he'd taken his eyes off the game, and then popped the cap off a fresh beer. Simon didn't even do that much. He just puffed on his cigarette a few more times and rearranged a couple of the cards in his hand.

I opened up my magic. Papa's spell, the one I'd helped him spin, wound like cotton wool around the pair of them, thick enough to blind them both. Underneath that spell, Ben wanted to win the game. Simon wanted another beer, and another cigarette, and a whole set of other things. I steered my knowing away from them, fast. I was going to have to rinse my brain out after this.

Papa'd showed me how to be careful. I was careful now. They weren't giving me a whole lot of wishing to work with, but it was enough. I loosened the cotton-wool spell, thinned it down to gauze, leaving just the lightest veil behind, just enough to fool my father that the magic was still in place if he happened to glance at them.

This is for Jack, I thought toward them. *This is for Jack.*

Ben grunted and tossed down another card. Simon swore and swigged more beer. I went into our room and closed the door behind me.

13

Mama's in the Kitchen, Messin' All Around

Mama did not take it well when I told her Papa said not to wait up. Not that she complained or anything. She just moved briskly around the room, unfolding the dressing screen so each of us would have some privacy for changing into the pajamas waiting in the dresser drawers, turning down the sheets, and determinedly not looking out the windows or listening at the door for my father's step in the hall.

Papa didn't come back for hours. I know because I couldn't fall asleep. I was dog tired, but between everything that had happened with Touhy, and then with Papa, my thoughts wouldn't settle down long enough to let me find any sleep. I just lay in my comfortable bed, stared at train lights flashing past outside, and counted Jack's snores for what felt like hours. When I couldn't take that anymore, I

144

turned onto my other side and stared at the mirror hanging over the dresser. It wasn't cracked anymore. I watched its darkened surface, waiting to see my grandmother again. But nothing moved in there, and nothing moved in there, and the longer nothing moved in there, the tighter my insides knotted together, because there should have been something. And the more nothing there was, the more worried I got.

When I finally did hear Papa moving outside the door, I shut my eyes fast and tried to make my breathing all even. It was a pretty bad acting job, but he didn't seem to notice. He just slipped across the room and helped himself to some pajamas. I heard him move behind the screen, and then the soft creak of the mattress as he climbed into bed beside Mama.

"Is everything all right, Daniel?" she whispered.

"As right as it can be, Margaret."

"Which is to say, not very."

He let out a long, slow sigh. "We'll find our way."

There was a long pause, and then Mama whispered, "How?"

I squeezed my eyes shut. Why couldn't I be asleep? I didn't want to hear this.

"I don't know yet," he answered. "I wish I did."

"Me too."

I heard the sound of a soft kiss, and a smile crept into my father's voice. "Well, I'll just have to make it come true, then, won't I?"

They were silent after that, and I got tired of keeping my eyes squeezed so tight. Slowly, the dark in my head rose up.

I didn't so much fall asleep as slide into a long, dim nightmare filled with voices, all trying to tell me something that would save my life. But I couldn't understand any of them. It went on and on until I woke up sweating and ready to scream.

It took me a good hundred or so hard heartbeats to believe I really was still in the apartment, and that the sun was up. But there was Jack still snoring on his sofa, and there was Papa curled up under the counterpane on his half of the double bed.

Mama was nowhere to be seen, but I heard some soft clanking on the other side of the door. Then I smelled hot butter and heard something I hadn't heard in months.

Mama was singing.

"Let the Midnight Special, shine a light on me.
Let the Midnight Special, shine its ever-lovin' light . . ."

I got up slowly so I wouldn't creak the springs, carefully dressed in a white blouse and green skirt Papa'd magicked into being for me, and tiptoed out into the front room.

Mama had clearly been up for hours. She'd also been busy as a queen bee, working her own brand of magic. That greasy little kitchen was clean as a new day. Ben and Simon were sitting at the table, wolfing down huge stacks of griddle cakes with blackstrap molasses. And that wasn't all. There was steak and eggs on their plates too. A bottle of fresh milk stood between them along with a battered coffeepot. More coffee percolated on the stove.

"Good morning, Callie," said Mama brightly. She bent

down, humming, opened the oven door, and pulled out a cake tin. I suddenly lost the ability to swallow and Mama laughed.

"I suppose you thought I'd forgotten," she said, setting the tin onto an overturned plate so the cake inside could cool. "Happy birthday, honey." She kissed the top of my head. "I couldn't let it go without at least a little something."

"How . . . how . . ." I gestured helplessly at the table. The kitchen was full of so many good smells that my stomach was ready to sit up and beg.

Mama smiled. "That nice Mrs. Burnstein downstairs, she told me where the grocer's is. I'll send your father around later to settle the bill."

"You got credit out of Old Man Grenke?" exclaimed Ben around a big bite of steak. "Lady, you're a miracle worker."

"And you shouldn't talk with your mouth full," Mama answered, but she did slide another couple of griddle cakes onto Ben's plate. Simon jabbed out with his fork, trying to grab one off the top, and Mama smacked the back of his hand with her spatula.

"Hey!" he shouted.

"None of that!" she snapped back. "You mind your manners, or no more for you."

"Yes, Mrs. LeRoux," mumbled Simon apologetically.

My jaw dropped open. Mama looked at me. I closed it before I could catch flies. Mama picked up another frying pan and laid another gorgeous, shimmery sunny-side-up egg onto Simon's plate, nudged the coffeepot toward him, and turned back to the stove.

"Sit down, Callie, I'll get you some breakfast."

I sat. The table had been fresh scrubbed and the smell of bleach mixed with the cooking smells. There was a lace place mat, and a clean napkin, and a white china plate. I had the wild idea Mama must have magicked the table somehow. Then she slid a couple of fried eggs and a fresh, crisp griddle cake onto my plate and I stopped caring where any of it came from, or who I was sitting with. I just grabbed up my knife, dug into the butter, poured on the molasses, and started eating.

Out of the corner of my eye I saw Mama wink.

"Is that steak and eggs I smell?" Papa came out the bedroom door, looking fresh as any daisy. He kissed Mama on the cheek, and sat himself down with a nod at the Hollander brothers. He shook out his napkin and let Mama fill his plate. "Why, thank you, Mrs. LeRoux."

Disbelief shivered through me. It tickled. This wasn't happening. It couldn't be happening. With all the disasters past, present, and future looming just outside the door, I couldn't actually be sitting here having breakfast with my parents. Mama was now taking one of the empty chairs, and helping herself to griddle cakes, and letting Papa pour her out a cup of coffee and add a drop of milk, like he knew just how she took it.

Jack came out of our room, rubbing his eyes. He looked

toward his brothers and froze. He saw, he understood, and he covered it up with a great imitation of one of his jaw-cracking yawns. I gave him a little nod, and he gave me one back and mouthed, *Thank you.*

Jack dropped into a chair and forked himself up a couple of griddle cakes and a piece of steak. "Did I hear right?" he asked innocently. "It's Callie's birthday?" His eyes kind of slid over Papa straight to Mama.

"It is," said Mama. "She's fifteen today."

"Happy birthday!"

"To Callie!" Papa raised his coffee cup, and the Hollander brothers, made more mellow by Mama's cooking than all the magic an Unseelie prince could muster, did the same.

I raised my glass of milk to them. Jack was grinning at me. I felt a blush beginning at the roots of my hair. But before it had a chance to work itself up into a full-fledged burn, the apartment door banged open to let in a stranger: a squat little man with a battered derby on his head and a big, black cigar clamped tight in his lantern jaw.

"Benny, Sy . . ." He saw us at the breakfast table and stopped dead. "What the hell's all this?" Mama puckered her face up, and the man chewed angrily on his cigar a few times.

Ben swallowed his mouthful of flapjack. "Mornin', Mr. Sweeny."

Mr. Sweeny did not seem to hear. "I said, what the hell's all this?" And he said it with his teeth clenched around his cigar. My breath hitched up. I couldn't help it. Papa'd be watching for how the Hollander brothers reacted. If they said too much, he'd know something was up.

"Ain't nothin'," Ben said quickly and I could breathe again. "Me an' Sy, we's ready to go, ain't we, Sy?" Ben tossed down his napkin and smacked his brother's arm. "Thanks for the breakfast, Mrs. LeRoux. Anybody cooks like you can come by anytime. Come on, Sy, Mr. Sweeny's waiting." The brothers grabbed their hats and hustled out. Mr. Sweeny glowered at the breakfast table, chewed his cigar at us one more time, and left with the brothers, letting the door slam shut behind him.

That was when I noticed all the blood had drained from Jack's face.

"Who was that?" I asked.

"That was trouble," said Jack to his breakfast plate. "Sweeny's a . . . well, he kept the local bootleggers in line back during Prohibition. Hired muscle for whoever needed it . . ." He eyed the door, and I knew he was thinking about his two huge brothers and maybe especially Ben's scarred hands. "Probably don't want to know what line he's in now."

"Well, we'll deal with that in its turn." Mama drank some more coffee. "Oh, and Daniel, I'll need some money for the grocer."

Papa chuckled and shook his head. "Margaret, you are a wonder. The whole of the fae world is after us, and possibly a portion of the human world too, and you're worried about the grocery bill."

"Daniel, I will not have us leave town owing. Besides, if

I can't produce a dinner for Benjamin and Simon, they may forget about being so polite about having us to stay."

I waited for Papa to tell her what we'd done to them, but he just shrugged elaborately and gave a long sigh. "Well, what can I say to that?"

"You say 'yes, dear,'" Mama replied promptly.

Papa kissed her cheek. "Yes, dear."

I felt strange. I'd never had this before, a minute to sit at the table with my family, my whole family, and Jack. To sit and eat and talk, and just . . . just *be*. I wanted to sink into it and be happy. Last night didn't mean so much after all. Neither did what had been done, and undone, with the Hollander brothers. Papa had to be careful, didn't he? He was just trying to look out for me and Mama. That was what he was supposed to do. If he went a little overboard, that was okay. It was all fixed now. I wanted to believe that. I almost did believe it. Because right here was everything I'd wanted for so long. I glanced over at Jack. Almost everything, anyway.

Jack, on the other hand, had gone kind of quiet. He kept watching my parents like he was hoping no one would notice him watching. I knew this couldn't be comfortable for him, having my folks sitting here smiling at each other when he'd found out only yesterday his folks were dead. I just didn't know what to do about it.

"Now," said Papa as he filled his coffee cup, yet again. Who knew fairy princes liked coffee so much? "We have a safe haven that should last us a few days. But we do need to move on from here, and to do that, we need two things." He blew on the coffee and sipped. "First, we need to find out what the situation is between the courts, so we know who's on our tail and how close they are. We also need some ready money for when we get to New York." Papa said this last directly to Mama. "There are people I want to talk to about the first, and as for the second . . ." He smiled. "Fortunately, Chicago is well situated to supply a musician with paying work. I should be able to find a club that will pay for a night's playing. Both these things, though, mean I have to be out and about today." He took another swallow of coffee and set the cup down on the saucer with a sharp click. "I had thought to ask you all to stay inside while I'm gone, but it occurs to me that would be a rather naive request." I started blushing again, but for an entirely different set of reasons. "So, if any of you do go out, I ask you to take this with you."

Papa reached in his pocket and brought out a handful of what looked like marbles and laid them on the table. It wasn't until I picked one of the glass-and-gold spheres up that I saw it shone gently with the light of the fairy lands.

"What is it?" asked Jack, turning one marble over in his fingers. They were just a little warmer than they should have been, and just a little lighter than if they'd really been glass.

"Think of it as a bit of wish made solid." Papa picked up the last one, laid it in Mama's palm, and wrapped her fingers around it. "If you are in trouble, or if you believe I might be, break it. I will be drawn to you."

My parents sat there for a long time like that, looking at

each other like they'd forgotten Jack and I were in the room. I could almost feel the promise flowing between them. I was sure Papa was really saying, *I won't vanish this time. I won't let them trap me away from you ever again.*

Jack, on the other hand, looked at his wishing marble like it had started going bad a few days ago. But he did slide it into his pocket. "Thanks."

I thought about asking Papa whom he planned to talk to, but decided against it. I really didn't want to hear him not answering one of my questions again. I wanted to keep the good feeling that surrounded us. I put my marble in my skirt pocket.

"Excellent." Papa stood up. "I'll be back in time for supper." He gave Mama an extra-long kiss. When at last he could stand to break away, he winked at me and picked up his hat, settled it low over his forehead, and left us there.

"Well." Mama got up from the table like she couldn't stand sitting still anymore, which she probably couldn't. I found myself wondering about the last time he'd left her, back before I was born, and what he'd said then and how she'd felt. "If you two will help me with these dishes, we'll have this all cleared up in two shakes."

We did. None of us said anything much. Mama just hummed and cleaned, like with enough noise and soapsuds, she could fill the hole made by my father's leaving.

Finally, we got the last dish dried and put away, and the dish towels all neatly hung up. Jack, though, took an extra-long time drying his hands on the last one.

"Listen, Callie, Mrs. LeRoux . . . I gotta go take care of some . . . stuff."

"You want me to come with you?" I asked immediately. The thought of being left alone with Mama was suddenly driving something close to panic under my skin.

"Uh, no," said Jack without even looking at me. "I just gotta . . . I'll see you at supper, okay? Thanks for the breakfast, Mrs. LeRoux. It was terrific."

And Jack was gone too. The door shut behind him as solidly as it had behind Papa. I couldn't believe Jack had just gone and left me like that. He didn't even try to come up with an explanation. Worry settled in. He was mad at Papa, and at me. Just how mad was he? And what was he gonna do about it? Jack was the person I knew best in the world, or at least that's what I'd thought. Now I wasn't so sure.

None of this was helped by the fact that I was alone with my mother for the first time since this whole long nightmare began. As soon as I turned around, I'd have to say something to her, and I had no idea what it should be. I had too many feelings jumbled up inside me, and not one of them would settle down enough for me to take hold of. The longer I stood there, the less I wanted to turn around at all.

"Oh, Callie," Mama breathed. "Just look at you."

I was sure she meant look at your skin, how brown it is. Look at your hair, all kinky and woolly and black. Look at all my work to make you into a white girl undone.

"You've grown into such a fine young lady while I've been away."

I about choked on my own thoughts. "You think so?"

She nodded. "I do."

We were silent again. Slowly, I realized there was only one thing I really wanted to say to her. It was the one question that had been boiling inside me since this whole long nightmare began. Until I asked it, I wasn't ever going to really sort out any kind of understanding of my life, or hers.

"Why didn't you tell me? About Papa?"

Mama let out a huge sigh. The strength seemed to leave her with all that breath, and she sat down heavily in the nearest chair. "Callie, you can't imagine how many times I've asked myself the same question." Slowly, she ran her thin hands across her hair, slicking it down and away from her creased-up forehead. "For a while I told myself you were just too young. Then I told myself that you were already keeping so many secrets, it wasn't fair to ask you to carry one more. After that I told myself if he never came back . . . if he never came back . . ." She shook her head and stared down at her fresh-scrubbed table. "But the truth is, I thought if you knew about them . . . about the king and queen and the Midnight Throne, that you had magic inside you, you'd want to find them." She lifted her tired eyes. "I was afraid you'd leave me, Callie."

I wanted to throw my arms around her. I wanted to hug her and say it was okay. We were together now and I'd never leave her alone.

But I didn't do any of those things. I couldn't. There was a whole well of anger inside me, and I didn't know where it came from or what it was doing there. But it bubbled up until I was full to overflowing just from looking at my skinny, worn-out mother sitting in this borrowed kitchen.

"You lied so you could keep hold of me," I croaked. "You're just like the rest of them."

"No, Callie, never. I . . ." She stopped. She didn't look at me. She plucked at a tear in the lace place mat, trying to get the edges to match up. "When I was little, there was a girl I went to school with . . . Rebecca Swenson. Her father was a no-good. Always on the bum. This was before the depression, you understand, when being out of work wasn't something that just . . . happened to a man. Mr. Swenson would come back every so often, take her mother's money, knock her around a bit, and run off again. Everybody knew about it. My parents felt sorry for Becky. Mother would let her work in the kitchen for a little money, and regular meals.

"But . . . Becky would spin these stories about her papa being a traveling man, and how he was off in some big city, like Memphis or New York. Whenever she got something new, a ribbon or new shoes—and it wasn't often—she'd parade around telling everybody how her father had sent her the present. It got to the point where she really believed what she was saying. It made me angry to hear her going on about it. I don't know why, exactly, but it did. One day . . . one day I just couldn't stand it anymore. I yelled at her to stop it. I told her that her father was a bum and everybody knew it, and the reason he wasn't home was that he was probably

dead in a ditch. I'll never forget the look on her face. . . ."
Mama's voice wavered. "She ran out of the kitchen, and I
never saw her again. No one did. At least, they never said. I
think . . . there were rumors . . . she'd killed herself." She
stopped. "That day you turned on me, when you yelled at
me, that I was crazy . . . all I could think of was Becky and
how she'd talked herself into believing her own lies about
her father. I was afraid . . . I was afraid I'd done the same
thing. That I really was crazy, that I really had killed you by
keeping you in the dust." She lifted her eyes. "That's why I
had you play the piano and break the protection. I had to
know if it was real or if I'd . . . if I'd just . . ."

She was trying. I felt it. Now, in this little space of time
where there was just me and her. She was trying to explain
and to say she was sorry. I wanted to forgive her, right then
and all at once. I hated the anger that was all knotted up inside me. But it had been there for so long and had been built
up so big over years of wishing and wondering and being
afraid that it wasn't going to shift itself anytime soon, not for
all my wishing, or hers.

But at least she was ready to talk. I shuffled my questions
around in my mind, with more than a little guilt, because I
knew I was trying to pump her for information, like Jack had
tried to with Papa.

"Did he tell you anything about . . . about the Unseelies?"

"Not much. He had to show me enough magic to prove
what he said, of course, and he did his best to explain that his

people were powerful, and that he had to make a clean break with them or there would be more complications to a situation that was already more than a little complicated." Her smile was weak and had no warmth in it at all.

"How about the Halfers . . . the Undone?" I asked the question fast, before I could talk myself out of it. "Did he ever say anything about them?"

"I never heard about them before now. Callie," said Mama, suddenly stern, "what are you thinking?"

"I just wondered." I was lying and doing it badly, of course. "If he'd said anything, because, well, your baby . . . me . . . I'm . . ."

She took my hand and squeezed, as if contact could force belief into me. "He didn't know about you, Callie. When he left, neither one of us knew I was pregnant. And you are nothing like those creatures."

"How do you know? You don't know what they are." *You don't know what I am either.* I bit my lip again. *Stop this,* I told myself. Things were getting better. I had to shut up now, before they jumped the track again.

"I know they tried to kill you and then they snatched you away from us," said Mama quietly. "Even without that, your father says they are dangerous."

"But you don't know why!"

"It doesn't matter why, Callie." Mama pushed herself to her feet. "I've seen what they are capable of with my own eyes and that's more than enough."

Her voice had turned to iron, and there was more iron behind her eyes. She really didn't care why Touhy or Dan Ryan or even Stripling had done what they'd done. She didn't care whether the Seelies or the Unseelies were behind it. She just saw yet more danger to me and Papa. If I kept on trying to push her into seeing what was on the far side of that danger, we'd end up shouting at each other, again. I didn't think I could stand that.

So I closed my mouth and turned away. My eyes were stinging. But I couldn't tell if the tears were building up because Mama wouldn't understand what I was feeling and thinking, or because I couldn't seem to manage to just tell her about it.

"Callie." Mama moved up behind me and laid her hands on my shoulders. "It's all right, Callie," she said. "There have been so many mistakes . . . we'll just have to do our best. But promise me you'll try, all right?"

"I promise," I said, and I felt that promise take hold inside me. With a start, I realized I was glad for it. Maybe it would get me to do what I couldn't seem to do on my own. Maybe it would find me the words to tell her what I was thinking.

Mama held out her hand, and this time I took it and let her pull me close so we could put our arms around each other and just hold on for a time.

"So." Mama finally let go and smoothed her dress down. "What shall we do first? Wash the windows? The whole room needs a good dusting and . . ." She stopped and watched me shifting my weight from side to side. "You want to go out too."

I nodded. Mama gave a wan smile. "And if I asked you to stay? If I said it was dangerous?"

I shifted my weight and looked out the filthy window. Mama sighed and smoothed her hair back again. "And that's the way it is. Here." She held out a scrap of paper. "I had Mrs. Burnstein write down the telephone number. Will you at least call if . . . if you need anything?"

I took the paper and tucked it into my pocket. I was going to need to start carrying a purse. I had wishes and presents and now my mother holding out an attempt to touch me without holding on too tight, and I didn't know where to keep it all.

She tried to smile. "Go. I've got plenty to do. There's no reason this can't be a decent place." By decent, of course, she meant clean.

I started for the door. I shouldn't have looked back, but I did, and saw her sit down heavily. Thin, alone, and bone tired, my mama stared out the grimy window, and I felt her wondering if any of us was coming back.

14

I'm Reckless

Thing was, as soon as I got onto the street, I had a problem. I didn't know which way I should be headed. Jack was long gone, and I didn't know the first thing about the city around me. I tried to put on a face like I knew what I was doing, so the skinny kids and hard-eyed old ladies wouldn't stare too much, and started walking.

I might have been on my own, but there wasn't any reason I actually had to be lost. If I was stuck with being an Unseelie princess, I might as well get some use out of it. I put my hand into my skirt pocket and touched Jack's notebook. Then I eased open my magic.

Jack Holland, I thought. *Jack, where are you?*

Probably, I should have just waited for Jack to come home. But I was worried. It just wasn't like him to do a little stammering and take off. He should have spun some kind of story, no matter what he was up to. And sometimes he got ideas stuck in his head that weren't the best kind, especially when he was mad. He could get really stubborn about them too. Besides, I needed to talk to him without any chance of my parents overhearing. I still had this idea I'd come up with out on the porch while we'd been talking to Touhy, and I was itching to hear how it sounded out loud. It made sense, I was sure it did, but I could already tell Papa wasn't going to like it. To have any chance of getting my parents to give it a try, I needed Jack to back me up.

Jack, where are you?

And just like that, I knew. I couldn't see him, exactly, but I knew where he was all the same. More than that, I knew the way he'd walked to get there. I felt it in my bones, and there was nothing in this whole city that could shake it out of me.

I smiled to myself, and started walking.

I probably shouldn't have been so confident about slinging my magic around after just one real lesson. It sure did feel strange at first, to be so certain about where to go without knowing the first thing about the streets or the buildings. But after a couple blocks, I'd settled into it. With my magic open, I could feel more of the currents around me than ever. This time it wasn't just the wishes and feelings of the people I was aware of, it was the city itself. I could feel the boundaries Papa had talked about, the places where territory and feeling began and ended. There were buried histories here, layers of life and wish and creation piled up like Mama's griddle cakes. They pushed and pulled on the people who moved through them. The city was living jewels and pretty puzzle pieces under my fingers. It was dazzling and chaotic, but it all fit together, and I found myself scrabbling at the pattern, trying to understand it. Was this what the full-blood fairies felt like when they came to the human world? If it was, I could understand how they might become fascinated by it. Even when I passed the newsstand and saw the papers with headlines screaming MGM OFFERS REWARD FOR INFORMATION ABOUT VANISHED STAR, it was just one more piece of the shimmering whole.

I was grinning and I knew it. I had Jack's present in one pocket and my papa's wish in the other, and my magic in my bones. I knew just where I should be going. I could feel the tug of the right path under the soles of my shoes. I could take on the world.

It was the cool of the metal door handle under my hand that brought me to myself, hard and sudden. I knuckled my eyes and stared around me.

Sooty brick buildings crowded on either side, and sooty striped awnings stuck out over doorways that didn't need them because the sun wasn't ever making it down here anyhow. The store in front of me had its shade pulled down and LESTER & SHALE painted on the glass in neat black lettering. The green door had been freshly painted and had another shade pulled down behind its double row of square glass panes and the CLOSED sign hung out.

I'd walked right down this alley off the main street, and I had my hand on the curving brass handle. I heard all the city noises, the voices, and the traffic, and I smelled all the smog and the trash. It was hot. I was perspiring. And I wasn't anywhere near Jack.

I'd done it again. I'd trusted my magic, and it had taken me right out of my good sense. Somebody'd reeled me in to this place like a fish on a line, and I hadn't even noticed. I didn't even know what part of the city I was in.

Then I saw how one of the door's glass panes had been smashed out, right above its handle. I lifted my hand back slow. The door was open, just a crack. You wouldn't even notice unless you were standing right up close, like I was now.

"You came," said a voice from inside. "By my blood and bones, you came."

The door swung open and I jumped back at the same time. The man on the other side stood swaying on his feet. He was a fairy, and he was trying to pull an illusion over himself, but he wasn't doing a very good job of it. He kept flickering. In one eyeblink, he was a bald, wrinkled little white man in a cardigan sweater. In the next, he was a black man in a torn-up suit, hunched over and breathing hard. One hand was shoved in his coat pocket, and the other clutched a black cane with a handle made out of the biggest diamond ever seen.

I recognized that cane. "I know you."

He didn't answer right away, and I felt something I never had from a Seelie or an Unseelie either: shame. It was like I'd caught him with his shirttail hanging out. He bent low, and lower, and I realized he was trying to bow.

"We met, once," he said. "At the Kansas City gate. I am major domo to the Midnight Throne, and their Unseelie majesties." He tried to bow again, but he shivered so much doing it, I was afraid he was going to fall flat on his face. He was wearing a gray shirt and a dark suit with a bright red vest. The front of the vest was splotchy. Something wet had been splashed all over it.

"Will Your Highness be pleased to step inside?" He turned toward the shop. He didn't pull his one hand out of his pocket. The one that held the cane was covered in a white glove, and it was damp-stained like his vest.

The major domo noticed how I hadn't moved. The news he worked for my grandparents did not give me any reason at all to walk anywhere with him, let alone into someplace where the door could be locked behind me. Truth was, I was a lot closer to running away than following. He probably figured that out because he started shaking all over so bad that if he'd been human, I would have thought he had the ague.

"I swear by my true name you will come to no harm from me or my errand," he said, his words low and urgent. Perspiration dripped down his shining cheeks. "I am specifically forbidden by my nature and my office from working harm against you. *Please,* Your Highness."

He was telling the truth. I could feel it, like I could feel the effort it was taking for him to stand there. But I didn't trust any of it. After all the mistakes I'd made and all the trouble I'd met, how could I? But I didn't run. I kind of sidled up to that doorway, one hand in my own pocket so I could hang on to Papa's glass marble of a wish. I put my other palm up to the threshold, and waited to feel the twisty lock-and-key sensation that meant this was a door out of the world. But there was nothing. This was a regular human shop on a regular human street.

The major domo's right knee buckled and he caught himself. I felt the shame curling out of him again, cold and sad. If this was a trap, somebody was pouring it on pretty thick. But then, that was what they did, wasn't it?

"You go first," I said.

Major inclined his head, and turned, slowly. His cane thumped heavily on the floorboards as he moved. He was hurting. I wanted to feel sorry for him, but I didn't dare. But I did take a deep breath and step over the threshold to walk inside.

Lester & Shale was a bookstore. The smells of paper, ink, and dust surrounded me. High shelves were crammed solidly together and towered over the dim, narrow aisles like the buildings towered over the alley outside. Every shelf was stuffed full of books: all kinds of books, from battered paperbacks to faded magazines with torn and curling covers to antique leather-bound volumes—some as narrow as my pinky finger and some as broad as my whole hand. Maybe half of them were actually in English. Books had been laid flat to fill the spaces above the books that stood upright. More books were piled on the floor between the shelves and yet more books spilled out of cardboard boxes and wooden crates in the corners. At the same time, something important was missing.

"There ain't no gate here."

"Not here, no. But . . . places such as this, so full of heart and imaginings . . . They welcome our kind and can be made useful." Major thumped and shuffled to the tiny desk at the end of the aisle. Even this was piled high with books and magazines. "You will forgive me, Your Highness." He groped for the leather-backed chair and sat down, laying his cane on the desk. "I'm afraid . . . it has been a long journey."

I looked around me. My ability to hold on to my suspicions was wearing thin, but I knotted it tight and held on.

"So, where's the owner?"

Major's mouth twitched. He might have been trying to smile. "Taking his lunchtime walk in the park," he said. "I expect it will be a little longer today than usual." He must have seen the look on my face because he added, "But not by much."

He was still telling the truth, which was heading into miracle territory. I'd probably never had such a straightforward conversation with a fairy man, and I was counting my father in that. "And you've got a message or something from my grandparents, is that it?" I prompted.

"Yes." Major groped one-handed among the papers on the desk, and winced. He tried to draw back, but I caught his hand. I wanted to see what he had hold of. But his hand was empty. What made him wince was pain.

His glove had been slashed open, and that wasn't all. A gash stretched across his smooth, brown palm. The liquid that filled the cut wasn't red, like blood. It was clear, like water but with a weak silver shine to it, and I could see down to the bird-thin bones underneath. The light of the fairy lands running out of his veins, trickling onto the papers and the scarred wooden desk.

He snatched his hand away and shoved it under the desk. "My apologies," he said.

"That's okay," I whispered as I let him go. I blinked at his damp vest, and his damp coat. I swallowed hard and made up my mind. I didn't trust him and I wasn't going to trust him. But I wasn't going to leave him like this either, and if that made me a chump, well, that was the way it was going to be.

I took a deep breath and opened my magic. There was nobody near but me and him, but there were all those books, all that work and love and feeling bound into paper and marked out by ink. Tapping into a static book wasn't as easy as tapping into living music, but there were a whole lot of them to work with and that kind of made up for it.

Be whole, I wished toward Major. *Be well.*

Major shuddered, he hunched up even tighter and gasped, and for a second I was scared I'd hurt him worse and tried to shut the wish down. But then his breathing eased, and he lifted his right hand. The glove was still shredded, but the skin underneath was whole, except for one thin white scar. When he lifted his eyes to me, they were bright with moonlight and starlight like they should have been.

"Thank you, Your Highness." He drew himself up tall and straight, and when he bowed this time it was a crisp, sharp gesture.

"You're welcome." I nodded back, already hoping this had not been another mistake. "Now, what's this message?"

Major gave another bow, and lifted a folded paper out from among the piles of magazines, bills, and receipts. It was thick, cream-colored parchment tied up with a red ribbon. He held it out toward me. This time I backed up.

"Oh, no. I am not touching that." Last time I had fairy paper in my hands, it did not go so good for me. "Every time my grandparents get near me, they try to haul me in."

Major sighed. "Their Majesties were afraid you would say something of the kind. They apologize, Your Highness, for past indiscretions. Truly. If you would just . . ."

"I said no! You want me to know what it says, you read it out." I folded my arms and waited.

Major sighed, but bowed, again. He broke the seal and unfolded the letter. I thought he would start reading, but he didn't. He turned the paper toward me.

The other side of the paper was covered in a layer of shining gold. The dim shop light touched it, striking sparks, and bringing up reflections. Being how they were fairy creations, those reflections moved.

There's a stone wall at the edge of the Unseelie country,

wrapped round with emerald-and-ruby vines. The stones are living goblins, and the vines are their arms, all linked together so they can keep out anybody who ain't been invited. That wall shimmered in the golden reflection, except the stones had been split open and the clear silver blood flowed out of them. Other stones wrapped their vine arms around their colleagues, and tossed them away, splitting them open. Little white-winged creatures crowded around the broken stones, pure and perfect and shining, just like the pretty, little-girl fairies you see in a picture book, and they were drinking up the silver blood where it poured out. Other shining beings rode past on white horses, their robes trailing into that silver blood, and their banners flapping in the breeze. Every one of them wore a golden mask beneath a golden helmet.

They will be here soon, whispered my grandmother's voice from the page. *The army is retreating to the emerald fields. Please, please, you must come. If you do not close the gates, we cannot hold.*

I reached out toward that page, as if I could touch my grandmother's hand. At the last second, I remembered, and snatched it back. Major winced as if I'd struck him.

"How?" I croaked. "How are they getting in so easy?"

"We were all betrayed," he told me. "You most of all."

"Mightily," added a man's cheerful voice back in the aisles. "And to top it off, Bad Luck Girl, you're both too late."

15

And the Boys Will Drag You Down

There were three of them, one to block each aisle of the shop. They were all white men with white hair and white mustaches, dressed up swell in new suits and two-toned shoes with white hats on their heads and watch chains on their white vests. They could have been bankers, or gangsters. The one who spoke out came up the center aisle, and he stood close enough to me that I could see a little charm in the shape of a golden mask dangling from that chain.

"Stay back!" I shouted to Major, and yanked Papa's wish out of my pocket.

"Oh, no, you don't!" Magic lashed out, fast and strong, and the wish was gone from my hand. The middle man of the three held it up in his thick fingers. Then he popped it into his mouth and swallowed it whole.

"Mmm." He licked his pale pink lips slowly. "Tasty."

His two friends snickered and stepped out into the light. Before I could take another breath, Major had ducked around in front of me and he had his black cane held up high.

"No further," he whispered, soft and dangerous. "No further or I will make an end of you all, I so swear."

"Now, brother," said the middle of the three. "What is this? We've just come to bring you news of the peace."

"Peace?" Major sneered.

"Peace," repeated the middle man. "And victory. The Midnight Throne calls you back to your service, brother," he said to the Major. "You hear it now."

Magic filled those words, thick and smothering and honey-sweet. I jumped back like I thought I could dodge it. But this wasn't for me. This was for the major domo. The light flickered in his eyes, and his anger melted like ice in July. He lowered his black cane to the floor, and he smiled. I could feel the relief in him as he bent into one of his crisp bows.

"That's it, brother." The middle man stepped forward, hand out.

Quick as thinking, Major whipped that diamond-handled cane around and brought it down hard on the middle man's wrist. His scream ended in a harsh gurgle as Major jabbed the tip into his throat.

"Run!" Major shouted to me. "Run, Highness!"

I didn't bother answering that one. I snatched up the feeling swirling through the shop around me, and I shoved back hard. Hard enough to rattle the shelves. The left-hand man looked up and raised his arm and his magic. And I grabbed up the Webster's Dictionary off the desk and threw it at him.

Lefty ducked and swore. I grabbed up another book, and the right-hand man tackled me, hard.

We rolled over, with me screaming and kicking and jabbing my fingers at his eyes and twisting on his ears and him screaming too. My magic lashed out on its own, looking for something it could grab and twist, because I was wishing for help too. Any kind of help.

What it found was the papers and books on the desk, the ones where Major's blood had spilled and smeared. They twitched and jerked upright and flapped open, bills and receipts and books, and even that dictionary. They rose up, flapping like giant paper birds in a high wind. While I was distracted, Right Hand got hold of my arm and tried to twist it up behind me. I screamed, and those flying books dropped down, right on his head. He let go to bat them away. I shinnied out from under him and shoved my foot hard in his stomach on the way out. Or near his stomach, anyway.

Major was dancing like a prizefighter in front of the desk, beating back both Lefty and Middle Man with his diamond cane and hollering curses at the top of his lungs. The papers must have noticed too, because they swooped down to plaster themselves against the bad guys' faces, blinding them. Smothering them. Major flipped his cane around in his hand, so he was swinging with that huge diamond at their knees and their skulls.

I had time to let out one whoop before my feet shot out from under me. I slammed hard against the floor and all the breath left me like it wasn't ever coming back. Right Hand reared up over me, his fist bunched up tight and his magic pinning me down hard. The Webster's Dictionary jumped at his head and bounced back a good six inches away. He laughed and swung down, but instead of my head, he hit a big pillow of paper that had balled itself in front of me. I shouted, and rolled, and kicked, and scrambled away. The dictionary fell to the floor and flapped open, releasing a cloud of words. They swarmed around Right Hand's head like big black wasps, diving for his eyes, and getting into his ears and up his nose, and right down his throat when he tried to scream. He fell back coughing, spitting, and swatting. I levered myself to my feet, a whole swarm of loose paper scrunched up around my ankles.

But while my books and my papers had rescued me, they'd left Major alone. One of the fairy toughs had Major's arm twisted around behind him. The other had his cane, and he swung the diamond handle down with a sick, wet crunch.

Run, I heard Major's voice pleading in my head. *Run, Highness.*

Middle Man raised the cane again. The next blow snapped Major's head back and his voice went suddenly, horribly silent. Lefty turned on me and held up his hand. Fire spurted from each finger and Lefty grinned.

I ran. I slammed out the door and into the alley. I pelted away from the main street and into the shadows. It was a twisting maze back there. I turned left and right without any kind of plan. I glanced back. Two fairy men ran behind me, and they were gaining. My papers swirled at my feet and my back. They flopped into the fairy men's faces, then jammed under their shoes and made them skid. Words buzzed and clouded around their heads. But papers tore and crumpled, and the wind blew the words aside. My magic tried to keep them together, and I had to save most of my concentration for running, but they kept on trying, and they did slow those murderers down.

Why had I ever liked this city? There were too many holes and cubbies and dead ends. I didn't know where to go. There were too many places for people and things to hide and spring out. At least in Kansas, if something bad was going to roll down over you, you could see it coming. Here, there was nothing but alleys and doorways and traffic and fences, and with all my magic senses, I couldn't tell what was behind any of them. I couldn't think clearly, my head was so full of the sight of Major going limp and still. It brought back the sight of Ivy lying dead on the white marble deck and Shimmy falling dead in the mud. I'd done it again, again, again. Another person tried to help me; another person wound up dead.

The difference was, last time there'd been a fairy court,

and a king, and my family to get out of the way. This time there were just two murderers following me. Just two, and I had nobody else to get out of the way now.

That thought opened up a kind of grim determination inside me. I dodged around the next corner and came face to face with a wooden fence. A little group of words buzzed straight past me and down, showing me where one board had been broken off at the bottom. I fell flat on my belly and shinnied through it and came up in the dusty backyard of a tenement neighborhood, kind of like Jack's, with the crowded clapboard houses, all three stories high with peaked roofs and porches out back.

One porch, a dug-out, concrete-lined patch, led to a basement door. I sent a strong thought to my following flock and all the words and pages dropped to the ground, scattering themselves among the other trash just lying there. I jumped down onto the dug-out porch, crouched by the wall, and waited, gathering a little knot of magic tight inside me.

"Come on, come on, you big dummies," I muttered. "You saw which way I went. Get in here."

A wind whirled hard through that little yard. The fence rocked, and creaked, and fell, puffing up a big cloud of dust. The murderers stepped through. And I saw how I'd made another huge mistake. Because they weren't alone anymore.

I wasn't the only one who could gather up the bits and pieces around me. I'd thought it was my words and pages that had slowed them down, but now I saw they'd been taking the time to work a little magic of their own. They'd made friends with the trash from the alley, and the junk and the rags and the rotted garbage rolled and roiled around them as they stepped over the fallen fence. The stink was unbelievable, and so was the noise. My papers out there cringed backward, and so did I.

"Well, well," said Middle Man. "Better go get her, boys."

Lefty called out some words I didn't understand and the trash piled itself up, folding and fitting and tucking together until that restless pile took on the form of a bear, rearing up on its hind legs. My words tried to swarm around it, but they just made it angry, so it roared and galloped forward, heading straight for me.

But as I scrambled backward, that bear was reeling back, like it had slammed into a wall. I straightened up and blinked. Lefty was shouting again. The trash bear slammed forward again, snarling and clawing at thin air, and the words buzzed furiously. But none of them—not the fairy men, not the bear, not my words—could get any closer. I pushed myself up against the building wall, so I was in plain view, and still not one of them could reach me.

Relief bubbled up and made me stupid. I stuck my tongue out at the murderers.

Right Hand and Lefty snarled and stormed forward. The bear and the wasps fell back. The fairy toughs linked hands and magic, and shoved their free hands right up to whatever barrier filled the space between the porch timbers. I grabbed at what little feeling and magic I had in there with me and got ready to fight for my life.

Turned out I needn't have bothered.

Both fairy men stood there for one split second. I could see them plain. Then the whole space outlined by the porch timbers filled with something thick and white, like a fog rising up from the ground. Except this fog had weight, and it wrapped around them, winding tight around their heads and limbs. They screamed and howled, but that fog filled their mouths to smother their cries and drag them both down to the ground.

I watched them kicking and struggling under that foggy white binding. But not for long. The lumps that had been the murderers slumped against the ground, growing smaller and smaller under that thick white blanket, until there was nothing left of them at all.

The trash bear wavered for a moment, and then burst apart. Junk and rot and refuse tumbled away across the dusty yard. My words buzzed aimlessly for a moment, and then dropped onto the ground, clattering like pebbles. Just more trash to fill up that dusty yard.

My throat tightened up. Slowly, I pushed myself to my feet. I wiped my hands on my skirt. I had no idea what just happened, but I had a very clear idea that I should not stay here on this little sunken porch. The coast looked clear. I couldn't feel any magic hanging around this porch space with me. Time to get good and gone.

But as soon as I reached the steps that led up to the yard, I tripped and fell. Dirty concrete bit my knees and I gasped in pain. I shoved myself back to my feet and tried again to run up the steps, and tripped again, fell again, and banged my knees again.

Fear crawled onto my back and I forced myself to stay calm. I tried to vault over the cement wall into the yard, but my hands slipped right off the edge and I was back on my knees. This time the concrete drew blood and I bit my tongue hard.

The hairs on the back of my neck stood up before I even heard the creak of the hinges. The cellar door was opening behind me.

"Come in, Callie LeRoux." The voice from inside the cellar creaked as badly as the rusty hinges. "Let's get a look at you."

Not on your life.

I stood up, and anger rallied my magic. I swung out with it, feeling for edges and cracks in whatever magic wall was holding me in. But there was nothing I could get hold of. I could still feel the world out there, with all its motion and jigsaw puzzle pieces, but I couldn't get to it. I was stuck.

The whole time, somebody in the dark beyond that open door at my back laughed at me. They chuckled and cackled and they wouldn't quit.

I tried again. I ran and I jumped up the steps. I pushed and shoved with my magic and my bare hands in every direction as hard as I knew how. Nothing happened, except I skinned my knees and my palms up real good and got myself all out of breath.

"Oh, get in here, gal," said the voice at last. "I ain't gonna eat you. Yet."

My heart was in my mouth. Sweat dripped in my eyes and stung. I was breathing so hard it blotted out the traffic noise. The weathered door was open onto a threshold so dark I couldn't see anything except the cobwebs in the splintery corners of the door frame.

I didn't want to go in there. Every door I walked through just made things worse.

But there was nothing else I could do. I wiped my upper lip with the back of my hand, straightened my shoulders, and remembered I was my mother's daughter. I lifted my chin high and stepped inside.

16

Up Jumped Aunt Hagar

The smell of damp, dirt, and old sewer surrounded me like the dark. A spider scuttled across my shoe and I jumped back, banging against the cellar wall and sending a shower of dirt down on my own head. I shrieked and swatted the air around me and got hands full of cobwebs. A spider scampered up my arm and I shrieked again and swatted at it.

And the cackling laughter rose up again. Anger and shame burned away my fear. How could a couple spiders and a little dirt be getting to me like this? I was not gonna make myself any more ridiculous in front of . . . of . . . whatever it was in here with me.

The dim light drifting in through the open door showed where there was a naked lightbulb overhead and a cobwebbed chain hanging down. I lifted up my scraped hand and pulled the chain. There was a chink, and the light came on.

I saw the ruined basement around me, its floor littered with trash, leaves, and scraps of rotted wood. But in the back corner, there was another room altogether, almost another world. It was a tidy place, with a fire in a fieldstone hearth and a clean rag rug on the floor. There was a handmade rocking chair and a carved table. The white-haired woman in the rocking chair was stick thin with skin a color somewhere between umber and bronze. Her long, knobby fingers worked a set of knitting needles as delicate as tree twigs. A huge spill of pure white spread across her lap and around her shoulders like a snowy shawl, except she was still knitting it. Instead of the yarn coming up from a ball like it should, it was coming down to her from a hundred different directions.

It was coming from each and every one of the spiderwebs that hung in the old beams over her tidy space of a room.

This was wrong, very wrong. This neat, petite old woman sat here drawing cobwebs onto herself to knit into a blanket. I wanted to back away. In fact, I did, until I bumped into the door that had shut behind me without making a sound.

"So much for the famous Callie LeRoux." Her sunken lips pursed. A quick hand darted out from under the white blanket and caught the slack spider thread up for her busy needles. At first her eyes were rich brown human eyes, but as they narrowed, I caught a shift, and for one second, I was looking into the stars. I felt a strange twist of nerves and a rush of relief at the same time. Whoever this was, she wasn't the fairy kind. I'd seen eyes like this before.

"Yes, ma'am," I said, trying to remember my manners. Once I'd started dealing in magic, I learned pretty quick there were people around you that you had better be polite to. I would have bet everything I owned she was one of them. "Um, you wouldn't by any chance know an old Indian called Baya, would you?" I asked. "Or a porter named Daddy Joe?"

"Ah. Now, they did say you was a sharp one. I guess they might be right at that." She held up the bit of white she was working on and ran her thumb over it. The pattern shimmered silkily in the light of her fire. It was beautiful, like the stars or flowing water is beautiful. All at once, I felt sure it held all the mysteries of the city around us. I wanted more than anything to move closer, to see it more clearly. When I did, maybe I'd finally understand.

I shut my eyes fast and the old woman chuckled again. "Sharp enough, anyhow. Not terrible quick, but you do get there."

The needles started clacking again. I took a risk and cracked my eyelids. She'd lowered her knitting and was busy casting on while the needles worked back and forth. "Um, I don't know what I should call you, ma'am." That was something else I'd learned. You never asked somebody like this their name directly. It might make them mad.

The old woman considered. "You can call me Aunt Nancy for the purposes of our conversing here."

"Yes, ma'am. And . . . and I guess I should thank you for helping me out with . . . them." I gestured toward the door.

Aunt Nancy sniffed. "Didn't do it for you, gal. They didn't ask my permission to go stomping through my city, did they? No more did you," she added, each word as pointed as her needles.

"Uh, I . . . uh . . . I'm sorry, ma'am. I didn't know . . ."

"Ha! Didn't think to ask. Don't worry. Your daddy was here this morning, all smiles and pretty words and if you please."

"Oh. Ah. Um. Good."

"Good enough for working days, anyhow. But I wanted a look at you for my own self, as you're the one who seems to be causing all this fuss."

I didn't want her looking at me. Her kind could see way too much. The last couple of times had gone pretty well, but then I'd been helping out some. This time . . . this time I was nothing but a problem. I shifted my weight and tried to think what I could do to get myself out of here. I wondered what Papa would say. "To what do I owe the honor of being invited here today?"

"Hee. That's right, Bad Luck Girl, you pay attention to your papa's pretty talk. He'll show you all the tricks. Train you up to be just like him."

One of these days I was going to learn to think quietly. I just wished that day would come soon. Aunt Nancy nodded with satisfaction. Her needles clacked fast and light, a sound like claws scrabbling inside the walls. Above and around us the spiders spun their webs for her to draw down. I swallowed fear and impatience. "Ma'am, I don't mean any disrespect, but if you've got something you want to say to me, I'd be glad to hear it."

"Got someplace to be, have you?" She jutted out her sharp jaw in disapproval. Her hand waved toward the distant door and her needles trembled as she worked. "All this comin' and goin'. I got kinfolk need looking after here. Can't have your people just trampling all over them, now can I?"

"We're just passing through, ma'am."

"Are you, now? 'Cause to these eyes it sure looks like you're fixin' to stay put."

So she'd been spying on me, on us. That touched the last dying spark of my patience. I walked up to the edge of that rag rug. A spider climbed out of the braids and moved, slow and long-legged, toward my shoe. My toes curled up and I had to fight the urge to stomp on it.

"What do you want? You could've left me alone easy enough or stayed hid. Why'd you want me to know about you?"

"To find out what you'd do," she answered. "Why else? Everybody watchin' the Bad Luck Girl. Everybody waitin' to see which road it's gonna be, ain't they?"

"Yeah, and everybody and their uncle's got an opinion. What's yours?"

"Hee-hee. Everybody and their uncle. That's a good one, comin' from you. But it's a fair question." She tapped her jutting chin thoughtfully as her dexterous fingers counted stitches on her delicate needles. That was when I realized what was wrong. That hand—that free hand that pulled the spider yarn and jabbed and gestured—that was a third hand, and there were two more closing the white shawl neatly around her, as if to keep out the chill.

It took every nerve I had in the whole of my body not to shrink away.

"I think as long as you remember who you really are, you'll do all right," Aunt Nancy said, counting stitches with two of her hands, while the other two held her needles, and another looped spider yarn around its index finger. "The question is, will you do that? Yes," she said to herself. "That is most certainly the question."

"Does this question have an answer?"

Her star eyes glittered at me, and I felt very small and very light, as if one of her spiders could have picked me up and carried me off.

"I believe it does."

"You wouldn't be interested in sharing it by any chance?"

"You'll hear it when you need to, gal."

I was getting real fed up with magic people. Couldn't even one of them talk in a straight line—spiders, coyotes, fairies, Halfers, none of them. I stepped hard on my temper, and leaned in for good measure, to make sure it stayed down.

"Well, if that's all, then, ma'am, with your permission, I'll just be getting along."

"Looking for your beau?"

"He's not my . . . !" I stopped and pulled back hard on my words, and my embarrassment. "I need to make sure he's okay. It's a big city and you never know who's around, do you?" I made sure I was looking straight at her when I said that last bit. But inside I was thinking how I'd been found. Everybody knew about Jack at least as well as they knew about me. They might be out looking for him too. I needed to know he was still okay.

Aunt Nancy gave an odd little puckered grin and for the first time, I felt something ease inside me. "Better give the boy his privacy just now." She pointed one of her needles toward the fire.

In the next eyeblink, I wasn't looking at a fire anymore, I was looking right through it, and on the other side, I saw Jack. He was standing in a cemetery, his head bowed. That place was filled with death and the knowledge of death, and it was old and close and deeply familiar. The headstones were huge, narrow slabs covered with the blocky writing I couldn't read and six-pointed stars that had been blackened by soot and years. So had the paved paths between them, and the grass on the graves.

Jack stood in front of a set of three gravestones. Unlike most of the others, these were still clean and polished. Jack had his back to the path, and his head bowed. He was praying.

". . . toosh'b'chatah v'nechematah, da'ameeran b'al'mah, v'eemru: Amein . . ."

Those were his family's graves. Jack had lit out of the house without saying anything so he could visit his dead.

"Why didn't you tell me?" I whispered to Jack's image. "Don't you trust me?"

"Maybe he should be asking you that," said Aunt Nancy.

She was right. I hadn't even stopped to think that Jack might have gone out to visit his parents' graves. Of course he'd want to do that. I would have. But I'd be darned if I was going to let the old woman behind me scold me into shame. "I do trust him," I muttered.

"Sure you do. You trust him just like you trust your mama and daddy. So much you didn't tell none of 'em where you wanted to go or what you was thinkin' 'bout this mornin'. Oh, no. Miss Callie knows best. She can go out on her own, just fine. Nobody needs to know *her* business. She can go out and leave her Mama alone and it'll be all right. She's got *important* things to do."

"That's not fair!"

"Ain't it?" She puckered up her shriveled mouth and counted her stitches with four of those long-fingered hands. "Well, well, you don't say so?"

On the other side of Aunt Nancy's fire, Jack stiffened for a second, like he knew he was being watched. I pulled back, guilty. I was intruding. Aunt Nancy was right. I didn't like it, but I couldn't deny it. I should have waited and trusted. After all this time, I should have known him better.

Behind me, Aunt Nancy's needles clicked twice, and Jack's shoulders relaxed.

"Oseh shalom bim'romav hu ya'aseh shalom"—he bowed his head again—*"aleinu v'al kol Yis'ra'eil v'im'ru. Amein."*

Jack stood silent for a bit. Then he let out a breath it felt like he'd been holding for a long time. He picked up two stones off the gravel path and carefully placed one on each of the first two tombstones. Last of all, he took the marble Papa'd given him out of his pocket, and laid it on the third tombstone.

"Oh, Jack," I breathed. Because he couldn't have said more clearly he didn't trust Papa if he'd shouted it from the rooftop. It hurt. I understood it, but it hurt bad.

Aunt Nancy snapped two of her knobby fingers, and the fire was just a fire again. "Now, if you take my advice, you'll leave that young man to himself a bit and get on home to your mother."

I almost asked why. Almost. She was looking at me again, and letting me see her star-filled eyes. "I'll do that. Thank you."

She clucked her tongue, but thoughtfully this time. "You remember who you are, Bad Luck Girl, and you'll do all right."

"I don't know who I am."

"Yes, you do. You just afraid to admit it."

"Yes, ma'am," I said, because there was no other answer. "Thank you, ma'am."

Aunt Nancy shook her head and clicked her needles and I walked out of there and up the steps as easily as I would out of any other cellar under any other building anyplace in the world. The papers were still rattling aimlessly around the fence. There were bugs buzzing low around the dust.

Not bugs. Words. The words and the papers were still alive, and now that I'd come out, they all came flocking up to me, rustling and humming, waiting for me to tell them what to do. The papers crept over my shoe tops and words landed on my shoulders and the backs of my hands.

This was not good. I could not go home like this, with a bunch of words and papers crowding around me like the strangest cluster of stray kittens ever seen. I knew Aunt Nancy was in there laughing at me. I shut my jaw hard enough to make my teeth click. I couldn't hang around here. I had to get back to the house and Mama, fast. People like Aunt Nancy did not say things just to hear themselves talk. Something was going to happen, and I had to be there. I had to think of something. I could probably wish the whole bundle of paper and ink dead, and maybe I should, but that felt wrong somehow. I mean, I was responsible for it being alive in the first place.

An idea hit me. I pulled Jack's notebook out of my pocket and opened it. "All right, all of you, inside."

They did it too. The words plastered themselves to the pages and the papers folded themselves up into tiny scraps and slotted themselves between the notebook pages. It was a minute's struggle to close the book, but I managed and stuffed it back in my pocket.

I let myself out the yard gate this time, and onto the shady street. It was only when I closed the gate firmly behind me that I started to run.

17

Mama Don't Allow

My ankles hurt. My cheeks burned. I was wheezing like a bad engine and still a couple of blocks from the Hollanders' when I heard the crowd. Up ahead out of sight, people yelled and swore and called names, and there were a whole lot of them.

They were around the corner, where I needed to go. I stopped and leaned against the lamppost, digging the heel of my hand into my side to slow down my spreading cramp. I tried hard to think of a detour. But I didn't know any of these streets and didn't want to try my magic just now. That had taken me enough strange places today.

I sucked in a long, whooping breath, and ran around the corner.

Up ahead, the sidewalk was one mass of people. Men and women shifted around so they could jam closer together. They were booing and yelling. Some had fists in the air, or pointed fingers. I swerved into traffic, ignored the honks, and jumped over the curb onto the sidewalk. The roar of the crowd behind me redoubled.

"Shame on you, Ben Hollander!" screamed someone. "Shame on your family!"

I tripped hard and almost fell. The crowd was screaming again. I was close to tears, but I turned around anyway, and this time I made myself look at what was happening.

The crowd had gathered in front of one of the narrow clapboard apartment buildings. The door had been flung open and Ben Hollander was coming down the stairs, shoving a woman in front of him. She stumbled across the porch, and I saw she had a bundle that could only have been a baby clutched tight to her chest. The cigar-chewing boss man, Sweeny, was there too, standing guard on the porch with his arms folded.

"Go on wid youz!" bellowed Sweeny over the heads of the crowd. "You ain't gonna pay, you ain't gonna stay!"

Ben pushed the woman and her baby down the porch steps, straight into the arms of some of the women who had gathered as part of the crowd. He had a bundle of clothes under his arm, and he flung them right out into the crowd. They booed loudly and he brushed his chin at them. Sy was there too, coming down the stairs lugging a mattress. He heaved it over the side of the porch, which set up another roar from the crowd.

I knew what this was. This was an eviction. Some landlord had hired Sweeny, Ben, and Sy to toss the family and all their things into the street. That woman, whoever she was, didn't own the house, so if she couldn't make the rent, she could be thrown out anytime. Or maybe she had owned it and missed the payments, so the bank was foreclosing. I couldn't see the woman's face for the crowd, but I knew exactly the kind of confused, lost look she'd have. I'd seen it on neighbors' faces back in Slow Run when the sheriff came to take their keys. Sick to my stomach, I bit my lip and turned away. There'd been nothing I could do then, and there was nothing I could do now. I had to get back to Mama.

Except it turned out Mama was already there.

"Benjamin Hollander, you stop this at once!"

Mama's voice rang steady and clear over the noise of the crowd. So loud, clear, and unexpected, in fact, that the crowd shut up. All together, that suddenly silent crowd turned to see my mama striding up the sidewalk, a shopping basket slung over each arm.

Oh, no. Not now. Not this time. Please, no, no, no, NO!

Mama hadn't noticed me yet. She just marched up the street like nothing was ever going to stop her. Even from where I stood, I could see the set of her jaw. All her attention was focused on the Hollander brothers as the crowd parted and she climbed those steps. I scrunched down to make myself as small as I could. I ducked and squeezed and shoved between the people in the crowd until I came up close to the porch.

Mama still didn't see me. She stood in front of Ben. Simon was in the doorway, a pile of bed linens in his bulky arms.

"What do you think you are doing to this poor woman?" Mama demanded. "Simon! You take those things back upstairs at once!"

"Mrs. LeRoux," said Ben carefully. "This ain't none of your business."

"And it shouldn't be any of yours," she said right back. "Now get back upstairs with that, Simon."

Simon Hollander's cigarette drooped and so did his shoulders. He turned around and, I swear to you, he would have done what Mama said, if Sweeny hadn't been there.

"Who is this broad?" Sweeny yanked his cigar out of his mouth and spat. "Get your ass off this porch, lady. This is a legal eviction."

Slowly and delicately, Mama set down her full market baskets. "If this is a legal eviction, Mr. Sweeny, you can show me the papers." She held out one neatly gloved hand.

Sweeny's face flushed a purple color that couldn't be healthy for anybody. "I told you to get . . ."

"And I told you, if this is a legal eviction, you must have the papers to prove it. Let's see them." Mama wasn't moving. But the crowd around me shifted, muttering and closing ranks.

"Papers!" someone shouted, and the rest of them took up the chant. An ugliness ran between them, fire hot, stone hard, and sickly sour. "Papers! Papers!"

"Mama. Mama, please," I murmured and leaned hard on the words as I pushed my way between the people gathered in front of the house. "Don't do this."

She couldn't possibly have heard me, but she turned all the same, and saw me standing by the steps. "Callie!" She frowned. I waited for her to move, to get off that porch and come down to me. But she didn't. "You go home now, there's a good girl. Mr. Sweeny? I'm waiting."

I knew what she was doing. This was what she always did. Whether it was feeding hoboes off the trains or buying up things from the "dime auctions" when a neighbor went bust, this was what Mama did. She tried to get her strong back between people and their trouble. But this wasn't Slow Run. I shoved my way through the last line of bodies and up the steps. Nobody here knew us. It didn't matter she'd been able to sweet talk that Mrs. Burnstein or that Old Man Grenke. We were strangers in a hard, strange land, and if things got bad, nobody was gonna care what happened to us.

Especially not Mr. Sweeny, who stalked up to her, his chin trembling from the buildup of pure mean inside.

"You're crazy, that's what you are!" Sweeny swiped at the air with his cigar. "Benny, get her and the brat outta here." He stood back, and he waited.

Ben shook himself and slouched into the space Sweeny had left open in front of Mama. "You should just go now, Mrs. LeRoux. Me and Sy, we got to finish our business here, and we cannot have no trouble."

Mama ignored him. And me. I climbed up onto the porch and tugged at her elbow. But it was like pulling at a statue.

"Mr. Sweeny." Mama stepped sideways so she could

look him right in the eye. "If you cannot produce those papers, I have to assume this is not in fact a legal eviction, and I will be forced to call the police."

"Papers! Papers!" the crowd shouted. "Sweeny, show the papers!" The baby was wailing as loud as any of them. Their anger got through my fairy senses and burned the underside of my bones.

So did Ben Hollander's. "I told you to get home!" Ben grabbed me by the arm and the next thing I knew, the world spun and I toppled down the steps into the arms of some lady in a black dress who smelled like garlic and cigarettes.

Up on the porch, Mama spun around and backhanded Ben Hollander right across the face. The crowd booed and jeered, but the brothers had already swung into action. Simon dropped the linens he carried and grabbed Mama's arm. Benny's fist drove straight into her stomach. Mama doubled over without making a sound. Simon let her fall to her knees.

The world went silent. The world went red. I didn't feel myself move. I was back on that porch and on my knees beside Mama. Her mouth was gaping open as she tried to breathe, but she couldn't. Her eyes near popped out of her skull from the pain, and she was heaving like she was trying to gasp for air and vomit at the same time. I wrapped my arms around her shoulders.

"You're gonna be sorry for this, Benjamin Hollander," I was saying. "You too, Simon Hollander! You're gonna be sorry you were ever born!"

The brothers' eyes widened as the magic in my words lashed out. I had no shape for them, no intent, only my anger and that one wish. They were both going to be so, so sorry.

Right then Benny Hollander started to cry. Simon stared at him for one second, his jaw flapping so loose the cigarette tumbled to the ground. Then he started to cry too, his teeth ground tight around the place his cigarette used to be as the fat tears rolled down his cheeks.

The crowd fell silent, stunned by the sight of two muscled thugs sobbing like the biggest pair of babies Chicago ever produced. Then somebody chuckled, and somebody else guffawed, and the laughter rose up as loud and as mean as the shouting had been a minute ago.

"What the hell's the matter with you two?" Sweeny stomped up to Benny and shoved him. Benny just cried harder and the crowd jeered. Sweeny pushed on Simon's shoulder, and Simon stumbled backward, and howled. Tears dripped off Simon's jaw. Ben buried his face in his hands and his shoulders shook. Even through the red and scorching anger that had hold of me, I felt the sorrow overwhelming them and it felt sweet. Truly, terribly, deeply sweet.

I smiled and tightened my arm around Mama's shoulders.

"Callie," she croaked. "Get me out of here."

I tried to stand her up, but I staggered. I'd gone lightheaded and wobbly. The magic I'd used on top of everything that had already happened had taken all the wind out of me. It didn't matter. Someone else was beside us. More than one someone. Strangers—men and women both—gently helped Mama to her feet, and me with her. They guided us down the stairs to the sidewalk, murmuring soothing words. Two other women gathered up her market baskets. The men formed a wedge to walk us through the crowd, which was still jeering at the Hollanders. When I looked over my shoulder, I saw the evicted woman walk back up those steps, still carrying her baby.

"Well, Sweeny?" she said shrilly. "You got them papers?"

"Come on, *liebchen.*" One of the women turned my head forward. "We get your modder home. Where you live?"

We walked away, surrounded by those strangers. Behind us, it sounded like the crowd had surged up the porch. It sounded like Sweeny was yelling at them, and then there was just more yelling and no telling who was doing it or what they were saying. I didn't look. I didn't dare.

The strangers walked me and Mama all the way up into the Hollanders' building. Mrs. Burnstein poked her head out her door as soon as we got inside. She exclaimed something I couldn't understand, and one of the other women answered her. Next thing I knew, Mrs. Burnstein had gotten ahead of us on the stairs. She clucked and chattered, and, more important, opened the door of the apartment. She showed no surprise at the way the back room had been transformed. I didn't even know for sure if she could see it. All I did know was she was giving orders in whatever language they all spoke, and those other strangers were obeying. The women laid Mama down on the bed and shooed all the men out. Mrs. Burnstein shut the door and pulled the drapes. Together, grim faced and efficient, those women got Mama out of her dress. A dark blob of a bruise was already spreading across her stomach and more bruises were darkening her forearm where Simon had grabbed her. Mrs. Burnstein made an exclamation, and spread her hands across Mama's stomach.

"Is she okay?" I was cold. I was shaking and groping for my magic, but it wouldn't come. Why couldn't I get my hands around my power? Mama was dying. They'd killed her and I couldn't do anything to save her.

"She will be fine." Mrs. Burnstein laid one gnarled hand gently on Mama's arm over the bruises. "Nothing broken, thank God. And the swelling is not bad."

"Callie," Mama croaked.

I grabbed her hand. "I'm here. I'm right here."

"Did they—"

"No." I cut her off quickly. "Nobody hurt me. I'm fine. You rest. Mrs. Burnstein says you'll be okay."

"Yes, I will. Just as soon as I get my breath. Thank you. All of you. Callie, make sure . . ."

"Yes, Mama." I knew what she wanted me to do. We'd done this before, back in Kansas, when neighbors had come around to help. I knew how it worked. You accepted what you absolutely needed, and no more than that. You made sure everyone was thanked, and you offered coffee and whatever sweets were on hand. But most of all, you got them out of there as fast as was polite. You had to show you could take care of your own on your own, whether that was true or not.

It turned out these people understood that as well as anybody in Slow Run would have. The women let me walk them out into the front room, where the men were talking in low voices. I thanked them all for their help and I meant it down to my bones. I told them Mama would be fine and tried to mean that too. When I offered coffee, they all declined. They told me I was a good girl and that Mama was a brave woman and I should make sure she got her rest. I assured them I would, and I showed them all to the front door, Mrs. Burnstein included, even as she reminded me for the third time she was right downstairs if I needed anything.

I closed the door. I walked over to the dining table without knowing why and stood there staring at it. Mama had all but scrubbed the varnish off trying to get it clean. There was a smell of lemons.

I was shaking again. I grabbed the back of the nearest chair and squeezed it hard. I squeezed my eyes shut too. I couldn't cry. This was all my fault. If I hadn't un-magicked the Hollander brothers, they wouldn't have been able to hit Mama. If I hadn't gone off and left her alone, I'd've been there before the trouble even started. It was all my fault. But I would not cry. I had to get back in there and sit with Mama so she wouldn't be alone. I could *not* cry.

The door downstairs banged and heavy feet ran up the stairs. The sound of hoarse sobs came with them and I straightened up fast. The flat door slammed back, and Benny and Sy stumbled in. Their eyes and faces were red. Tears still streamed down their cheeks. Benny had a black eye. Simon was holding his wrist, and blood ran down from his flattened nose. They both stared at me, wild-eyed and weeping.

I turned around, walked into the back room, and shut the door.

18

Lowdown, Worried, and Blue

The Hollander brothers were still crying when Jack got in. I was in the back room, sitting next to the bed, but I heard him out there. Mama had let me cover her up with one of the sheets, despite how stuffy it had gotten, and now she was asleep, breathing deeply, with one hand sprawled across her stomach. In the other room, Jack was asking his brothers what was the matter. The only answer they gave was more hoarse sobs. Jack started shouting. I think he shook one of them, and they just kept on crying.

Jack barged into the back room.

"Callie! Something's wrong with . . ." He saw Mama in the bed and me in the chair and stopped dead. "What happened?"

"They . . . they were evicting somebody in the next street. Mama tried to stop them, and Ben hit her." Just thinking about it made my hands curl up tight into fists.

"God Almighty," whispered Jack. "Is she okay?"

"Just sleeping."

"Callie . . ." He glanced toward the door, and the sound of his crying brothers. "What did you do?"

I looked at him.

A kind of palsy took over Jack's face as expression and feeling chased their tails round inside him. He swayed on his feet. It was like he wanted to come closer to me at the same time as he wanted to get away, but he couldn't make himself do either.

I pulled the sheet up a little farther around Mama's shoulders.

"You're . . . you're gonna stop it, right?" said Jack. "I mean, what they did, it was lousy. They always were lousy, but your ma's gonna be all right, isn't she? You can stop it now."

"Jack," I whispered. "I don't think I can."

"Don't talk like that, Callie." He grabbed my arm. He was trying hard to force his voice to be cheerful, but what came out was worse than if he'd just given in and shouted at me. "I know you're upset, but we'll just make a wish out of it. Come on. You know how this works."

He pulled, but I didn't budge. "I thought I did. But this is different."

"What's different? How is it different?"

"I don't know. But it is."

One finger at a time, Jack let go of me. He pulled off his cap and scrubbed his head, hard, the way he did when he was trying to keep his feelings locked inside. "Look, look, I know you're mad, but you can't just leave them like that." Jack's calm was as weak and forced as the good cheer had been a second before, and the panic was showing through just as plain.

I twisted my fingers.

"Just come out and have a look, Callie," he pleaded. "You can stop this. I know you can. You were just mad. Please." He crouched down in front of me and took up both my hands in his. "They're lousy, but they're my *brothers*. You got to try."

He was scared. I didn't need any magic senses to feel it. He was as scared as I'd ever seen him, and I couldn't stand it, especially not with his hands holding mine. This was one more thing that was my fault. No matter what I thought about his brothers, I couldn't leave Jack so afraid.

I smoothed the sheet down over Mama, taking note of how her breathing was still deep and even. Then I followed Jack into the front room.

The smoky evening light shone red through the clean windows. Simon had fallen onto the sofa. The light turned his pale skin bloody. For the first time since I'd met him, he didn't have a cigarette between his teeth. Instead, he'd stuffed one fist into his mouth, trying to silence his own sobs. His half-moon eyes were screwed up tight, but the tears still trickled out of them.

As bad as Simon was, Ben was worse. Jack's oldest brother hunched in the corner, his knees pressed up against his chest and his bugged-out, bloodshot eyes staring at nothing. "I'm sorry," he whispered. "I'm sorry, I'm so sorry. I won't do it again. I promise. Please, I'm sorry."

It could have been funny, but it wasn't. The Hollander brothers were crying themselves into sickness and exhaustion and they couldn't stop. My magic was in charge of them now and there wasn't one thing they could do about it.

I tried to take a deep breath and calm down. Jack stared down at them, wide-eyed and pale, waiting for me to do something to fix what I'd already done to his brothers. I crouched down in front of Ben so I could see into his eyes. Why couldn't they look less like Jack's? I pried open my magic, and turned it outward toward both brothers.

Looking at Ben and Simon through my magic senses was like looking in a mirror. I saw myself there—my power and my wish. But I couldn't tell where the magic ended and the men began any more than I could have felt the edges of a reflection in glass. There wasn't any crack or fissure I could wedge my power into. This wish I'd made by accident was stronger than anything I'd done on purpose.

I closed my magic down slowly, and turned my face up to Jack.

"Oh, no," he breathed. "No, Callie. Try again."

I didn't get the chance. The front door opened, and Papa ran in.

"Where's your mother?" Papa asked. "Is she all right?"

"She's in our room. She . . ."

"I know." Papa tossed his hat aside and strode across the

room. I stood up, slowly. I was shaking again. I wanted to stop shaking. I wanted to know what to do, or at least how to explain. But of course I didn't need to explain. Papa'd probably known about the whole thing as soon as it happened.

Papa grabbed Simon's face in both hands and used his thumbs to pry the younger man's eyes open. Simon didn't even struggle. He just stared into my father's fairy eyes until Papa let him go. Simon fell back and buried his face in his hands again.

Papa hurried into the back room. We waited. My heart was in my mouth the whole time and I couldn't think of one word to say to Jack. He just paced in a tiny circle, scrubbing his head.

My father reemerged and closed the door behind him.

"She'll be out in a minute," he said.

I swallowed hard, trying to clear out some space in my head for words to get through. "Papa . . ."

"Not now, Callie. Just step back."

I did as I was told. In fact, I backed up until I bumped against the dining room table. Jack moved beside me, but not too close. This wasn't going to be one of those times when we held hands. That understanding cut clear through me, because it was the first time I really thought about how bad Jack would be hurt if Papa couldn't fix what I'd done, and soon.

Papa was coaxing Ben to his feet. Ben staggered after Papa, and let himself be placed on the sofa beside his brother. His eyes were wide and terrified. Whatever he stared at, it wasn't anything in that room. Oh, I'd done a real good job on him. Papa cupped one hand around each of the brother's heads. I felt the soothing magic he layered over them, soft and easy. Both the Hollanders blinked at him for a moment. They leaned closer together. Their streaming eyes fluttered shut. First Ben, then Simon drooped, and fell back, unconscious.

Papa lifted his hands away.

"What did you do to them?" asked Jack.

"I sent them to sleep. It's about all I can do right now."

"What do you mean all you can do?" Jack took one step forward. His hands were clenching and unclenching, looking for something to strangle. "Why don't you wish them better? What's the matter with you?"

"Jack, I'm sorry," said Papa gently. "This is a genuine transformation. It came from the heart, and it had all the power a member of the high court could throw into it." He didn't say "all the power Callie could throw." He didn't say "my daughter." But he knew who did this. He knew I'd undone the protection he'd laid down against Jack's brothers. I had put us all on the road to where we were now. "It cannot be undone with just one wish. It will take time, and it has to be worked very carefully if they're not to be damaged any further."

"Then let's get started!" said Jack. "What do we do? What do you need?"

"I can't," answered Papa. "Not now."

"Why not!"

"Because tonight, I have to go to work."

There aren't a lot of times I've seen Jack at a loss for words, but there he was, with his eyes popped out and his jaw hanging open. *"What!"*

"I managed to get in on a gig at the Black Bird tonight. Their man's out sick. It's good for thirty dollars, plus tips."

It was so strange to be standing here, talking about magic one second and work the next. It was even stranger because the magic was what felt real and normal, and the idea of working for pay felt like something from some old story. I might have laughed, except I was watching Jack slowly draw his shoulders back and pull himself up to his full height. He was a half inch taller than my father when he stood up straight like that, and his voice had gone horribly cold and even.

"So, you're just going to walk out of here and leave them like this?"

Papa didn't blink, and he didn't back down one inch, not in his words or the way he stood. "They will take no further harm. When I get back in the morning, I'll be able to start undoing what was done." Papa was still not looking at me. He faced Jack squarely. "Do you want me to rush the job? I could make things worse."

Jack closed his jaw with a sharp click. "I want you to *fix* this."

"I will. But tonight, I have to work. We need that money to get out of town."

"But you can just . . ."

That was all Papa's straining patience could take. "Will

you get it through your head that magic is not infinite?" he snapped. "The very nature of your world imposes limits on what it can do and how it can work. And trust me, Jack, you do not want me using my power while I am angry or impatient. You especially do not want me remembering your brothers assaulted my wife and daughter while I am trying to free their hearts!"

They were very close, almost nose to nose. I wanted to say something, but I didn't know what. Who could I stop? This was my fault. All of it. If I'd trusted Papa, if I hadn't tried to lift the protection . . . Jack wouldn't have been happy, but it would have been all right. If I hadn't gone out following Jack, I would have been here to help Mama and keep her from interfering with Sweeny's eviction. Mama wouldn't have been hurt, at least not by his brothers. What would I do if Jack took a swing? What would I do if Papa did? I didn't know. I didn't know at all.

"Daniel?"

Mama stood at the threshold of our room. If her voice was a little hoarse and she moved a little stiffly, she was at least upright and moving under her own steam.

"It's all right, Margaret," Papa said, without once looking away from Jack. "It will be just fine, won't it, Jack?"

The magic was quick this time. A single smooth twist in the tension that filled the space between Jack and my father. Jack blinked once. His shoulders slumped and he backed up a couple steps, looking down at his hands like he couldn't remember what they were for.

"Yeah. Yeah, I guess so." He looked at his brothers again, but I couldn't tell if he saw them properly now. "They're not going to get any worse, are they, Mr. LeRoux?"

"No." Papa's voice was gentle, but it was cold. "That much I can promise."

"Okay." Jack was giving in. I could feel him relaxing into Papa's little twist of power. He didn't even know it had happened. I imagine it felt fairly natural to him. Jack always tried to look on the brightest side.

The only problem was, this bright side wasn't Jack's.

Jack and Papa folded the Murphy bed down from the wall, and wrestled the Hollander brothers onto it. Mama made sure Ben and Simon were covered up then she set about making sandwiches for Papa to take to work. Jack stood by the piano, looking out the window.

I sat in one of the chairs at the table. I didn't know what to do. I didn't know what to think, beyond the fact that this was my fault, and no one was saying so. It was my bad ideas that created this disaster, with a little help from my bad luck. Now my father had magicked Jack, and Jack didn't even know it had happened. And I couldn't do anything about it, because if I tried to undo the knot my father had tied, Papa'd be angry at me again. Worse, Jack would be angry at me. He should be angry. It was wrong that he wasn't, because it meant his head and heart weren't his own anymore. Being around me had stolen the one thing from him that no one should have to lose. And that was my fault too, because my father had done this to him, and I hadn't stopped it.

So here we all were, trying to be normal about things, when none of us, not even Jack, knew what normal was.

Papa took the paper sack of sandwiches from Mama and kissed her cheek. "I'll be back in time for breakfast." He kissed my cheek as well. "Take care of your mother for me."

I nodded, but I couldn't answer. Because the only thing that came into my mind was a question. *Take care of Mama? Like I did this morning?*

If I was supposed to be taking care of Mama, she didn't see it that way. She started making up a pot of chili with beans, and a pan of biscuits. Jack sat down in one of the armchairs by the silent radiator, pulled out his battered notebook, and started writing. He didn't say anything to me, and I was glad. I didn't think I could stand it if he'd been all cool and cheerful, with me knowing where that cool came from. I thought about the notebook he'd given me.

". . . I was able to get the sugar for the icing," Mama was saying as she checked on the biscuits. "We'll have your cake tomorrow when your father's home. Fifteen! I can't believe it."

I couldn't believe it either. I didn't feel fifteen. I felt a thousand years old. A thousand bad-luck years old. Jack was sitting there, writing and whistling. Not five feet away, his brothers weren't even snoring in their enchanted sleep. What if Papa couldn't fix them? What if he couldn't even wake them up again? Jack wasn't the only one who hadn't figured on Papa's magic having limits. I mean, the Seelie king had gotten inside a castle and turned it into a dragon. How could there be anything magic couldn't do? How could there be anything my father couldn't do?

I shouldn't have thought that, because the next thought was what if he isn't telling the whole truth? Maybe he could have done something, but he just decided not to.

I lurched to my feet.

"I gotta . . . I'm gonna . . . I need to use the . . ." I didn't even bother trying to finish. I stumbled out the door.

I went downstairs as quiet as I could. I needed to get out. I needed time to think. Twilight had settled in outside and I could hear the voices of women shouting for their no-good kids. Those same women who had helped Mama, even though they didn't know us from Adam's off ox. I wrapped my arms around myself. It wasn't cold, but I needed something to hold on to, and there wasn't anybody else. I wandered down to the street's dead end, and past it, out onto the wasteland of clinker and gray dust heaps. It smelled like old tar and burnt-out ashes and shifted like the dust back in Kansas had under my shoes. The kids who used it as a playground ran past me, heading home to their dinners.

I trudged up the nearest pile, and back down the far side. The river stretched out in front of me, muddy brown and black in the last of the daylight. It lapped restlessly at the ashy bank. The crows and the gulls had gone off to roost someplace, and the bank was as quiet as anyplace in Chicago ever got. There was more city standing on the other side, and while I watched, its lights came on one at a time like stars. It looked almost pretty on that far bank.

Something rattled and shifted in the corner of my eye. I didn't turn my head. I already knew who it was. I felt it.

"There you are," said Touhy. The wind off the river buffeted her paper body, so she had to twist and turn to keep from being blown away. "I been waiting for you."

I couldn't muster any feeling about that. My heart and my head were both plain worn-out. "What made you think I'd show?"

Touhy gave her crinkling shrug. "Sooner or later it was gonna get to be too much for your human friend and he was gonna turn you out. It's not their fault. It's just the way it is. We're too strong for the humans, so they shove us away, and we're too ugly and strange for the courts, so they swallow us up."

"Jack didn't turn me out."

"Oh, yeah?" Touhy quick folded herself into a question mark and back into a scrap-paper girl again. "Then what are you doing out here?"

"Nothing. Thinking."

"So, you can think and follow me." She flipped and folded and shuffled until she became a patchwork arrow pointing downriver. "Come on."

"Why?"

Touhy folded herself back into the pink-and-paper-bag girl again and grinned. "So you can see what your old man's so afraid of."

I looked back toward the clinker piles. The smokestacks and the sawtoothed skyline jutted out of them like a smoking nightmare of a forest. I couldn't even see Jack's building from here. Not that it mattered. I couldn't go back there. I was the Bad Luck Girl. I couldn't bring any more of that onto Jack. If I was gone, my father would only have to worry about taking care of Mama, and neither of the fairy courts gave a darn about her. They could leave Chicago, and set up someplace else, and be safe. Maybe they could even go back to Kansas. Without me, or my family around, Jack could get back to being a normal human being with normal human problems. He wouldn't have to worry about magic or fairies or prophecies or anything. Him or his brothers.

I hunched my shoulders up to my ears and followed Touhy down the bank of that slow, black river, and I didn't look back.

19

When You're Down and Out

If I'd had room inside me for something other than my own misery, I might have been surprised that Touhy took us up to an El platform. As we climbed the two flights of stairs, she put on a complete young-lady shape. Her pink dress unfolded to a long, straight skirt. A matching cloche hat covered her straggly paper hair, and white gloves that were only slightly crumpled covered her wrinkled hands. By the time she pulled the fare out of her tissue-paper pocket, she could have been a girl around my age, maybe even a little older. Not that anybody was paying attention. The people around us on the platform were filled with their own plans and worries, or just trying to get home to their suppers.

That suited me fine. I huddled in my seat by the window and watched the skyscrapers flashing past. The train muffled up my magic, but I didn't care. I didn't care about anything, and that felt almost like freedom. I could feel the flat outline of Jack's birthday present notebook in my pocket. I told myself I'd get rid of it as soon as I found a good spot for the words and the papers. I didn't want anything of Jack's anymore.

Touhy and I got off the El on the good side of town. Stone town houses lined a broad and well-lit street. She took us across Lake Shore Drive and into a green stripe of open lawn she called Lincoln Park. People strolled on gravel paths between the fountains and the statues, enjoying the summer evening. Every last one of them ignored me and Touhy as completely as the folks on the train had.

Not everything was carefree, of course. We skirted the Hooverville shacks that hunched at the edge of the park. Men in thin shirts and battered hats bunched together around oil-drum fires and watched us warily as we walked past. I couldn't help looking for a tree in the middle of the shacks, just in case.

Past the Hooverville, Touhy turned us through a kind of maze made up of hedges and beds of flowers all shut down for the night. Out of sight of promenades and hoboes both, Touhy scrunched herself into a ball, and became the scrap-paper girl again. She tumbled along, twisting and turning for the sheer fun of it. The wind off the lake tossed her up high. Touhy spread herself out like a patchwork kite and glided on that fresh, cold breeze. Jealousy flashed through me to see her so happy with herself. I grit my teeth against the feeling, and broke into a trot to keep her in sight.

I didn't see the boundary we crossed, but I sure felt it. It was like walking into a wall of pure heat. I gasped and gagged and staggered backward. But Touhy wafted up behind, gave me a surprisingly hard shove, and I stumbled through.

"Don't the cops run into that?" I asked, rubbing my arms. Touhy laughed and tumbled past.

"It only gets solid if there's magic coming at it. For humans, it just . . . guides their eyes away."

I opened my mouth to ask another question, but it was cut off by a shout from up ahead.

"What says the 'ville? Fair?"

"Fair!" roared back a whole crowd of voices.

The voices were coming out of a cluster of the broad, sprawling trees. Their branches had been strung with lights; electric bulbs of all sizes and colors bobbed in the breeze alongside neon tubes and bits of electric sign. The colored lights and their shadows danced over a whole set of little houses. Some had been wedged into the crooks of the branches; others took shelter next to the sturdy trunks. They'd been built out of whatever came to hand, but what came to hand had been squared up and made tight with good roofs and brick chimneys.

"It's a Hooverville," I said, staring. "A Hooverville for Halfers."

Touhy was beside me again, little more than scraps and bits and a pair of green eyes. "It's home," she said. "Come on."

Touhy took me under the trees with their bobbing,

mixed-up lights. The breeze kicked up again and a smell I didn't know I'd been missing hit me—the full, dull, earthy smell of a farmyard. We passed a set of pens with cows, even a few sheep and one old horse. I could hear more voices, muttering, creaking, rumbling.

"What says the 'ville?" A man's dry voice rose above the others. "Fair?"

"Fair!" the others shouted back.

We cleared the last of the trees. On the far side of the Hooverville, somebody'd dug a shallow amphitheater out of the lawn. They'd lined it with benches, and those benches were lined with Halfers. There were more paper cutouts like Touhy, and people who might just as easily have been cats or rats or dogs or bugs. They sat with people made of stone, of bronze, and brass, of tree branches and tin cans, brick, and marble. I spotted Claremont, the glass-shard girl from Dan Ryan's gang. She sat with Cedar, and the girder boy, and Dan Ryan himself.

Halfers whispered and pointed as Touhy led me down the amphitheater aisle. Ryan glowered at me with his bright rat eyes, and fingered the burlap bag hanging from his rope belt. I tried to lift up my chin and get mad, but I was shaking too much inside to make it work.

Touhy kept nudging me along until we reached the end of a line of Halfers that snaked down to the bottom of the hollow. A table had been set up there, and three Halfers sat behind it. One was a man who might have been built from a fallen-down house. Splinters stuck out of him like quills and his shirt looked like it had been made from old shingles. The woman in the middle chair was mottled brown and white, with a black nose three times as long as anybody's should be. The last man reminded me of the Halfer Edison from Los Angeles, except he was smoother around the edges and glowed bright orange instead of silver.

All three of them were listening to a stooping black-and-gray Halfer that looked to be made of driftwood stuck together with tar. He, or maybe it was she, held a bawling calf on a halter.

"What did you pay?" the splintery man asked the wood-and-tar Halfer. His voice was the dry voice I'd heard before.

"The stockman's daughter has influenza," answered Tarry. "She'll start to get better when he kisses her good night."

There was some mumbling from the Halfers on the benches, and the splintery man behind the table lifted his voice to them. "What says the 'ville? Fair?"

"Fair!" The crowd, including Touhy, called back. A man shaped from brick and mortar came up to help Tarry lead the bawling calf away.

"Okay. Now, Halsted," the splintery man said. "What have you brought?"

"A pound of butter." Halsted had a man's voice and was mostly a pile of rumpled rags. He pulled a brown paper package out of what could have been a pocket, or a fold of his body. "And a bolt of cotton cloth." I couldn't even see where all that calico came from, but Halsted laid it on the table too.

"What did you pay?" asked Splintery Man.

"The shopkeeper's husband's been gambling to try to make the rent. Tonight he's going to win."

This brought on another round of mumbling before Splintery Man asked his question again. "What says the 'ville? Fair?"

"Fair!" the 'ville called again.

It went on like that. Touhy crowded close beside me, making sure I moved along with the line. By now the people at the table had seen me, and they were having a tough time keeping their minds on the rest of the parade. Everybody who wasn't outright staring at me was sneaking plenty of little glances. But it wasn't enough to disrupt business. The Halfers kept laying down what they'd gotten hold of. They brought food and clothes, kegs of nails, and scraps of about anything that could be scavenged off the streets. Every one of them named some kind of price that had been paid, and the Halferville accepted them all.

Finally, the line in front of me and Touhy cleared out. As Touhy led me the rest of the way forward, the noise the Halfers made was more like the clash of a train yard than a crowd of voices.

"All right, all right, settle down!" Splintery Man hammered his fist on the tabletop and it sounded just like a judge's gavel.

"Who's this, Touhy?" The mottled woman's skin rumpled almost like Touhy's did, but she wasn't paper like I'd thought at first. She was a bird lady, and covered in sparrow feathers.

"Seems pretty obvious, Ashland." The glowing man's voice sputtered like a radio when it's not quite tuned in to the station. "Looks like we got us the heir to the Midnight Throne."

"Well, well." The feathered woman—Ashland—looked down her long, curving nose at me. "Where did you ever find this, Touhy?"

That was too much for Dan Ryan. "Touhy didn't find her! I did!" He shot out of his seat. "She's mine!"

Touhy and I both ignored him.

"She wanted to see the 'ville," Touhy told the three at the table. "She's our kind, after all."

"The Bad Luck Girl wants to join us?" Ashland's feathery eyebrows knotted up tight.

"Callie," I said back. "I'm called Callie, and I don't plan on staying anywhere I'm not welcome."

Touhy shoved a crinkling elbow into my ribs. "She can help us, Calumet," she said to the splintery man. "She's got powers none of us do. She can get our people back."

The first thing I wanted to do was yell, at the Halfers and especially at Touhy. She might have warned me what she was bringing me into. Even if I had yelled, nobody'd have heard me. Everybody else had already started up their own shouting, and the air was full of clashing, clanging, rushing voices.

"What about Stripling?" Dan Ryan hollered above all the rest. "You all heard the story Edison sent down the line. This one"—he stabbed one long finger at me—"she stood around while her old man had a Halfer killed!"

"That was an accident!" I shouted back. "He didn't know." Except he did. He just hadn't cared.

Touhy elbowed me again. "It's not her old man standing here now, is it? When have we ever turned one of our kind away because of how they got made?"

"She's not our kind!" Dan Ryan spat. "Look at her! What kind of Halfer's got a face like that?"

The force of his words whirled me right around, and I planted my hands on my hips. "So your problem with me is I don't *look* right? That's what my papa says about you all."

I regretted those words the second I said them. The Halfers on the benches surged to their feet—or whatever they had under them—and started yelling all over again. They yelled at the three behind the table. They yelled at each other, at Dan Ryan, and at me. It felt like the crowd around the eviction when I'd magicked Ben and Simon.

"Enough!" Calumet's brittle shout crackled over the heads of the Halfer crowd and he banged his gavel hand so hard on the table something snapped. "Simmer down, all of you!"

Everybody must have been used to Calumet being in charge, because enough of them quieted down to make the rest notice they were shouting at their neighbors, and they quieted down too. Which left me standing in the center of a bunch of angry glaring magic folks, and wondering what kind of order Calumet, or feathery Miss Ashland, or Glowing Man would give next.

"Is that really what you're doing here, Bad Luck?" Calumet's splinters quivered under the collar of his shingle shirt, making me think of porcupines and other dangerous critters. "You've really come here to help us against the courts?"

I couldn't answer. I hadn't come here to do anything or help anybody. I'd come here to hide. But if I said that out loud, this could turn ugly. Uglier.

Ashland seemed to be thinking the same thing. She put her feathered hand on Calumet's shoulder, carefully. "This is going to take some time to sort out. If it's true this one . . . Bad Luck . . . is properly a Halfer, and she's here of her own free will, she deserves the protection of the 'ville just like any of our people." She said this straight to Dan Ryan, and all Dan Ryan's greasy black hair stood on end, but he kept his mouth shut. "That is, as long as she agrees to abide by *our* laws." This she said to me. She had gray eyes in her brown-and-white face, and they were warning me not to start any nonsense.

"What says the 'ville?" Calumet raised his dry voice. "Fair?"

There was a heartbeat of emptiness, but then the Halfers called back, "Fair." It was grudging, and it was fainter than it had been for the butter or the calf, but it was there.

Glowing Man made a noise somewhere between a snort and spitting. "All right, Touhy, you brought her here, you get to keep her. If she makes any trouble . . ."

"Thank you." Touhy wrapped her fragile hand around my elbow. "Come on, Bad Luck. You can stay with me while the council makes its decision."

I wanted to say something about the name she'd saddled me with. I wanted to say even more back to Dan Ryan about the way he looked at me as Touhy hustled me up the amphitheater aisle. But what was I gonna do? It wasn't like I had anywhere else to go.

Touhy, it turned out, lived in a tree house even smaller than the back room of Jack's tenement. Wires ran in through its window to hook up three electric lights hanging from the ceiling beams. Their light fell on a tidy white bed, a braided rug, a carved table, and a chair with an embroidered cushion. The walls were lined with shelves, and the shelves were lined with books. They were in bad shape—water rumpled, with covers missing, and pages burned or torn or chewed. Probably they'd been scavenged and mended as well as they could be, just like everything else in this place. Me included.

"Why're you doing this?" I asked, keeping my hand over the notebook in my pocket. The pages and words were rustling, like they wanted to come out and play.

Touhy didn't answer. She glided over to a dresser made of brass and copper. It even had a mirror fitted together from panes of pale colored glass, two yellow and two pink. She slid open a drawer and pulled out another couple of braided rugs and a lumpy green pillow. "Because no matter what kind of bee Dan Ryan's got in his bonnet, you are one of us," she said, spreading the rugs on the floor. "You're part magic, part not, and you sprang up in this world without nobody asking for you."

"That's what Halfers are? Just part magic and part not?"

She nodded. "The Seelies, the Unseelies, they come here and they scatter all their magic around, granting wishes and fooling humans. You get too much of it in one place, and eventually, you get one of us." She spread her arms, letting her trailing scraps flutter in the breeze.

I pulled my hand out of my pocket and tried not to feel those words and pages twisting around. "Um . . . yeah, but . . . are any of you . . . born?"

"You mean are we part human, like you? Some. Dan Ryan for instance."

My mouth shut hard at that, and Touhy's wrinkled face split into a big grin. "His father was a human soldier back in the old country, but his mother was a fairy lady. Seelie, I think. Anyhow, she left the baby and that sack with him when she went back to her country."

"But, but, he's . . ."

"He's what?" asked Touhy coldly. "He's ugly? Looks like a rat? You wait, Bad Luck. When this world mixes with our magic, we all change shape. You stay here, you'll change too."

My fingers twisted together. I'd grown up trying to hide

my bad hair, and keep my skin from turning too brown in the sun, so nobody'd guess I was the wrong color. I'd thought I'd gotten over thinking like that, but now it all came flooding back. What else would I have to hide if I stayed with the Halfers?

Touhy, apparently, didn't like my being so quiet. She drifted up to me, and poked a paper finger into my chest. "Listen, Bad Luck. I stuck my neck out to get you a fair hearing. Do not make me regret it."

I thought about swatting her hand away, but it seemed like too much trouble just then. "You stuck your neck out on your own. I didn't ask you to."

She just snorted, and the sound was like tearing paper. "You really think you're something special, don't you?"

"What?"

"Ooh, look at me!" Touhy's face flipped around, coming up with a bunch of arrows pointing at her eyes. "I'm the tragic little girl. Everybody's after me! Everybody hates me! I got to run away from it all." She slapped the back of her hand against her forehead. "You should be glad you came out pretty, Bad Luck. They wouldn't have been near as careful with you if you looked like one of us."

"Shut up!" I clenched my fists tight to my sides. "You got no idea what I've been through!"

I wanted to tell her the fairies weren't careful with the pretty ones. I wanted to tell her about Shimmy, and Ivy, who were both laid out dead somewhere because the courts couldn't be bothered to protect them. About Major, who'd been sent after me and was just as dead as the others. The courts used us all, however they needed to. But Touhy wasn't giving me the chance. She just unfolded to her full size and looked me right in the eye.

"I got no idea? You sure about that, Bad Luck?"

A strange, soft pressure leaned against my mind. Touhy was magic too, and she was showing me her memories, pushing them inside me whether I wanted them or not. She showed me being cold and scared and alone, of thinking she was the only thing like her in the whole world. She'd been almost killed in fires that broke out in the South Side slums. She remembered hard trying to find enough food, and enough decent feeling to survive on. She ran from the dark things that came to life when magic and smog mixed with blood down by the slaughterhouses. She ran from everything and everybody, until the splintery man, Calumet, found her and brought her here.

I turned away. I wanted to apologize, but I couldn't. Something inside me had hardened up too much for that. Mama probably would have called it stiff-necked pride, but I didn't want to think about that either.

Touhy crinkled and rustled behind me, whispering something I couldn't hear. Then she hopped into the air and drifted down slow, until she lay flat on the little rug pile. "Get some sleep. One way or another, you're gonna need it." She closed her eyes.

As if that was some kind of signal, the lights winked out. Not just in Touhy's little house, but all over the 'ville. I guess somebody'd thrown a central switch or some such. I sat down on the white bed. There was a feather mattress under the white wool blankets, all cozy and inviting. Touhy didn't think much of me, but here she was giving me her bed. I stared at the floor where the silver moonlight puddled on the rag rug. These people lived off the city and the people in it, but paid for what they took. That was a lot different from what I'd seen the Seelies do. Or the Unseelies.

I was dog tired, but I didn't lie down. Instead, I took Jack's battered notebook out of my pocket and looked at it. The wind blew in through the window, rustling Touhy and all her books on their shelves. I opened the notebook to a random page and squinted at it. There was plenty of moonlight, but I couldn't read the smeary pencil writing, at least not at first. A couple of my live words crawled out from under the page, and decided to help out by fitting themselves to those other words so they stood out better.

"I'm Dirty Dan, King of the Outlaws!" crowed the desperado. "The man who can lick me ain't been born!"

"We'll see about that!" In one swift movement the stranger drew his Colt .45 and fired off a single shot. Dirty Dan let out a bloodcurdling scream and . . .

I closed the book fast. I did not need to be hearing Jack's voice inside my mind. I looked at Touhy's shelves. I could tuck this book up there with all the others. It'd be better than throwing it away. It'd be safe here, and my pages and words would even be among friends. Would the words turn into Halfers if they hung around here long enough? Had I just made a whole bunch of new people? And here I was trying to figure out how fast I could get rid of them.

What would Jack think of that? I bit my lip and slid the notebook back into my pocket.

The wind blew in through the open window, bringing the smell of the lake and the rustle of the tree branches. Their dim reflections shifted in Touhy's four-paned mirror. I shouldn't have looked at them, not so soon after running my thoughts over the loose magic I carried in my pocket. Those reflections got me thinking about the war on the other side of the betwixt and between. I wondered if it was still going on, or if it was over, and if it was, who'd won. That got me wondering what Papa was doing now, and Mama, and Jack, even though I told myself I shouldn't be wondering about them. Ever.

Curiosity's a hard thing. It pushes and it pinches and it won't go away until you do what it wants. I could tell already, I wasn't getting any sleep until I had some answers.

Just once, I growled as I got to my feet. *This once only.*

I faced the mirror and opened my magic senses. Thing was, I didn't have a solid idea what I really wanted to see. So maybe that's why each one of those colored panes showed me something different. There was Dan Ryan, kicking up stones and sand in the dark by the black, restless waves of what had to be Lake Michigan. Tears ran down his dirty face. In the next pane, I saw the shining ruin that was the palace of the Midnight Throne. My uncle stood there, tall and proud in his fairy prince clothes and obsidian mask. Three goblins—squat stones with twisted vines for arms and gnarled roots for legs—scurried in. They dragged a Halfer with them. She was a thin, brittle woman who could have been made from glass, or ice. Uncle Shake smiled at her and then turned and bowed. Somebody else was in that room with him, but all I could see was the small, pale hand that beckoned to the Halfer woman. The anger drained from the woman's face, replaced by a terrible shining expression of hope. The goblins let go, and the Halfer walked forward to take that pale hand.

I dropped my gaze to the last pane, and there I saw Jack. He perched on the rail of the tenement balcony, one arm wrapped around the post. His mouth was moving and he was staring out at the glowing smokestacks. I knew what he was doing. Jack was singing. He was singing to me. Singing for me. I heard the words in my head, plain as day.

". . . *I wish I was a tiny sparrow,*
"*And I had wings, and I could fly.*
"*I'd fly away to my own true lover. . . .*"

But Jack's song froze, and his shoulders stiffened. He jumped off the railing to the balcony, turning around, turning right toward me. I clamped my magic shut, and the reflection winked out.

"Touhy?" I said to the dark.

"What?" she muttered.

"This place is protected, right?"

"Yeah. Can't nobody find us here."

"Good." I laid my palm over Jack's notebook. "Good."

20

He Didn't Wait for Me

Something was pulling on me. It had hold of my guts and my head and I was being dragged away.

"Engine, engine number nine, going down Chicago line . . ."

My eye snapped open. I shrieked and tumbled off the bed at the same time, coming down on my feet like some part of me had decided I was the world's biggest cat. My magic reared up all in an instant, slicing through the sick dragging sensation. Or almost through it.

"If the train should jump the track . . ."

I whipped around to the window. Dan Ryan crouched on a branch outside, his long toes wrapped around the swaying limb and his burlap sack open in his greasy hands. The first gray light of dawn was just sliding through the leaves, and he thought he'd caught me napping.

"What're you doing?" Touhy rolled off the bed in her

paper ball shape and planted herself in front of the balcony window.

"Outta my way!" snarled Dan Ryan. "Don't think I won't take you too, you traitor!"

"You leave her alone!" I scrambled over to Touhy's side.

Dan Ryan hissed and shook his sack. "You're getting in here, Callie LeRoux! You're getting in now and you're staying this time!"

He had a good piece of my name, and its power pushed hard. I actually stumbled forward a couple steps before I could reach out with my own magic and snap that summons in two. Dan Ryan growled a cuss word.

"Cut it out, Dan Ryan!" Touhy shouted. "You heard the council!"

Heads started poking out of windows around and below us. Somebody snapped the lights on.

Dan Ryan didn't care. He jumped straight through the open window, sack and all. I knocked Touhy sideways, and we both fell to the floor. I scrambled away, scared sick that I'd tear her. Ryan hit the bed, and the floor, and grabbed up the tail of Touhy's paper dress. I felt his fury, and I snatched it up and turned it around, putting the magic behind a solid swipe of my fist straight at Ryan's head. The notebook in my pocket shuddered hard, and all at once papers and words were flying everywhere. Ryan ducked my arm, but paper covered him and sent him stumbling backward while words buzzed angrily around his head. He lost his hold on his sack, and it landed on top of Touhy. She grabbed the bag in both hands and rolled herself up tight around it.

Dan Ryan cussed so hot he could have burned the place down. He scrabbled at my pages with hands and magic, getting clear enough that he could launch himself straight at us both. But a brown-and-white arm shot in through the window and grabbed his belt. Ashland yanked Ryan roughly backward so he banged against the wall.

"Enough!" Wood slammed on the balcony rail, and Calumet heaved himself over it to stand beside Ashland. His eyes were as hard and angry as his words. "Touhy!" He swatted at my swarming words. "Control these things!"

"Those aren't mine!" She pointed one paper finger at me. "They're hers!"

A blush crawled up my neck and bloomed across my face. I opened my notebook and sent a wish to the pages and words. They didn't want to come back. They liked it out here. It was way more fun than being shut up in some old book. I had to wish again. This time they came. I closed the notebook and tucked it away again. This was definitely going to be trouble sooner or later.

But there was more trouble standing right in front of me. All Ashland's feathers were ruffled up.

"Who started this?" Calumet's voice crackled with anger.

"Sorry, Calumet," said Touhy, but she didn't unroll herself. "Dan Ryan startled Bad Luck, and she took a swing at him."

"Yeah." Dan Ryan twisted around, yanking his rope belt out of Ashland's hand so he could get back on his feet. "I *startled* her."

That was the best they could do? I had to fight to keep my eyes from rolling. I guess I'd gotten too used to Jack's level of storytelling. Dan Ryan glowered at me. I glowered back. My gaze slid over to Touhy, who had poked her girl's face up out of her crumpled-up body. It was stupid, but some things are ground hard into you. Right then, with Ashland and Calumet towering over us, I plain and simple didn't want to be the tattletale. Plus, I couldn't forget that Dan Ryan's father had been taken by the Seelies, or the Unseelies. Could I really blame him for being angry and desperate?

"Sorry," I muttered instead. "I don't like being startled."

But Calumet wasn't buying it, not at any price. "Where's your sack, Dan Ryan?"

Dan Ryan shifted his glower over to Touhy. Touhy unrolled. The burlap bag fell onto the floor.

Ashland's black eyes glittered and she picked up the sack. Ryan winced like she'd pulled his hair, but she paid no mind. "So you three decided you'd just settle this among yourselves, did you?"

"Well, you weren't doing anything about it!" shouted Ryan. "How long are we gonna wait? They could all be dead already! We got her! We've got to use her *now*!"

"You are not the only person who's lost family." Calumet's splinters rose and fell on his back, in time with his hard breathing. "If we're lucky, we might just get one chance to strike back. If we waste it, we are all of us done for." He waited for that to have time to sink in. "Maybe the council should keep your sack if you can't handle it responsibly."

For the first time since I'd met him, I saw Dan Ryan look scared.

"No, it's okay," I said. "Give it to him. He won't try startling me again."

For a minute I thought the councilors were going to demand an explanation. I could feel their curiosity, and Touhy's, winding around my shoulders. But Ashland and Calumet just exchanged their own glance, and Ashland handed the sack to Dan Ryan. "Save it for important things," she said.

Ryan tucked the bag under his rope belt. "We are not done here," he told me. "Not by a long shot."

"Didn't think so," I muttered. We didn't get any further, though.

"Oy! Get Bad Luck down here!" A sizzling, hissing voice called up from below. "We got us a problem!"

"You mean another one," grumbled Calumet. "Touhy, when this is over, the council wants a word with you too."

That drew a grin from Dan Ryan nasty enough to almost make me forget I felt sorry for him and start up the fight again. If the Halferville councilors hadn't all been busy giving me the stink eye, I just might have. As it was, I slowly turned my back to show him I wasn't afraid of him at all, and followed Ashland to find out what kind of new trouble I was in.

* * *

Of course it was Jack. Who else would it be?

He stood a couple yards back from Halferville's magic shield. He had a handful of pebbles, and he was pitching them at that wall of heat, watching where they sizzled and fell to the ground. But as soon as I cleared the trees with the Halfers, Jack dropped his stones and charged forward, until the heat hit him and he had to fall back.

"Who's that?" demanded Glowing Man.

"He's a friend of Bad Luck's," said Touhy. I noticed she and Glowing Man kept a careful distance from each other.

"We figured that much," Glowing Man shot back. "What's he *doing* here?

Right then he was shouting. I could see his face, but I couldn't hear anything. I tried to mouth, *I'm fine. Go away!* but he just shook his head.

"How can he even see us?" muttered Calumet. He was giving me the stink eye again, and putting everything he had into it too. "He's full human."

"It's an accident," I said. "I made a wish for something else, and it stuck." Last night, I'd tried to tell myself my wish couldn't be that strong. The Halfers had good magic, and they knew what they were doing. My wish on Jack's eyesight couldn't really be stronger than their shield. Looks like I was wrong again.

Touhy rolled her eyes and muttered something about the high court I was pretty sure I didn't want to understand all the way.

"This is bad." Ashland's voice dropped to a nervous twitter as Jack cupped his hands around his mouth to shout some more. "He'll draw attention."

"You think so, do you?" sneered Glowing Man. "Bad Luck, whoever this is, you get rid of him."

I waved at Jack with both hands, gesturing for him to just leave. He squinted at me and backed up a step. And squinted again. When I didn't do anything else, he shook his head and took a run at the barrier. He slammed right up against it with his shoulder and bounced back hard. His shirt was smoking where it had hit, and a black patch spread across the upper arm.

"What are you, cracked?" I shouted. "Get out of here! You'll get hurt!"

But Jack just slammed that smoking shoulder against the Halferville shield again and again. His shirt was sparking and he had to slap at it before it actually started on fire.

"You can't get in here! Go away! Go home!" I waved my arms and made giant shooing motions. But Jack wasn't even looking at me. Instead, he fished out the notebook he always carried, scribbled something on a page, and held it up.

NOT GOING UNTIL YOU TALK TO ME.

I grabbed my notebook from my pocket and wished at the words. They came crawling out from between the pages and plastered themselves onto the paper.

I DON'T WANT TO TALK TO YOU. I held that up. Jack stared at the jostling words. Then he stared at me. He pointed at the book. I shrugged.

Jack made another note. This time he angled it toward Ashland.

SHE TALKS TO ME OR I GET THE COPS BACK HERE. AND PARKS DEPARTMENT. AND ANYBODY ELSE I CAN THINK OF.

"You wouldn't," I whispered. Jack folded his arms at me. He would. At the same time, I couldn't help noticing he was threatening to get the cops, who wouldn't even believe in the Halferville, and not my parents, who most certainly would.

"Can I get through this?" I asked the Halfers.

Calumet nodded at Glowing Man. Glowing Man's face— what face he had, anyhow—scrunched up and he pulled a brass key out from somewhere. He banged it against the barrier three times. I felt a rush of cool air and stepped straight into it.

The Halferville behind me was gone. There was nothing there but park lawn, and Jack standing in front of me.

"Well?" I said to him. "What do you want?"

"What do you think I want?" Jack stuffed his hands into his pockets, and I watched him trying not to work his way up to a shout. "I want to be sure you're okay."

"Well, I am."

Jack looked away, and then he looked over my shoulder. Probably he could still see the Halfers waiting on the other side of the shield, even if I couldn't. "Can we go someplace? Where we can get some privacy?"

I thought about saying no, or that nobody on the other side of the shield could hear us. But I really didn't want anybody even watching this, whatever this was going to turn out to be. So I started walking in the direction of the wind.

Jack fell into step beside me, tugging the brim of his cap down. We'd walked side by side like this for miles across the country, through the Dust Bowl, and into California and Los Angeles and Culver City, and back out again. I fought against how comfortable it was. I had to get used to missing this.

"You know your ma's tearing her hair out," said Jack finally. "Your pa lit out from that gig he found. Didn't even take his tips. He's been out hunting you all night."

We came to the top of a small hill, and I got my first look at Lake Michigan. I'd never seen so much water in my life. It stretched all the way out to the horizon and shone silver blue in the morning light. Sparks like the ones I saw in my father's fairy eyes danced across the rippling waves. The wind blew my tangled hair into my eyes. Pebbles and gravel covered the beach on the far side and twisted underfoot. The gulls screamed at each other and at me as they rose up from the stones.

"What did you tell my folks about where you were going?" I asked him.

"Nothing. Just said I'd be looking for you, same as them." Jack took hold of my shoulder and turned me to face him. "Why'd you run out on me, Callie? What happened?"

There was only one way I could think of to explain. I reached out with my magic and undid that little twist Papa had put in him, the one that kept him from getting too angry about what had happened to his brothers. Jack felt it go, and he knew what had been done, by Papa, and just now by me. He flushed white, then red. He stared at me, and this time I didn't flinch away.

"I couldn't stop him, Jack, and I didn't know what he was gonna do next."

"So you left me alone with him?"

"I thought he'd go away. Him and Mama both. I thought . . . I thought they'd leave you be."

"And what kinda good was that supposed to do me? Were you gonna come back afterward?"

Those words stopped every thought I had dead in its tracks. "What?"

"I've been going crazy looking for you, Callie! I thought Dan Ryan'd got you, or your uncle! You didn't even leave a note or anything. I thought . . . I thought you might already be dead!"

His voice cracked high and thin on the last word. His worry whipped around my head too hard for me to shut out, no matter how much I wanted to.

"I'm sorry," I whispered. The way he hunched up, thin and scared, and for a change looking younger than he was, it went straight to my heart and stuck there. "I just didn't want to hurt you anymore."

Jack aimed a kick at the ground, sending up a shower of dirt and pebbles. "Well, you did."

"I'm sorry." I was. I really, truly was.

"You said that already. Come on, Callie. Let's go home." He started trudging back the way we came. I stayed where I was. It took him a long minute to turn around. He was too used to me following wherever he led, I guess. So was I.

"I can't go with you," I said.

"What? Why not?"

I could not believe what I was hearing. Why did he have to pick now to get so stupid? "Why not? What about what I did to your brothers? What about what Papa did to you?"

"Yeah, well, if he's gonna stay, he's gonna have to make a few of those famous fairy promises. And he's gonna find a way to fix Ben and Simon." Jack paused. "You think maybe the Halfers could help?"

My jaw was flapping loose. I could taste the cool, damp wind at the back of my throat. "How can you possibly stand there talking like that?"

"Like what?"

"Like being around me isn't going to get you killed! Or worse!"

Jack let out a long sigh and had the nerve to look exasperated. "You saw my family, Callie. You saw how they live now, and believe me it used to be worse. You know what happened to Hannah. Maybe getting killed has been something I've walked with since I was born. At least with you, it's for something good. Something I choose."

He didn't mean it. He couldn't. This was just Jack being Jack and trying out all his charm on me. Except I couldn't feel the charm. I couldn't feel anything but honesty. Honesty, and a little worry. Jack was worried I might not believe him.

I stepped back. Pebbles ground under my shoes, making

me unsteady. Or maybe it was watching the worry flicker in Jack's eyes that was doing that.

"How can you even . . ."

"What?"

"Nothing." I shoved my hair back from my face. The wind blew it right back, and I shoved it down again.

"No. It's not nothing." Jack was right behind me. I could feel him there, warm and steady and much too close. "You started this, Callie LeRoux—you finish it."

It wasn't fair. He knew what names did to magic people. Except it wasn't my name that was making me want to talk. It was just Jack. I had to explain things to him now, before I lost my nerve. He had to understand so he would finally go away.

"How can you even know you feel anything real for me? What if it's just something my magic's doing to you?"

There. I'd said it. This was the fear that kept me up at night. This fear turned the twisty, wonderful feelings that bubbled up when Jack smiled into nothing but ash and worry. Because every time he looked at me, I knew I might be messing with his heart and head. I knew Jack might only care because I wanted him to. Because I wished him to.

"I wish it was," said Jack.

"What?"

"If what I feel about you is just something your magic's doing, then I wish it was real. Because it feels real, Callie, and it feels fine and I never want to lose it."

No. No. He wasn't saying this. He sure wasn't taking one

step closer so he could lift up my hand, which was so cold from the lake wind and from being afraid. He most definitely and truly wasn't still talking, saying things I'd barely had the nerve to dream I'd ever hear from him.

"Besides," he said with a sweet, small smile, "fairies need human feeling. You've said so. How do you know it's not me doing this to you?" His smile turned just the tiniest bit sly, and all the strength in me seemed to head for the hills. Oh, he was doing something to me all right, but it had nothing to do with wanting or wishing. Not the magic kind, anyway. But that sly, joking smile was already gone. What he said now, he meant. "Callie, you're the smartest, bravest, prettiest girl I've ever met, and if I haven't said so, it's because . . ."

A very uncomfortable idea crawled out of my tangled thoughts. "If you say it's because I'm a princess, Jack Holland, I will bust you in the mush."

Jack stared at me like I'd grown a second head. "It's because I was afraid you'd run out on me!"

Oh. A blush burned hard across my cheeks. It seemed to be catching, because Jack was blushing too. I'd never seen him look like that. And I'd sure never heard him stammering like he was now. Bits of sentences scattered like the stones when he kicked the ground. And he still hadn't let go of my hand.

"I wasn't sure . . . I didn't . . . I thought maybe it wouldn't be . . . you know . . . right. I mean, fourteen, and . . . I knew you'd never . . . never had a boyfriend or stepped out, or . . . I wanted to say something, or . . . spending so much time alone with you and wondering if maybe . . . if you might be thinking about me like that . . . you've got no idea how hard it was."

"Don't be too sure about that," I muttered.

Jack's eyes flipped open wide. "Really? You mean it?"

I couldn't answer. I was finding out all about what *tongue-tied* really meant and I didn't like it. A ghost of a smile flickered behind Jack's eyes. It faded fast, but only because something much stronger was taking its place—stronger and truer than any of his easy smiles or quick words.

"If I didn't say anything, it wasn't because I didn't feel anything, Callie. It was never that."

I didn't know what to do. I had to do something. I lifted my hand and let my fingertips brush across Jack's cheek. It was raspy. I never thought he might need to shave. I'd never seen him do it. I touched one of the freckles on his cheek. His skin was warm. His Adam's apple bobbed hard when he swallowed. I wondered if he wanted to kiss me. I wondered if I wanted to kiss him. At first I thought I didn't. Then I thought I did. Then I thought I couldn't. Then I thought maybe I could.

Jack smiled, soft and sweet, like he understood all that. Probably he did. He always understood me better than I figured on. He took my hand away from his face and squeezed my fingers gently.

"It doesn't matter where it comes from, Callie," he said softly. "What matters is what we *do* with it. Come back with me. We'll figure it out."

Right then I would have gone with him anywhere, and I couldn't think of a single reason not to. I followed him back toward the slope that separated the park from the beach, staring at his face like I'd been struck stone-blind. I was stumbling like it too, which just made him grin. Which got me annoyed, and wiped some of the haze away from my memory and pulled me up short.

"I can't."

Jack's sigh was pure impatience. "Now what?"

"The Halfers need my help."

"Talk sense, Callie. You can't be thinking of helping them after everything they've done to you."

"You heard Touhy the other night, Jack. And there's more to it." I told him about what I'd seen and heard, about Touhy and Dan Ryan and all the rest. I told him about the major domo and Aunt Nancy, and felt his anger flicker hot and hard that I hadn't told him before, but he sat on it fast.

"All right, all right," he muttered. "If you're gonna insist, we'll go talk to them. But we've got to let your parents know you're okay."

"Okay," I agreed, because I didn't want to start another whole argument. So much for my grand plans for running away and not putting anybody else in danger. *Darn you anyway, Jack Holland,* I thought grumpily. I kept my eyes pointed straight forward as we started walking again, just in case he took it into his head to smile at me again. But despite working my way down into a comfortable grumble, I couldn't help noticing the wind at our backs had shifted. Instead of fresh water and green grass, it filled with the smell of smog and slaughterhouse. I thought we'd left that all behind in Jack's old neighborhood.

Jack noticed it too, and glanced around. "What the . . . Do you see that?" He squinted up at the hazy blue.

"I don't see anything."

"It's like . . . maybe an airplane? But it's too low. Just there." He pointed. "Can't be a plane." He squinted hard. "There's a bunch of them. . . ."

I followed his finger and saw the clear blue sky hanging low over the lake. Jack shook his head. "I'm seeing things."

I went cold inside. "Yeah, you just might be." I put my hand on his arm. "You better wish I could see it too."

Jack did. I wrapped my magic around that wish and made it true. And all at once, I could see all he saw, and a little bit more.

It wasn't an airplane. It was a crow, stark black and gliding through the morning blue. And like Jack said, there were a lot of them. They wheeled and dove over one particular section of park. And I knew just which one.

"It's the Halfers," I said. "They're being attacked."

21

A Great Notion to Jump

We had no iron, or anything else to use for weapons. We had nothing but ourselves. We ran in anyway, ducking under tree branches and dodging around flower beds. Well, I dodged. Jack, with his long legs, vaulted right over them.

The crows gathered thick as flies overhead, darkening the sky. They were big—two or three times as big as ordinary birds, and ten times as black. They wheeled and dipped and when they got below a certain point, they'd vanish like they'd never existed. That was behind the barrier for the Halferville. They'd torn open the top somehow and were diving inside. It was impossibly silent. The spell I'd laid over Jack let him see, but neither one of us could hear. We were paying so much attention to the crows, we both slammed straight into the shield and bounced back. It wasn't hot anymore. It had gone cold, or been turned cold, but it was just as solid as ever.

"Can we get in?" bawled Jack.

I held my hands up in the air, clenched my teeth, and opened my magic. My hands and mind cringed as I pushed against the shield, which was now cold as ice in February. It was smooth as ice too, mostly. There were cracks. They were tiny, but they were real. I could slide my magic in and lean my strength behind it. I shook. Sweat prickled my scalp. This wasn't the right kind of gate for me to open. I had no natural gift for this, just brute force and cussedness. Just the fact that the people on the other side were being attacked like I'd been attacked, and they didn't have anybody else to help them.

The shield cracked open. Not much, just a little hole. We both lost some skin and raised some blisters squeezing through, but we made it, and we ran.

Halferville was in chaos. Dozens of voices screamed and shouted and the crows cawed in answer. Halfers ran for the shelter of the trees and shacks with the giant crows sailing in behind them. One of those birds lit onto the grass and it started to grow, like Mimi and the dog pack had grown, but it didn't stay bird shaped. It turned human shaped, with crow eyes in a gray face and trailing black robes. While I watched, a tin-can boy snatched a baby that looked like it was made of bread crumbs off the grass and took off running. One of the crow men stretched out curving, clawed hands to grab up the tin-can boy and the crumb baby and slide them into those robes like popping them into sacks.

Sacks. Where was Dan Ryan and his sack? I couldn't see him anywhere. Where were Touhy and the councilors?

Not everybody was running away. Halfers charged out of their houses with hatchets and hoes and whatever else had come to hand, hollering at the tops of their lungs. The crows didn't have the air to themselves either. Ashland stood on a shack roof, her arms raised as she cried out in a voice almost too high to hear at all. Sparrows wheeled in the sky, laughably small next to the dark carrion birds, but there were a whole lot of them, and they pecked and screamed their tiny, righteous rage.

There were rats too. Hordes of them, filthy and squealing, and worrying at the ankles of the robed man shapes. The crow men kicked them aside, but sometimes not fast enough, and if any crow man fell, he was covered over by a living flood of black and brown.

One robed man cawed sharp and high. He tossed the tarry Halfer I'd seen the night before high into the air for a crow to grab in its talons. The Halfer screamed, and Ashland screamed, sending her sparrows after him, but the crow was too fast, and it was lost in the smoggy blue. The crow man laughed and the crows overhead cawed.

Jack wasn't standing around. Somebody'd dropped a long-handled hoe. He scooped it up, running into the middle of a cluster of crow men who'd surrounded a couple of brick Halfers. Jack clobbered the nearest crow across the head, and reeled around to face the others.

An arrow whizzed past, trailing fire to sink deep in the heart of a crow as it swooped down. A gunshot exploded from one of the shacks, and then another. A crow man hollered and fell and a Halfer shouted in triumph, and there was another shot. A crow dropped out of the air and flopped onto the ground. Jack swore and ducked.

I heard Touhy shouting. She was leaning out her window and waving and pointing at me. I understood and yanked my notebook out of my pocket and shook it hard. Words and live pages scattered onto the wind.

Go, go! I told them. *Help Touhy!*

They swirled up into the sky, in time to meet Touhy as she spread herself on the breeze, gliding and screaming toward the nearest crow. She wrapped her body around its wings and held on tight, driving it to the ground where another Halfer could grab hold of it.

I turned in place. It was too much, too crazy. I didn't know what to do or how to do anything at all. I couldn't think what to grab or where to run next.

Then I saw Dan Ryan. He was stretched out on the ground by the sheep pen, and he wasn't moving. A crow man bent over him, ready to scoop him up. Everything suddenly became very clear and I took off running toward him. There was so much fear and anger swirling around, I almost didn't need to reach for it. I just grabbed and twisted one hard wish around it and swung out. I knocked that crow man back a good ten feet without breaking stride.

An idea hit me as hard as I'd hit the crow. When I'd ridden in that sack there'd been metal rattling around with me. Maybe here was something I could use. I yanked the sack off of Dan Ryan's rope belt. He stirred weakly. Blood trickled down his long face.

"Sorry." I jerked the mouth of his sack open and up-ended it.

A whole new flock of crows burst out of the sack, screaming at the top of their lungs and knocking me tail over tea-cup. I cussed hard as I sat up again and the crows cheered to see their friends.

But it wasn't just crows. Pigeons flew out of that sack and rats ran to join the others attacking the crow men. There was bread and cans and—oh, thank heaven—scrap iron. Half a junkyard's worth of scrap iron, nails, broken bars, and old pans poured out of that magic sack.

Jack appeared at my side. He didn't need any telling. He just grabbed up a rusty bolt, took aim, and hurled it at the nearest crow. The bird screamed and toppled toward the ground. It never hit. The sparrows swirled around it, and got it first.

Jack wasn't the only one who saw what was happening. A bunch of the Halfers grabbed up the busted, rusted iron, and ran hollering at the crows. Glowing Man snatched up a frying pan, and it went red hot in his hands. He was scream-ing orders to the archers in the trees, screaming at the wooden ones and the paper ones to fall back while fiery arrows rained down. The crow men didn't break. They flew at the Halfers, they grabbed them up, vanished them away.

"Engine, engine number nine!" I shouted, pulling together all the magic I could muster. "Going down Chicago line! If that train should jump the track, crows, crows, get in the sack!"

It wasn't easy. This wasn't my magic, and this sack didn't like me. I didn't have names to work with, but the nearest crow man vanished into Dan Ryan's bag. And I turned and I shouted, and the next one tumbled in, and the next.

"Duck!" hollered Jack, and I did. Something whistled over my head, and went *thwang!* A crow man hit the ground beside me. And I saw Jack standing over him, a metal bar with a curved end clutched in both hands.

"Crowbar?" I gasped. Jack grinned and turned, and waded back into the fight.

More Halfers grabbed up the scrap iron. Glowing Man was with them, shouting more orders. The Halfers spread out in a kind of formation, ringing around the crow men, driving them down into the hollow of the amphitheater. But their enemies were still birds, and they could still fly. Black-robed men jumped into the air, changing into birds again, with talons that could gouge and wicked sharp beaks that could stab. They wheeled out of the way of the bird shot and the arrows and came down screaming on the Halfer archers, tearing them from the trees and carrying them away. I felt one of my pages tear, and then another, and then a whole book's worth. More crows swallowed my words by the handful. Tears stood out in my eyes to feel them die, but I couldn't stop. I shook the sack and hollered the incantation and shoved the crow men in with all my might and magic. But the crows just kept on coming. I saw a crow man grab up Cedar and shove it under his robe. Ashland staggered on the roof where she stood and a crow dove low, aiming straight for her. A gun banged and the crow dodged, and it dove down again.

I opened the bag, and my mouth. Then I saw another crow shoot up into the air. This one had a squirming wad of paper in its claws.

"Touhy!" I shrieked, and I heard her scream in answer. But only just for a second. Then she was beyond hearing at all.

Jack grabbed my hand. I'd lost track of him, but he hadn't left my side. He'd gone dead white, but I knew that crazy look in his eye. He didn't like Touhy, but he wasn't going to let her be lost to these monsters, and he had a plan.

"Callie," he said. "I wish you could fly."

We stared at each other for a single heartbeat. Then I turned and took off at a run, my arms spread out to catch the wind and the force of Jack's wish behind me. I jumped.

And I flew.

The air hit hard, and the cold followed fast as I shoved head and shoulders through a wind that felt as near solid as the Halferville barrier had. But the wind was worse because it didn't stay still. It twisted around me, tangling me like ropes. It pushed me up one second, and dropped out from under me the next. The world was nothing but a colored blur on the other side of my tears. If there hadn't been so many crows, and they hadn't been so black against the blue sky, I never would have been able to follow them because I wouldn't have been able to see them.

But they were and I could. They made a black cloud straight in front of me, and I plowed through the wind after them. I tried not to think about what I'd do if any one of them turned around and came at me. It was taking every ounce of concentration and magic I had to keep after them. I had nothing left to fight with.

Slowly, slowly I started gaining on them. Smokestacks flashed by, and church steeples. I swear a carved angel turned its head when I skirted too close to its marble wing. The crows dropped lower and I pulled my arms in, kicking at the air like I was diving down to the bottom of a swimming pool. The wind was worse down here, funneled through solid walls of brick buildings, becoming a rushing river, and I was trying to force my way against the current.

The crows banked, and something brushed against my arm. Pain burst through me and I saw stars. When they cleared, I saw a sprawling hulk of a burnt-out building rushing to meet me. The crows flew into it like flakes of ash settling over a dead fire. I felt a familiar sensation blossoming inside me. I was near a gate. The crows were flying in and through. I stretched my magic out in front of me. I wobbled and the world tilted, but I had the edges, I had them . . .

Arms wrapped around my waist and the next thing I

knew, I plowed into the ground, toppling head over heels, fighting with someone big and heavy who was cussing and calling my name. But I finally got free and scrambled to my feet.

And I looked down at Papa, groaning and clutching his shoulder as he lay on the sooty steps of that burnt-out mansion.

22

Gonna Get Real Tough

"What are you *doing*?" I struggled to my feet.

"I could ask you the same thing." Papa wheezed and pushed himself up on his knees.

Crows screamed somewhere up ahead. So did Touhy. *Touhy.*

I hurt and I couldn't catch my breath, but I staggered up the steps toward that ruined house anyway.

"Callie!" Papa shouted. I ignored him. If he wanted me, he could follow me.

He did, faster than I would have figured. He grabbed me by the arm and spun me around. "Callie, you stop this, now."

"No!" I shook him off. "They got Touhy! And Dan Ryan and Ashland! I can't leave them!"

"Daughter, listen to me carefully." Papa had lost his hat somewhere, and his fairy eyes shone bright, even in that broad city daylight. "You are coming with me. I will spell-bind your arms and legs so you can't move yourself without permission for a month if I have to. But you will come. Do I make myself clear?"

He did. His words and his will dropped like stones against my thoughts. Maybe if I'd been whole and strong, I could have shifted him, but I wasn't. I was banged up, exhausted, and out of breath, and I was pretty sure I was bleeding on my arms and forehead. And Touhy and Dan Ryan and who-knew-how-many others were gone. I could feel it. I stared at the burnt-out building they'd vanished into. It had been a mansion once, but now all its arched windows were broken and blind. Ash and soot turned its sides black, and the roof was nothing but a mass of broken timber. The gate was in there. I could feel that too, and the crows had taken their prisoners to the other side of it.

It hadn't been enough. We'd fought back with everything we had, and they'd still gotten snatched right out of their home. And I didn't even know who had them.

"I'll find you," I said to whatever waited on the other side of those ruined doors. "I will."

"No." My father cut me off solid and sharp just as I finished the word.

"Whaddaya mean no?"

"I mean no." He raised his face, checking the wind and the light. I could feel his every nerve standing on end. "As soon as we've gotten Jack and your mother, we're leaving.

The Midnight Throne has fallen. I felt it," he added in a whisper, his shining eyes drifting toward that old, ruined mansion. "I felt my parents' will swallowed whole."

I closed my mouth. His fear was cold and it woke up all the fear I hadn't had time to feel yet. I wanted to run, just like he said. Run fast and run far.

But I couldn't. "They took friends of mine, Papa. I can't leave them."

"You have to. Callie, don't you understand?" He jabbed his finger toward the broken house. "You've been seen. They know you're here now. They know we're all here. We have to run before they come back!"

But run where? Where was left?

"I know you feel for these Undone . . . ," Papa was saying.

"Halfers. They call themselves Halfers." My thoughts were stumbling in all kinds of directions. I thought about my pages and my words. I didn't even have names for any of them. I didn't know for sure what they even were, but they'd given themselves up to help me, and the Halferville. And it still hadn't been enough.

Papa waved his hand hard, the gesture showing how little this mattered to him. "Whatever they are called, they have nothing to do with us. We have to get your mother and Jack and get out of this city. When we've found a safe place . . ."

I shook my head. New understanding was rising up in me, slow and quiet, like the dust rising in the distance. "There is nowhere safe," I said. "You know that, Papa. Same as me." It was here. I saw it. It spread across the horizon of my thoughts and I was never getting away from it, not ever. "We both tried running away. You abdicated. I lit out. It didn't work and it isn't ever going to work. We have to turn around, Papa. We have to face this. All of it."

Papa lifted his hand like he was going to tug on his hat brim, but when it wasn't there, he smoothed down his close-cropped hair. I'd stunned him, but not for long. "How do you suggest we do that?" The contempt in his words smacked hard against my new understanding. "We're alone here."

"We've got each other. And Jack, and Mama. That's a lot right there."

"Not anything like enough to defeat the Seelie army if their king takes it into his head to send them through that gate in the next thirty seconds." Papa grabbed my hand again. "We are getting out of here. *Now.*"

For a second I thought he was going to magic me, but he just pulled me down the old, uneven steps behind him.

"Wait, Papa. Stop."

"Wait?" he rounded on me. "Wait for what? For the corbies to come back and find us? Or perhaps we should wait for these Undone you've taken such a shine to?"

Which was just about enough of that. "Stop it!" I yanked my hand out of his. We both stood there in the middle of the sidewalk, with the traffic rattling past and the clouds scuttling overhead. Just an ordinary city street on an ordinary city day. But there was nothing ordinary about what I had to say next. I walked up to my father, and looked him right in the face. I could feel the Unseelie light shining behind my own eyes and I wanted to make sure he saw it there. "You're as bad as the rest. You look at them and see something different and ugly, something that doesn't fit. Well, I don't fit either, Papa. Maybe, just maybe it's because I don't fit that I've got this power the courts are falling over themselves to get hold of. Just imagine what kind of power the rest of the Halfers have!"

"What power could they possibly have? They've got no place, no country, no true shape. They barely even have names!"

"They work together," I shot back. "They care about each other."

"And you think you can make use of this happy Undone family?"

"I don't want to use them. But I might be able to talk them into helping us. Or Jack might. Jack's good at that." I paused. "I thought we could make a deal with the courts. Get them all to sit down like the League of Nations. I'd promise them I'd leave the gates how they are as long as they promised to leave us alone. But that's never going to happen. Even if they did let us go, they'll keep making things miserable for . . . too many other people. We have to fight back, Papa."

"Fight?" he breathed. "You actually believe you and a gaggle of scraps and bones held together with a little spilled blood and careless wishing can take on the high courts and all their power?"

I didn't answer. What could I say? He was right. I was standing a block away from the gate to the fairy country, and I was talking about nothing less than a full-blown, flat-out war with a whole world's worth of power that I barely understood. Papa stared down at me for one second longer. Then he turned on his heel and marched away, so I had to run to catch up.

"Where are you going?"

"Back to your mother. Maybe you won't be so anxious to charge into a new fire fight when you see the state you've already thrown her into."

That shut me up, and fast. Papa didn't bother to squelch any of the grim satisfaction that oozed out of him as he led me around the corner.

There was a cab parked next to the curb, and the driver leaned on the fender, whistling. I could tell by the staticky feel around him, he'd been magicked, and I tried not to wince. As Papa strode forward, the cabbie jumped up and opened the car door. Papa stood back, making sure I climbed in first.

Mama was in the backseat. She sat bolt upright, both hands wrapped tight around her clutch purse. She didn't look at me as I scooted across the seat. It took a second for my eyes to adjust to the dim inside of the cab, but when I did, I saw the tears streaming silently down her cheeks. Papa climbed in behind us, and signaled to the cabbie to drive. The man pulled away from the curb, without once looking back to ask us where to go.

"Mama," I croaked. "I'm s—"

She shook her head, but she didn't turn her eyes toward me. "Anything else, Callie." A tear dripped off her chin, and another followed it. "I could have stood anything else. But you vanished. No one could find you. Not your father. Not Jack. You. Just. Vanished."

"It won't happen again. I pr—"

"Don't," she said heavily. "Not another magic promise. No more, Callie. I'm done with it."

I wanted to tell her it wasn't my fault. I wanted to tell her she wasn't being fair. I wanted to yell something really, truly awful, so she would *have* to look at me. I wanted to swear to her with all the magic in me that I'd never make another mistake this bad. I'd never leave her alone again. I wanted to find the one word, any word, that would make it all right, that would finally end this mess between us so she would wrap her arms around me again, and she'd just be Mama and I'd just be Callie and none of the rest of it—not the magic, not the craziness, none of it—would ever have happened.

But that word didn't exist. Perhaps it would one day, but right now all I had was the truth. "I'm finished running," I said. "I thought I could get clear . . . that I could get you clear of it. But I was wrong. The only way we're ever going to get clear is to fight."

She still didn't look at me. Not for a long time. Then she took in a deep breath and let it all out. And she did look at me. Then she looked at Papa.

"Daniel?" she said.

"No, Margaret," he said back.

"But she's right, Daniel," said Mama. "They won't stop. Ever. It's only a matter of time before they kill us, or worse." And when Mama said *worse,* she knew what she was talking about. Papa knew it too. I put my hand over hers. She grabbed my fingers and held on tight.

Papa turned his face away and stared out the window for a long time. I could feel his magic prowling through the confined space of the cab. I could feel him hating the metal and the confusion that surrounded him and wishing for a way out.

"I've got a plan," I told him, told them both.

"And why do I suspect it involves the . . . Halfers?" said Papa.

"Because they're the only help we've got."

He was quiet for a long time after that. When he spoke again, his words were slow and very tired.

"Callie, if I asked you, as your father, to come away now for your mother's sake . . ." He looked over my head to Mama. "Would you?"

I squeezed Mama's hand and felt her answering pressure. She was telling me to go ahead and speak the truth.

So I did. "No," I said.

Slowly, Papa dragged that prowling feeling deep inside himself and closed the door against it. Whatever was going on inside him now, I could only feel the barest brush of emotion and magic. "Could I have expected any less after . . . after all?" he asked the window glass. He waited for an answer, but none came and he bowed his head. "All right, then, Callie. We'll go." He lifted his eyes to Mama. "For better or for worse, we'll go together."

The cabbie dropped us off at Lincoln Park and drove away without asking for his fare. I remembered the Halfers and their meeting the night before, and felt like a real cheapskate. I'd have to find a way to pay him back. If I lived long enough.

It didn't take long to find the Halferville barrier, or to tell that it was still cracked open. I led my parents through to the other side, and to a disaster area.

Houses were torn open. Electric poles lay crisscrossed on the ground like giant pickup sticks. The stink of blood and burning still hung in the air, so did the magic. Halfers had been laid out on stretchers and blankets in the middle of the 'ville. Others had been covered over in quilts, with their people sitting stupefied beside them. Some of those covered-over figures were just too small.

But what I saw most clearly was that Jack was there, and Jack was okay. He manned the handle of an old-fashioned pump, helping fill basins with clean water so some scrap-and-string Halfers could carry them over to the wounded on their blankets. He saw me too, and he left them all. I opened my arms. I didn't care about who might see. I just wrapped myself around him so we could hold each other tight.

"You're okay," he breathed, pressing his cheek against the top of my head. "You're okay."

I couldn't talk around the lump in my throat, so I just nodded and hugged him harder.

"What's *he* doing here?"

Jack and I broke apart like somebody fired off a shot. But it wasn't us being talked about. Calumet and Glowing Man had stood up from where they'd been sitting with the wounded, and they faced my father. They weren't the only ones either. It seemed like every Halfer who could still stand was crowding around, and most of them had pieces of iron in their fists.

Papa just pulled himself up straight. Magic and anger swirled slowly through him, and he had plenty of both.

"You said she was going after Touhy and Dan Ryan," said Glowing Man to Jack. "We believed you."

"She did," answered Jack. "These are her parents, Mr. and Mrs. LeRoux."

"Mr. LeRoux." Calumet drew Papa's name out slowly, like he wanted to make sure he didn't miss any of it. "We've heard about you. The shame of the high court."

Papa's eyes flashed like summer lightning. "What did you call me?"

"Please, Mr. LeRoux," said Jack. "Please, Calumet. Nobody's the enemy here. What happened, Callie?"

"I did try to save them," I said to Calumet, and the others. "But the . . . the corbies got through the gate before I could stop them."

"Before you could stop them," Glowing Man sneered.

"Aren't you the one who can close the gates? Why didn't you use this famous magic of yours?"

"You will speak to my daughter with respect, Undone," snapped Papa.

"Or what?" Glowing Man moved his hand out from behind his back. He was holding a butcher's cleaver, and it shone white hot.

"Wait, Dearborn," said Jack. "Just for one second. Callie knows what's what. She wouldn't have brought her father here without a good reason. Right, Callie?"

I nodded. Everyone was looking at me now, Jack most of all. I felt him sending out his trust, and his love. I wished he'd stop it. I couldn't think for feeling when he did that. And I had to think. I had to walk straight and steady up to Calumet and the glowing man, Dearborn.

"We're here to take the fight to the courts," I said. "All of us are. I know how we can do it, and we can do it so they'll never see it coming. But we need your help. Touhy and Dan Ryan and the others . . . they need all our help."

"All our help?" said Dearborn to Papa.

But it was Mama who answered. "It's not what anyone wants, but we've been left with no choice. I think you can appreciate that, Mr. . . . Dearborn, is it?"

Dearborn stared at Mama like he'd never seen her sort before. Maybe he hadn't. She was an original, my mama, standing there in the middle of a crowd of living bits and pieces and taking it all in stride. Actually, now that I came to think of it, she was an awful lot like Jack in that way.

Calumet turned around and faced the Halfers. "What says the 'ville? Do we fight?"

The feeling in the roar that answered could have knocked me flat. They would fight. They would all fight. I just had to hope it wouldn't be for nothing. I bit my lip, and tried not to feel the anger trembling through my father. He'd get used to this. He had to.

"So," said Jack to me. "What's the plan?"

23

See What Careless Love

Of course nothing happened right away. There was a whole lot of talking to be done first. My parents and Jack and I had to sit down with what was left of the Halferville Council in what was left of splintery Calumet's house so I could explain my plan. Then everybody needed a chance to pick it over, add to it, and argue about this and that until the sun went down. Then, because Calumet and Dearborn insisted, we had to take ourselves out to the Halfer amphitheater and explain everything all over again to the Halfers who were well enough to sit up and listen. There, they had to shout and argue and pick it over some more until the moon rose above the trees, and it felt like there was nothing left of my plan but bare bones.

Much as I hated the idea, I might just have to apologize to Dan Ryan when I saw him again. Now I knew how flat-out crazy-making the council's way of doing things felt. All I wanted was for us to get moving. We needed time, we needed to pull everything together, but we had no time and we couldn't move. We had to agree. We had to make sure of every little point. We had to get through all the sniping and griping and shouting about just what Papa was even doing there. Papa wasn't helping anything by insisting that Mama should get to safety before we did anything. He even tried to get me on his side by saying Jack could take her out on the train, maybe to Detroit, or maybe all the way to New York. I wanted to agree, more than anything, but we needed them both in the Halferville. Even if I had agreed, it wouldn't have done any good. Neither one of them would have left without being magicked, and even then they would have come right back on the next train.

Other than that, though, Papa held tight to his temper and let everybody else do the talking. I was kind of proud of him. He still didn't like the people around him. He sure didn't trust them. I could feel it in the flicker of the light behind his eyes, and in each of the few words he did speak. But he stayed polite and kept his cool, and I was grateful for it.

By the time the meeting broke up, dawn had come around again. Most everybody headed back to the houses that were still standing to try to get a couple hours' sleep. Papa, though, said he'd stay up a bit.

"In fact, if you will permit," he said to Calumet and Dearborn, "I might be of some use helping with your wounded."

Both councilors looked startled. Then they looked suspicious. Papa waited.

It was Calumet who reached a decision first. "Thank you." He spoke the words like he was having to drag them out of the dark. "That would be most welcome."

"I'll go with you," said Dearborn to Papa.

"I'd expect no less." Papa stood aside and let Dearborn walk away first. He gave me a last look, saying we'd talk soon, and I nodded back.

Calumet rubbed his eyes very carefully with his wooden fingers. "You can have Touhy's place, for now," he told me. "You remember where it is?"

I did remember, and I took Jack and Mama over to the base of the tree. But when Mama realized she'd have to climb the trunk to get to our borrowed quarters, she put her foot down.

"I don't wish to seem ungrateful, but I've no intention of turning squirrel at this late date."

That drew a tired smile from Calumet. "I'm sure we can find a space nearer the ground, Mrs. LeRoux. Fifty-four?" He called to a passing Halfer who looked like she'd sprung to life from an assortment of ribbons and wrapping paper. "Can we find Mrs. LeRoux some space?"

Mama made her manners and said her thanks, and then looked over her shoulder at me, but she did follow the ribbony Halfer. Jack, in the meantime, was yawning like he was going to split his head in two.

"You'd better go with her," I said to him. "Get some rest. We're all going to need it."

Jack brushed the knuckle of one finger against my cheek, and suddenly nothing felt like it could be all that bad. "Okay, Callie. We'll play this your way."

"Thank you, Jack," I whispered. I had a thousand other things I needed to say to him. But looking up into his eyes just then, I knew even those thousand weren't ever going to cover it. "Thank you for everything."

He grinned and I swear, I couldn't find any breath in me anywhere. But that grin was gone just as quick, and he looked around uneasily. "Callie . . . you're sure about your Pa?"

"What do you mean?"

"You're sure . . . You're sure what side he's on?"

This was not what I needed to hear from Jack right now. Especially after sitting next to Papa for hours, knowing the whole time how very badly he did not want to be here, and how often he wished he could think of a way out.

"I have to be sure," I said. "We're all out of choices, and time. I . . ."

"What?" He was standing very close. By now he had to know how that made it hard for me to think, and see straight. In fact, I was starting to think he enjoyed it. "You what?"

"I hate how there's no time," I told him. "I just want one day where there's not another danger or another fight coming up. I want . . ." I wanted to know what to say, but I wasn't getting that either. So I just took Jack's hand and held it.

"We'll get there, Callie," said Jack softly. "And that's a promise from me."

He kissed me. Right on the lips. It was so soft and so quick, he was already walking away before I was even sure it had happened. Jack swung his arms over his head and adjusted his cap and ducked out of sight between the trees, heading toward the sunrise.

I couldn't move. I couldn't have moved if somebody'd set fire to my shoes. I guess I did find my hands and feet eventually, because I was able to climb up the ladder to Touhy's room. That's if I didn't fly.

Once inside, though, reality came back in a cold rush. The little room had not escaped the fight. The bed was on its side and the covers had been shredded. All the books had been torn off the shelves and they lay in tattered heaps in the middle of the room. A few of my words were creeping around the edges of the pile, nosing at the pages, but none of them moved. My eyes stung and I fished in my pocket for Jack's notebook. When I opened it up and whistled, the words tucked themselves inside, and they felt glad to be coming home. I didn't want to think about that. There were a whole lot of things I didn't want to think about. Like what might be happening to Touhy and Ashland now, and even Dan Ryan. I shivered and wrapped my arms around myself.

Soft footsteps sounded on the balcony.

"Jack?" I whipped around.

But it wasn't Jack. My father ducked in through Touhy's low doorway.

"Jack?" His eyebrows lifted. "Hmm. I can see I'm going to have to have a talk with that young man about his intentions. Soon."

I dipped my head to try to hide the blush. I don't know why I bothered. My father could feel my embarrassment as clearly as I could hear him chuckle.

"Is it bad out there?" I asked.

"You saw it." He kicked at the loose papers with his toe.

"We're going to need to do something about Ben and Simon too," I said. "This is going to take a while here."

"Your mother thought of that. She's going to call Mrs. Burnstein. The hospital may be the best place for them both, while they're asleep."

"Did you tell Jack?"

"Your mother did. He agrees." I met Papa's eyes. "He agrees, Callie," Papa repeated. "No tricks. Not this time."

"So?" I blew out a sigh.

"So." He sighed right back. "I know this might be unexpected, but . . . I thought I might spare your mother, just a little."

Quick as thinking, Papa passed his broad, smooth hand over my forehead. *I'm sorry it's come to this, daughter,* he said into my mind. *I truly am.*

Music swirled through me. I didn't hear it. I felt it. It went straight into my brain and whirled around my thoughts, catching them up and scattering them far and wide.

It wasn't long before I had no thoughts left.

* * *

273

I blinked. Bright, hot daylight streamed over Touhy's balcony rail. A wave of dizziness overtook me and I staggered. Papa caught my elbow.

"Are you all right, Callie?" he asked.

"I . . . yeah. Sorry. We were talking . . ." I blinked again. "We were talking . . ."

"About how it's time for us to get going," he said. "If we're to present your idea of a League of Nations–style meeting to the courts themselves, we need to do it before they decide to make another attack on the Halferville." He jerked his chin out the window. "I'll give your Halfers this. They don't lack for courage. The corbies have emptied whole towns when they're set loose. However, I don't think Dearborn's patience with me will hold for another such raid."

"Right." I remembered now. We'd been up all night talking the plan over. The Halfers had not been happy, but they'd agreed in the end. Especially once I promised I'd make getting back all the hostages part of any bargain. Things had broken up so we could get some sleep. Now Papa had come to get me, because I'd slept a little too long.

"Jack and your mother are waiting below," Papa said. "They wanted to walk to the gate with us."

"As if we'd be able to stop them."

He smiled back. "As if. Now"—he held up one finger—"we can't look weak. Or like we're doing this on the spur of the moment. If we meet anyone, you let me do the talking, you understand? As the heir to the Midnight Throne, you are the greater power. If you address another power directly, not only will you be lowering yourself, you'll be opening yourself up to scrutiny and giving them a chance to see what's really going on inside you. That gives them the chance to find something they can use against you."

"Okay. I think I understand."

"Good girl," he said softly. He was holding something tight inside. I could feel it, but I couldn't reach it, and I knew he didn't want me to. It was too big, whatever it was. I decided I'd better let it go. We had too much else to do.

The gate and its ruined mansion stood in the part of the city Jack called Bronzeville. We walked the whole long way there, me, my parents, and Jack. Bronzeville was the section of the city where most of the Negroes lived. The city of Chicago might not have Jim Crow, but it did make sure that people of color kept to certain neighborhoods, even more than the Poles or the Irish or the Hungarians or the Jews. It was crowded and noisy and smoky, just like the other parts of Chicago I'd seen, only here the people around us mostly had skin that was some shade of brown—from creamy gold to sandy brown to shining midnight black, and every tone and variant in between. We passed big stores and small stores, apartments, restaurants and diners, luncheonettes and night-clubs, bars, and church after church after church. Big churches, small churches, churches that were nothing more than storefronts with painted windows and stood right next door to "policy" shops that Jack said were gambling dives. And not once did anybody on those crowded, hot summer sidewalks look at us like we might not belong.

We could have ridden the El ourselves to make this trip, or gotten a cab, but nobody wanted Papa going into this at anything less than his best. He sure looked the part. He'd made himself a sharp gray suit with a snap-brim fedora and a dark tie and shined shoes. We'd all been dressed up to match, clean and pressed as if we were headed into one of those churches. Mama was in her blue flowered dress, and I was in my straight skirt, white blouse, and cloche hat. Jack was back in his white flannels and dress shirt. Papa took Mama's arm and strolled down that sidewalk like he was already king of the world. Folks nodded to them as they passed, and Papa touched his hat to them in return. Even Mama got a ghost of a smile on her face to be looked at with respect by the white-gloved ladies out walking with their own men.

I was sure there were problems with this part of town, and if we stayed, they'd turn up soon enough, but I knew I'd never forget this feeling. For this little bit of time, in this place, I was free to walk out with my parents and with Jack, and none of us had to hide. I tried to tell myself there would be other days like this, in other places. But I couldn't forget those days would only come on the other side of this one. And only if we all lived.

Way too soon we were all standing at the steps of the

burnt-out mansion, staring up at the broken door. I could feel the gate in there, wide open and waiting. That made me shiver. I'd been through two other city gates—The Unseelie gate in Kansas City and the Seelie gate in Los Angeles. Those had been whole, living places and I'd known who they belonged to. I looked up at this gate, and I didn't know a darned thing. That added on a fresh shovelful of fear that I really could have done without.

Papa gave me a glance, then led Mama a little ways down the street. I watched while he took up both her hands and leaned in to whisper to her, but only for a second. They deserved some privacy.

The problem with turning away from my parents was it left me turned toward Jack, with all my doubt and all my worry.

"You'll be careful, won't you?" Jack said. "I don't . . ." He stopped, and I watched him change his mind and decide to finish that sentence anyway. "I don't like that I'm not gonna be with you."

"I don't like it either." I couldn't look him in the eye. It made me go too wobbly inside. It made me want to grab hold of him and never let go, and I couldn't do that. Not yet. "You've got to promise me you'll look out for Mama till we get back."

"Course I will." He tapped my shoulder with his fist. Then he opened his hand and ran his palm down my shoulder, and down my arm to my hand. My heart thudded hard against my ribs. I had forgotten something, something really important. I felt it in Jack's warm touch, but I couldn't reach it.

"Ready, Callie?" said Papa behind me. He and Mama still held hands. Mama only let go so she could give me a big hug. I hugged her back as tight as I could.

"We'll be back as fast as we can," I said. "I promise. I really do. It won't be like last time. I won't let it."

Mama's whole face tightened up, and I didn't want to feel how close to tears she was. "I know you'll take care of each other. When you get back, you and I will have a proper talk."

"Yeah, I'd like that. I just . . ."

Mama's hold on me loosened. She ducked her head, trying to catch my gaze. "What is it, Callie?"

"Mama," I whispered. "I'm scared."

I'd thought she might cry, but she didn't. She pulled herself up straight and proud. Had I thought Papa looked like the king of the world before? Here in front of a doorway to another whole country, Mama looked like its queen. "I know you're scared, honey," she said. "But don't you give them the satisfaction of seeing it. You weren't even supposed to exist, but here you are, after the worst they could throw at you. You've already beaten them all. You remember that, and you hold your head up high."

I hugged her. There was nothing else I could do. I crushed her to me tight, as if I could draw her right inside my skin and carry her away with me. Mama hugged me back just as hard. When we could finally stand to let each other go, I stepped away from Mama so she could go to Papa and they could kiss once more, a kiss that was as long and as close as that hug.

Jack's hand stole out and I felt his fingers wrap around mine and squeeze. I closed my eyes and drew that feeling down deep too.

Then Papa faced me. He held out his arm and I laid my hand on it. He and I alone walked up those steps to the blackened doors. I felt Jack receding. I felt Mama slipping away like she'd never been. I did not let myself look back.

Past the foyer waited a burnt-out threshold. Tattered gray curtains hung from the ceiling. I pushed past them and they were cold, soft, and damp as old fog, and I shuddered. The shadows had their own way here, and I could barely make out anything but lumps of dark and the old smells of wet trash and rot.

I hesitated, trying to find my footing in the dark, and trying to fight down the tide of fear lifting up around my heart. I felt Papa's magic sort of settle itself around me like a comfortable old coat, offering warmth and protection against all weathers, flood tide included.

Which way, my daughter? he asked in my mind.

The big, old fairy gates don't come in just one piece. There's a kind of front porch that opens onto the human world. We were past that now. Then there's a big space where the worlds sort of blend together. It was like the betwixt and between, except the fairies who held the gate kind of moved in their furniture and hung drapes. That was where we were now. I turned in place, using my magic to feel carefully around me. There were memories trapped in this place along with the dark. The house had been ruined when it burned, and the gate had been badly damaged, but it hadn't been closed. Not quite. There was still a crack. And cracks could be widened. Ruin could be cleared. Somebody had done just that. It had taken a long time, but they'd done it. But I couldn't see who they were. I couldn't feel the shine or the midnight of them to know if it was the Seelies or the Unseelies who'd opened this gate, and were waiting for us to walk through.

Papa saw all this flickering through my head. *It doesn't matter now, daughter. What matters is that we need to go farther in. Which way is it?*

I bit my lip, and started walking again.

A long hallway led farther into the house. Eventually, it opened into a gallery that stretched out in either direction, like a letter *T.* Cobwebs trailed down from the ceiling and clumped up in the corners. There was one old chair, turned on its back, its stuffing trailing out. Another threshold opened in front of us. A heavy, half-burnt beam slanted across it and we had to duck underneath.

On the other side, there used to be a dining room. Whatever fire had taken this place, it had broken the heavy table down the middle and reduced the carved chairs to charred frames. There was a heap of ashy splinters in the middle of the floor, like somebody'd grabbed what was left of the cabinets and chairs to use as kindling for a campfire, ignoring the soot-streaked fireplace.

A pair of doors waited on the far side of the ruined room. Once there had been glass in their frames, and they had looked out onto a garden. When we'd walked into this house, it had been a sunny afternoon. Out in that garden, though, it was nighttime. I couldn't tell if we'd been in here that long or if it was just always night out there.

A warm wind blew through the few sharp shards that still glittered in the burnt-out mullions, but this wasn't any smoggy Chicago breeze. This was warm and smelled of sweet dreams. This was the wind from the fairy lands. It was nothing so much as a current of pure magic, and it flowed straight into my veins.

Papa let out a long, slow breath. He leaned into that wind from his faraway home and breathed deep. I felt his magic stirring restlessly, yearning, sad. Lonely.

Papa?

He was a long time answering.

I'll be all right, he said, but he had to pull his attention a long way back to do it. *But we have to be extra careful from here on out.*

We walked forward, treading gently on the creaking boards. Things skittered and scurried between the heaps of trash. In the corner lay something all heaped up and dirty gray that looked like a fur rug that had been kicked aside. There was a broken sideboard hunched up in the dark. An old painting had fallen on its face beside a heap of white rags and wrinkled leather. Something sparkled on the floor. It was a lady's brooch, like a bright orchid made of a hundred tiny diamonds. How could this have been left here? I was sure I'd seen it before. I was about to bend over and reach for it when a flash of red caught my eye. Something long and snaky had been draped across one of the heaps of half-burnt papers. Like a rope, except not quite.

It was a dog's leash. Now I remembered where I'd seen that pin.

Don't look, daughter. Keep walking. But Papa's mind was too close to mine, and I understood, because he did. The shaggy thing I'd thought was an old rug, and that wrinkled pile of white and leather scraps, they weren't just trash. They were all that was left of Mimi and her mistress.

"They failed me," said a light, clear voice. "And they paid the price."

A girl stepped out of the shadows. She was white and about my age, with a sunny smile and golden curls. She wore a long pink wraparound skirt and a pretty matching striped top. Or, it would have been pretty if it hadn't had the huge dark stain splattered all over the bodice and waist.

I knew her. She was Ivy Bright, and she was supposed to be dead.

"She *is* dead," said Papa out loud. "This, daughter, is our host. This is the Seelie king."

"Hello, Callie," said the Seelie king in Ivy's sunny, happy voice. He clasped her little white hands together joyfully. "It's so good to see you again."

"That it is, Your Majesty," said a man's voice from deeper in the dark. "That it most certainly is."

I didn't want to know that voice. I didn't want to lift my eyes from Ivy's pale, dead face. Because things were only going to get worse when I did. My uncle Shake stepped out of the dark to stand beside the Seelie king.

24

The Man Come
to Take You Away

Uncle Shake was all decked out in his fairy prince clothes. His black-and-silver cloak swept back from his shoulders, and that mask with its silver veins and mirror eyes gleamed against his clear brown skin, covering the face I knew was so badly scarred. At the sight of Uncle Shake, Papa's whole self shifted. His arm tightened to pin my hand close to his side, and his magic closed around mine. But the touch of that magic had changed. Before, it had surrounded me with strength and protection. Now there was just a kind of slick softness.

The Seelie king, from inside Ivy, took Shake's hand in both of hers and smiled up at him, putting all Ivy's little-girl charm into the expression. I wanted to scream. I wanted to smack that pretty little face, with magic and bare hands. I wanted to smack it hard enough to knock the Seelie king right out of his dead daughter's skin. He'd set her up to die. He'd made me shoot her down. Now he dragged her body out of the grave to stand here and smile for him. There was not enough anger in any world for this. I pure and plain wanted that creature inside Ivy's skin to die.

Slowly, the shock bled out of me, and I was very aware of something else. Papa stood still in front of these two mismatched monsters, holding me in place. He was full of contempt as he looked at his brother and the Seelie king, but there wasn't any surprise in him. None at all.

"You knew," I whispered. "You knew and you still walked us in here."

"And how could I have stopped you, daughter?" Papa said the words cheerfully, like he was letting me in on some kind of good joke. "You were so determined to come and save your Halfer friends, what was I to do?"

Shake wagged his head back and forth slowly. "It's just shocking the sort of company these children do keep nowadays."

"Yes, isn't it?" Papa replied, just as serious. "It's not entirely her fault, of course. She wasn't raised with any proper discrimination."

"You should have brought her back before," said Shake. "It would have saved so much unpleasantness."

For an answer, my father slowly winked one bright eye.

The bottom dropped out of my heart, and even Shake stood speechless for a second. Then Shake threw back his head and busted out laughing.

"You sly dog, Donchail! You planned this from the beginning!"

Donchail. Shake was using Papa's fairy name. His true name. The one that could break any disguise and work magic over the owner. In response, Papa smiled broadly, showing all his straight white teeth. He bowed to my uncle, and to the Seelie king.

No. No. This wasn't happening. It wasn't true. It couldn't be.

My uncle kept right on laughing. Papa joined in, his laugh shaking him right down to his shoes, and me with it, because he still hadn't let go.

"Glory to you, brother!" Shake slapped Papa's shoulder. "You had me completely fooled! I actually thought you'd been infected with love for that woman. But you were just getting the child off her! You knew it would shift the power!"

Papa bowed. "The laws change if I am no longer the heir," he said. "So much more becomes possible, and so much more can happen out of sight. As you know full well, brother."

No, no, no. I reached my thoughts out to my father, but it was like reaching to a glass wall. He was gone from me. I couldn't touch him, even though he still had hold of me. I guess he felt me trying, because he looked down at me. The smile my father turned toward me was filled with sunlight. It said that everything was all right, finally.

"Please, no," I whispered. "No, Papa."

The Seelie king reached out Ivy's hands and grabbed mine. "Oh, yes, Callie. Don't you see? Your father's arranged *everything*. Now you can come home with me, and we'll be best friends forever and ever."

Ivy's hands were cold and soft, like clay or mud, like anything but human hands. I clapped my hand over my mouth to muffle the scream that wanted to bust out of me. I yanked my hand back from the Seelie king, and I lurched into a run.

Or I would have, if Papa had gotten out of the way.

"Uh-uh, daughter." Papa wrapped his hand around my wrist, and he squeezed, hard. "It's not good manners to turn your back on a king."

I didn't stop to think. I stomped on his foot and shoved an elbow in his stomach for good measure. Papa doubled over and his grip slipped. I ran through the burnt-out library, racing for the door and the human world.

But I wound up running smack into the arms of a crow man.

Black robes wrapped around me, strangling and smothering. I hauled on my magic, wishing for them to tear, and they did, a little. I kicked, and punched, and yanked, and I did break free, just in time to see that the crow man wasn't alone. More of the flock flapped in through the broken windows. They settled among the heaps of trash and turned from black birds to robed men. They had red eyes and gray faces and black, crooked fingers. They snickered and chuckled and knotted those fingers in my hair and around my arms and my ankles. They hoisted me high and didn't care I was screaming as they carried me right back to the Unseelie brothers and their Seelie king.

The corbies set me down in front of Papa, who laid his hand on my head. "Now, daughter, was that smart?" he asked, his voice soft and disappointed. "Did you really think we'd be allowed to leave the party so soon?" He turned his hand back and forth, forcing me to shake my head no. Then he said to Shake and the Seelie king, "She won't do that again, brother, you'll see."

"I don't know, Donchail. She has a way of surprising us all." Those words had a sharp edge. Shake was remembering everything I'd done to him so far. I remembered too. I wanted to do it all again, and double it. But between my papa's hand closed over my scalp and all the corbies crowding up at my back, I could barely move. When I reached out with my magic, I couldn't even find Uncle Shake. All I felt was the crow men, wicked, tricky, bony, and hungry. Always hungry.

"She'll mind," Papa was saying. "I'll see to it. After all, I must have some employment now that I've returned."

"Ah! Now we come to the little hitch in your long plan, brother." Shake—Lorcan—tilted his head. I couldn't see his eyes behind the mask's mirror lenses, but I could still feel his gaze crawling across me, and my father. He was looking for weakness, and promising it would not be forgiven when he found it. But Papa just stood under that slow scrutiny, and kept on smiling.

"Well, well," said my uncle thoughtfully. "But you must understand, such decisions are not up to me." He nodded toward the Seelie king.

The Seelie king wasn't looking at Papa. He—she—he was looking at me through Ivy's dead, damp eyes. He walked forward slowly, bringing the smell of old blood and gunpowder. My stomach lurched and I admit I cringed, but that just pressed me into the soft, skin-warm robes of the crow men at my back. They chortled and grabbed hold of me that much harder.

"I could kill you now, you know," said Ivy's voice happily. "You have no idea how much trouble you've caused with your running around, your crude manners, and your nasty, ugly little friends. I could kill you dead and the law would allow it, for what you did to me." He said it all thoughtful, like Ivy was considering which dress to wear.

"Majesty, we spoke on this," remarked Shake. "There are formalities to be observed, are there not? It would not do to leave any little . . . loopholes open."

"Hmm." The king made Ivy tap her chin and then sighed. "Yes, I expect you're right."

The king inside Ivy waved her hand. The crow men fell back, letting go of me so suddenly, I dropped to my hands and knees on the soot-stained floor. I scrambled to my feet again, as fast as I could, but I was aching all over, and angry red marks covered my arms where they'd held me.

"Well, Donchail." The king made Ivy sigh. "Since you say she'll mind you, Your Ex-Highness, you can take charge of your daughter, until we get back at least."

"Thank you, Majesty." Papa grabbed my arm before I could see which way to try to run. He bowed again to the Seelie king. "I assure you, your trust in me will not be without its reward."

"Hmmm," said Ivy again. "Well, we'll see about that."

Shake seemed less than happy about this pronouncement. "Don't think we're done, Donchail," he said to Papa. "You've won the hand, but you still owe me for these scars of mine." He ran his fingertips down the edge of his mask. "And a few other things."

"You may be very sure, Lorcan, my brother. I returned here ready to pay you back in full for all that's been done."

The king rolled Ivy's eyes. "Boys," she said to me as if I was supposed to understand. "Now come along, all of you. We can't be standing around here anymore. There's simply too much to do."

The king held out Ivy's arm, and Shake took it, just like Papa had taken mine back on the sidewalk, when we left Mama and Jack behind. When Papa took my arm this time, it was nowhere near so polite, and he dragged me along behind.

"Wait. Papa. Please. Stop." I had to find a way to reach him, to buy time enough to figure out how to get away. "What about Mama?"

"What about her?" answered Papa lightly, cheerfully.

"She still has your young Mr. Holland. They'll be fine. Those two are just like peas in a pod." He gave those words a nasty slide and my stomach clenched up.

"It wasn't real, any of it." I said it out loud, so I'd never forget it. "You never loved her."

Papa leaned in close, his fairy eyes suddenly hard as diamonds. "What do you think?" he hissed. "Am I with her? Am I taking her away from all this, as the saying goes? No. I'm here with you and with *them,* on my way back home. How much do you think I could possibly feel for her?"

"His Majesty is waiting, Donchail," called Shake. He and the Seelie king stood in front of the broken glass doors that looked like they led to the old garden.

"I apologize, but there's just one more thing." Papa put his hand into my skirt pocket. "I'll hold on to this." He tucked the notebook Jack had given me into his jacket. "It's too small and cheap a thing for Princess Calliope to be carrying about her person."

That did it. What little calm I'd been able to pull together broke in two, and I kicked out again. This time, though, Papa was ready for me. He stepped sideways and back, twisting my arm firmly around behind me, so the more I struggled, the more it hurt.

Shake pushed the door open for the Seelie king and the king made Ivy walk on through into the ash-covered garden. Papa followed, marching me in front of him.

The Great Chicago Fire had happened over fifty years ago, but that garden smelled of fresh smoke and crackled with heat. The plants were as blackened and broken as the inside of the house, but fresh sparks shone on the edges of the ashy leaves. But that was only for a little ways. As we walked, I felt the last of the human world melting away into the magic of the Unseelie country. It filled me with the comfortable sensation of coming to a place that knew me inside and out. Up ahead was the world where I fit, completely and without question. Part of me was already aching to get closer. It didn't want me to try to drag my feet. It wanted me to hurry up. When I got there, I'd be given something I didn't even know had been kept away from me. When I got there, I'd finally have all my magic, all myself.

Think about Jack, I ordered myself. *Think about Jack and Mama. Got to get away, got to get back to them.*

That helped. A little. My eyes had adjusted to the dark and silver shadows of this place. I could see the rough stone wall that traced the border of the Unseelie lands. It was jumbled and broken from where the armies had come through, but some of the guardian stones were still alive, and they were opening clay-gray eyes. They were afraid, but they were also happy. Of course they were hungry too, like every other fairy I'd met who wasn't one of the kings. They were thinking how they'd done their work well. Maybe today they'd be fed.

The Seelie king waved Ivy's hand. The stone goblins cringed and fell back, widening the nearest gap in the wall. It would be beautiful on the other side of that wall, as beautiful and perfect as the first ray of sunlight on a winter morning, or the light of the full moon over the water.

I clamped my eyes shut. I didn't want to see. I didn't want to feel the curiosity, or worse, the longing, bubbling through me. I didn't want to understand that the whole world beyond the wall had missed me.

"Oh, isn't that cute!" exclaimed Ivy's voice. "She wants to be surprised!" There was a little giggle, but then that pretty little-girl voice turned hard.

"Open your eyes," she, he, it commanded. "Open them, Calliope Margaret LeRoux deMinuit. Open them up, Heir to the Midnight Throne, Bad Luck Girl, Prophecy Girl."

There was a sharp twisting inside my heart, like a knife blade slicing deep. The Seelie king knew my names. My uncle, who'd been at my side and in my head, had given him all of my names that he'd found out, and my names opened my eyes.

And just like that, I was home.

25

So Sweet, So Cold, So Fair

The human world is alive, but it's nothing like the life in the fairy world. I couldn't touch that world the way I could touch the world around me now. I couldn't know it instantly, couldn't feel each atom of it like I could feel my fingers and toes, and move them about just as easily. This world was beautiful. It was everything and everywhere I wanted to be. There was no more helplessness or confusion for me here, and there never would be again. I was a part of everything. The Unseelie land was what I was, and who I was and would be forever.

"You should close the gate, Callie," said my uncle. "We don't want any uninvited guests at your homecoming, do we?"

As soon as those words reached me, I agreed with them. No. We certainly did not. I understood that instantly and completely, and I knew the Seelie king agreed as well. I turned lightly on my toes, and just as lightly, I reached out with my powers. I found the ragged edges of that ratty, broken gate that led to Chicago and the human world. I pulled it shut and turned the key.

My father smiled down at me, approval shining in his eyes. I took his hand so together we could follow the king and my uncle as they led us farther into our home.

We passed through the Bone Forest first. Trees with mottled, pale trunks drew down the light from the stars so it pulsed in the ripples of their white bark and the veins of their thick, pale leaves. Ferns made of smoke clustered around their roots. White moss curled and billowed like the morning mist over bone trees that had broken and been left to fall. The ground itself held a thousand thousand separate lives in its insects and the grains of its dark loam.

Next came the Emerald Fields, and the Ebony Road that would lead us to the Twilight Gardens. I knew the name of each place we passed through. I knew how they'd been born and all the lives that made them up. I could have walked through them with my own eyes closed, because there were other eyes everywhere and they all belonged to me.

Not all life held the shape of plants or insects. Those were the lesser of our kind. There were people too. My true kindred, the Unseelie, were all tall and beautiful, with the light of our world in their eyes. Like my father. Their skin was midnight or ochre or amber or sand or pure white. Some had translucent wings and carried the scent of jasmine or hyacinth with them. Others were like the purest, most perfect ideal of the human form. My uncle wanted all these to see our passage to the palace of the Midnight Throne, and they came at his wish. They lined the Ebony Road. The Seelie king made Ivy's mouth smile and Ivy's hand wave, and the Unseelie nobles cheered. But as soon as we passed by, they all fell silent. I thought about glancing back to see what was going on behind us, but that idea didn't last, and I never did see.

Beyond the Twilight Gardens waited the palace of the Midnight Throne, but not in its full glory. There had been resistance to the Seelie king's arrival, and it had broken the palace apart. The towers were cracked like the oldest trees in the Bone Forest, and smoke moss and blood ivy were already crawling up their sides. The great star dome of the center was broken open like an eggshell, and I thought I saw the memory of crow men rising out of it toward the indigo sky, which held both the stars and the distant promise of full night. A sadness hung about the broken palace, but that was no surprise to me. I'd known it was coming, after all, just like I knew the road to the palace and all its history.

No one was concerned much with my reactions just then. My uncle and the Seelie king were looking at my father. Papa gazed at that shattered palace, seeing it both for the first time and the hundredth, because he was wholly a part of the Unseelie Lands, just like me. He was sad but accepting, just like me. What were the king and my uncle finding to look at? We were all one and the same here. None of us could surprise the other. That was a human thing, and we'd left all human things far behind.

We entered the palace through the Blue Moon gates, and the First Hall, and the Great Hall, and the Antechamber. The guards, servants, and messengers scurried or stumped or glided past the stones that had fallen from the dome and the moss and mist creeping through the cracked walls. Ten guards pushed open the great doors to the Throne Room, even though those doors were cracked so badly we could have stepped through without effort.

The Throne Room was made of midnight-black marble shot through with veins of starlight, so it looked like the stone had captured lightning in its heart. Like everything else, the room was alive, though badly wounded from the war. It hoped if it held out long enough, it would be fed. The dais at the far end of the great room was still in one piece, though. So were the two thrones carved from pure darkness, one for the king and one for the queen. My grandparents were also in one piece. Mostly.

The king and queen of the Midnight Throne sat as still as wooden puppets in their places of honor. I could feel they were alive. But they'd been cut off from the land and pushed deep down into themselves until they couldn't even see up anymore. Their heads lolled on their shoulders, their eyes were wide open, and their jaws gaped. They looked so funny I had to laugh.

"You're gonna catch flies!" I giggled. I couldn't remember

who'd said that to me, but they'd said it a lot, and I liked the sound of it.

Grandma's diamond crown had slipped down over one ear and that only made her look funnier. I nudged at it with a flick of magic, and it fell clattering to the stone floor. My uncle laughed and with an even lighter flick, sent the crown rolling across the floor to scatter a pile of tough, papery leaves that had fallen from the new bone trees sprouting outside.

There was memory here too. It cowered between the shadows and the shining marble. In memory, Grandfather barred the door against his own army after the Seelie king had turned it against him. Grandmother stationed herself on the dais, and raised her spear, because they already knew the doors would not hold. The door split open with enormous thunder, so the Seelie king in the skin of his lovely, golden dead daughter could walk through, with my uncle right beside him. The king spoke my grandparents' names; Faelen, Twilight Lord, King of the Midnight Throne. Luigsech, Midnight's Consort, Twilight's Queen, Daughter of the Ebony Road and the Bone Forest. All his will and desire infused those words. He wished that they would fall into their thrones, unable to move until someone said those names again. Because the Seelie king wished it, because he knew the names, and because he was the strongest here, that was exactly what happened.

"Why?" asked Papa. The word echoed back and forth in

that broken chamber, and the stones themselves strained to listen. "Why leave them alive at all?"

"Because it would not do for Princess Calliope to take on her heritage before we're sure she's ready," said my uncle. "While our parents live, the throne is theirs, not hers, and wiser heads can act as regents for her."

"Of course." Papa smiled. "Just how it should be. We must be completely certain all things are in readiness before we make the final move, mustn't we?"

"Oh, yes," agreed the Seelie king. "They were careless, those two. They kept themselves too sated, too happy, and dabbled too much in the dangers of creation." Ivy's head shook sadly. "They gave their names to others." He meant my uncle, of course, and my father a little, but mostly my uncle. "You should always keep one name back." The king was looking at me, but I couldn't understand why. I did know my grandparents had been careless, and now they were funny. I started to laugh again, but an uncomfortable sensation rumbled through me, and I pressed my hands to my stomach.

"What's the matter, Callie? Hungry?" asked my uncle.

"They are . . . They're hungry." I meant my grandparents. Cut off from the magic of the Unseelie country, they were slowly starving. But it wasn't just them. "The whole world is hungry. Why are they hungry?"

"What else will keep them in line?" asked the Seelie king mildly. "If the lesser ones are fed, they'll only grow stronger.

If we let them be strong, what will stop them from challenging us if they feel like it?"

I felt my face scrunch up. I was seeing something from far away. A crowd of mismade creatures gathering around a table. They were talking about payment for what they'd taken. I was thinking about a white boy and a dusty street and the shame of not having payment for food. . . .

Why was I thinking of such ugly things?

"Do you want to feed them, Your Highness?" my uncle asked. "And perhaps you'd like something to eat for yourself?"

Another image flashed through my mind. I saw the goblin stones split open and pale Seelies scooping up the life as it ran out of them like liquid silver. My uncle laughed, and the vision was gone. "Oh, no, Your Highness. That is for the lesser ones. For us, there are much daintier foods."

"But so soon?" murmured my father. "We just arrived. Perhaps she should see her room first."

"I disagree," said the Seelie king. "I think Her Highness should see the Kitchen Garden."

So, of course we went to the Kitchen Garden, which was less a garden and more a greenhouse. A bunch of its frosted panes had shattered, but some were still whole, and they shone down bright daylight for the garden. There were gardeners—lean and knob-jointed Unseelies with broad, forked hands for digging, or scissor fingers for pruning. They picked their way between beds of earth that held the fruit trees and ordered rows of plants. Not that all of them looked like the plants I'd gotten used to in the human world. One tree had the shape of a bearded man with boots and a sword in his arm that had become a branch and hung now with bloodred cherries. I knew as soon as I looked at him that he was Feodor Alexi Alexeovich. In another bed, a mottled brown-and-white woman stretched out on the earth like she'd lain down for a nap. She was Berta. Mushrooms sprouted from her, in a way that made me think of feathers. Another tree had gotten itself tangled. A long, colorful strip of paper twined around it like a vine. The tree held the paper tightly, though it rattled in the breeze like it was trying to get free. Bunches of grapes dangled from twisting paper stems. I couldn't see anything left of her real shape, she'd been twisted so tight, but I knew this paper was named Tola. I'd called her and Berta both something else before, but that didn't matter now. They couldn't hide their real names from us here. They weren't strong enough. Neither were any of the others. I looked at the beds that stretched out for long yards in every direction. Many were filled with trees and plants. Every one of them had a name, and every one grew a new fruit or other tasty treat. Some were empty, though, nothing but bare dirt waiting to be planted over.

"We know you came here planning to bargain for your Undone, Callie," said my uncle. "But you can see now that simply isn't possible, can't you?"

Of course it was. Had I ever had such a silly plan? I couldn't take the food from my family and my king.

"What do you think, Callie? Are you still hungry?" The

king turned Ivy's face toward me. The blue of her eyes was only a thin ring around her black, blank pupils. "Maybe you should try the grapes."

I moved forward. The purple grapes looked sweet and ripe, and I really was hungry. I stretched up on my toes, but stopped. Something was clouding my vision. Another memory. A memory of the hot sun on my back and watching while bark closed over my fingertips. Slowly, I settled back down on my heels. Why didn't I pull the grapes? What was the matter with me?

"Not ready," said the Seelie king softly. "Not yet, but almost. There's still something we don't have." Ivy's mouth smiled. "You should go to your room, Your Highness. There's going to be a dance tonight, to welcome you home, and you want to be ready, don't you?"

Of course I did. I didn't want anything else. I especially did not want to look back to see who was trying to scream. They had nothing to do with me.

There is no time in the fairy lands. No sunrise or sunset. Everything bleeds together, just like a dream. I danced with the Unseelie nobles in a dress of diamonds and stars with a diamond tiara on my head. I sat at a table that stretched out under the bone trees and watched those trees bowing to my uncle and the Seelie king.

Eventually, I walked out with my uncle and the king all across the Emerald Fields and up the Scarlet Hills. There, we could see all the way to the border of the Unseelie land, where the twilight shadows ended and the pure white cliffs waited. That was the Seelie country. It hadn't always been there, of course. Fairy lands were as fluid as magic and could travel as easily as wishes and dreams, if their rulers wanted them to. The Seelie land had rolled right up to the border when the king won the war over my grandparents, but it couldn't come any farther. It was pushing against a barrier, but there was no way through. There could be, of course. I could make one if I reached out. I knew where to touch and turn to open the way up wide, or close it down so small a mouse wouldn't have been able to wedge a whisker through. It was strange that that other country was struggling to discover a thing I could see with one glance. It was funny.

"Open the gate, Calliope Margaret LeRoux deMinuit," the king made Ivy say. "Open the gate to the Seelie land."

"Why?"

"Because I want you to," answered Ivy's voice. "Prophecy Girl, Bad Luck Girl. Open the gate."

That confused me. "But it's perfect here. What do you need with that old place?"

The Seelie king was angry. I felt it burning all around me, and I didn't like it. It reminded me of all kinds of things from long ago and far away, beyond the borders of the Unseelie country, and I didn't want to think about any of them, ever again.

"Not yet," my uncle said. "Not quite."

"Why not?" Ivy stamped her foot. "What's left? How many names can she possibly have?"

"We will find out," said my uncle. "It will happen. She cannot keep the secret from us forever."

And that was how it went. My uncle walked me round and round the Unseelie lands. This country was a simple, ordered place, not like the jumbled-up chaos of the human world. There was the forest, the field, the hills, the road, the two gardens, and the palace. All was as it should be, and my uncle showed me everything, great and small. He let me walk alone sometimes, through the forest, over the fields, and up the hills. We even walked all the way back to the spot where I'd locked the other gate, the one that led to the human city. All the time, he watched me. I could feel him watching me as clearly as I could feel all the other hungry lives that made up our home. He especially watched when I went down to the Kitchen Garden and reached for the grapes, and came a little closer each time.

Usually, the Seelie king met me in the broken greenhouse. When he did, he made Ivy's voice ask, "Who are you? What is your name?"

Each time I answered, "Calliope Margaret LeRoux de-Minuit, Prophecy Girl, Bad Luck Girl, Heir to the Midnight Throne." Because those were the names that came to me. I couldn't think what else I was supposed to say. I just knew my uncle and the king wanted me to remember something more. But I hadn't brought any other names with me from the human world, and I didn't know anything more about myself than what they shared with me.

One time, I wandered into the Throne Room to see the Seelie king standing in front of my grandparents. He was angry at them. Even though the heart of their kingdom was crumbling around them, there was still something between them and him, and he hated that. He was so angry at them he wanted to swallow them whole. But he couldn't. They couldn't move, they couldn't speak, but this country still belonged to them. He'd have to kill them to take it away, but if he killed them, the Unseelie country would come to me, not him, and he didn't want that either. Not yet. I watched for a while, because the hate was something new and it was interesting in its way. But it got familiar after a time, and I wandered away again.

Once it was certain I knew every inch of the world, and every inch of it knew me, I was allowed to walk as I chose. But it was strange. If my uncle and the Seelie king weren't with me, I frequently didn't want to walk outside at all. I sat in my silver chamber, or I just wandered through the palace. I noted without surprise that new trees and new ivy had grown since I'd last been by. They drank their sustenance from the starving stones, slowly hollowing them out. Even if the Seelie lands never rolled over this place, the palace would eventually dissolve into the trees and ivy and smoke moss. If I opened the gate to the Seelie land, it would happen that much sooner. That would be different. It would be nice to see something different, I thought. Maybe one day. Maybe soon.

* * *

Sometimes when I sat in my silver chamber, I saw things in the reflections on the polished floor and the smooth curve of the bedposts. There was only starlight and twilight, so those reflections weren't very bright, and they didn't last long. But I liked it when I could see them, because they were new and different. They didn't fit the world around me, though, and I liked that part less.

Sometimes, I saw a human boy with blue eyes in a frail house talking seriously with ugly creatures. They wanted to listen to him, but they were afraid. He kept on talking anyway, which was silly of him, but it made me sad for some reason. I didn't watch him that much.

Other times, I saw a green place where a thin human woman moved among more of the ugly creatures. They were clustered around kettles of hot oil. They tossed lumps of pale dough into the golden liquid so it bubbled violently. It was interesting for a while, but not for long, and I turned my eyes away.

One time, as I wandered through the palace, I found my father. He sat in a golden chamber, much like my silver one. In fact, he never left it. The Seelie king and my uncle wanted him to stay here, so he did. He didn't come to the dances or the feasts, the hills, the gardens, or the fields. I never wondered why. He didn't need to be near me, after all. I always knew where he was. So did they.

But now that I saw him with my actual eyes, I saw he was

writing in a book. Something rippled through me, and I realized it was surprise. I could see the book, but couldn't touch it, not the way I could touch the stones and the trees, and the guards and the servants. It was different. I moved closer, and I read,

. . . ready. The last ones coming in . . .

They've had three days already. No time left and only one more name. If they find it before . . .

My father snapped the book shut, and tucked it away in his golden robes, and that fast, it was gone from my mind.

"I dreamed of this," he said to me. "In that other place. I dreamed of being whole again, just like this."

He wasn't making any sense. But he kept on. "I was angry for a while when I first got here. That's what the other place does to us. It pulls our kind away from what we are. It cuts us off from the power and the hunger. We become just like them. It's the love, you see, Callie," he said. "There's no hunger left where the love is."

"How charming," said my uncle from behind me. He laid both his hands on my shoulders. "How very, very charming. Now, remember what we spoke of."

They'd been talking. I frowned. Had I known that? I must have. I just hadn't been paying attention.

"Of course." My father smiled. "Daughter, tell me your final name."

I frowned harder. "But you know all my names." Why were we even talking about this?

"Not all," said my father softly. "There's one left. Tell it to me, as your father, and then I will be able to walk with you and help you to your throne and help you rule. It has been promised. But you must tell it to me."

He wanted it. He really did, and so, of course, I wanted it too. The whole of the Unseelie country was sure there was another name belonging to me, so I was certain too. But I didn't know what it could be. I couldn't see it anywhere; I couldn't feel it anywhere. If I had known it, it was all gone now.

My father was looking at me and his eyes were dim as the darkness between the stars. He wanted something from me, but I couldn't tell what. He was as hungry as all the others around us, but it wasn't the same kind of hunger. It had a different weight and texture. It was tied up in me, the frail woman, and the blue-eyed human boy, and the three days they'd lived away off in the human world. It kept him separate enough from me that I didn't understand and that made me angry.

"Maybe it's in that book," I muttered.

"Book?" said my uncle. "There's a book here?"

26

Leavin' This Morning

"Tell me about your father's book, little niece," ordered my uncle.

I frowned. My uncle wanted me to tell him what I'd seen since I walked in here. Why? There was no separation between us here. That was the nature of our home, and its promise. Why would he need me to talk when he ought to already know everything that had happened?

My father smiled. "I think my brother is playing a game with us."

My uncle did not answer this. He turned his glittering mask to me. "What was he doing when you came in here, Callie? Who was he talking to? You need to answer me."

I giggled. "What's that for?" my uncle snapped.

"You can't see." I giggled again. "You took that fancy mask from the Seelie king, and you still can't see."

"He can't see?" said my father softly. "Not even a little?"

What was the matter with these two? "Of course not. It's all in the memories, Papa, haven't you looked?" My grandparents had cut across one eye when he rebelled the first time so he wouldn't see what they were planning, and then across the other as punishment when he rebelled the second time.

"No." Papa narrowed his two good, whole eyes at my uncle. "I didn't see that. I must not have looked carefully enough." There was something wrong with the way he said that, like he was suddenly speaking from a great distance. "What is it humans say?" he went on. "None so blind as those who will not see?"

My uncle didn't like that. I felt his annoyance like a harsh curl of smoke on the wind. A spot of tarnish crept across the golden floor from under his faint shadow.

"Come out of here, Callie," said my uncle. "The Seelie king wants us."

What was he talking about? I always knew when the king wanted me somewhere, and I didn't know that now. I stared at my uncle, and saw my own eyes reflected back in his mirrors. For one second, those eyes looked stormy blue, and worried. I blinked. My uncle didn't feel close anymore. His anger was pulling him away from me, even though he was mostly angry at my father. That tarnish beneath his feet spread farther, and turned darker. I felt squirmy. Maybe if I told my uncle about the book, he wouldn't be so angry.

"What is this book?" said my uncle. "Where did you see this book?"

"Why, it's just the notebook, brother." My father pulled the battered object out of his robes. "The one I'm holding for her. You saw me take it when we came here."

"Of course," my uncle answered. "What I can't understand is why you'd keep such a shabby thing. Why don't you give it here?" He extended his hand.

"If you want it, you're welcome to take it." My father held the book high up in the air.

My uncle's hand stayed where it was. His head tilted up and down. The air around him curdled, like the tarnish forming around his shadow. I waited to feel him see the book my father was holding in plain sight. But he didn't, and a new thread of feeling ran through his anger. Fear.

"Blind," my father whispered. "You are blind, and the king will not let you heal. What were you promised, brother? That you'd be whole again as soon as the Seelie king was safe on our parents' throne? Or would it only be when the Seelie country devoured our own?"

Anger swirled between them, sharp, hot, and bright, until the whole room shivered and the wall behind my father bubbled uneasily. Liquid gold dripped down toward the floor.

I didn't know what to do. I could feel everything that was happening, but I couldn't form any intention. No one had told me what I should do. I didn't like feeling helpless. It reminded me too much of things back beyond the gate, and that only made the helplessness worse. I felt the gold softening under me, beginning to bubble and melt like the wall behind my father and the tarnish stretching out from my uncle's shadow.

Happy birthday . . .

My head lifted up and my eyes opened. I hadn't even realized I'd closed them.

"No," whispered my father. "Not now. Not yet."

Happy birthday to you . . .

Someone was singing. It wasn't pretty, like the music the Unseelies made. It was jangly and offbeat. Even downright ugly. It wasn't even all that new, but I hadn't heard a sound like that since I came here, and I turned toward it.

. . . dear Callie . . .

That's right. I remembered. It was my birthday. It had been, anyway. Back in the world beyond the gate, where there was time and boundaries and endings. This was new. No one had sung my name since I'd come here. I wanted to see who was doing it now. I turned all the way around and walked out of the room, stumbling a little, because the marble floor had a new crack.

"Oh, you sly dog, Donchail," breathed my uncle. I felt him reach his intention out to find the Seelie king. He meant to direct the king's attention to the singing.

In answer, my father dove out of his chair and tackled him.

I whirled around. Surprise rattled the stones around me. This was definitely new. My uncle shouted, but my father planted his broad hands across his brother's face and I felt my father wish. He wished so hard the golden walls cracked open to let molten metal pour down like blood.

"Go on, Callie," said my father. I heard his voice was calm, but with my eyes I saw him struggling with my uncle, bearing down against him with all his strength. My uncle raged, twisting the room around them. But he wasn't strong enough.

A thunderclap echoed through the palace, and the mask split in two. My uncle screamed.

"Go see who's singing," my father ordered me.

I wanted to, but not as happily as I'd wanted other things since I'd been here. This wanting was colder but at the same time more familiar. I drifted confused through the shattered corridor, past the growing trees and spreading moss. I wondered if my uncle or the Seelie king would mind my going. He didn't usually mind me walking alone, but he could get angry about strange things. I didn't think the Seelie king was going to like it when he found out my father had broken that pretty mask. He didn't like ugly things, and my uncle was very ugly underneath.

How old are you now? The voices were singing now. It was harder to hear. The anger from my father and my uncle was so strong it almost drowned out that faint and shaky sound. *How old are you now?*

How old was I? I had been fourteen. No, I'd been fifteen, just not for very long. That was important. There was a reason that was important. I'd know what the reason was in a minute. When I got to the end of the Ebony Road. When I got back to the Bone Forest, and past the wall, to the gate I'd closed on the way home.

But I'd been right. The Seelie king was angry. The forest at my back trembled with his anger, and the trees groaned as the ground rippled around them. The guardian stones rolled this way and that in confusion. I wished for the border wall to let me out. They stared at me with their hungry gray eyes, but they weren't strong enough to refuse.

On the other side of the wall, on the other side of the sealed-up gate, the singing kept on as if nothing was wrong at all.

How old are you now, dear Callie?

The king's anger was reaching for me. It stretched out of the palace, down the road, and through the forest. It smelled like burning and it shriveled what it touched. My feet started to hurry almost without my wishing for it, and the realization trickled slowly through me that I was afraid. I would shrivel if the king's anger caught up with me. It might turn me all funny-looking like my grandparents, or put me in one room like my father, or scar me up like my uncle. I didn't want any of that. I was running now. I stretched out my power and found the seam where I'd sealed the gate shut. I slowed down long enough to touch its lock with my magic.

The gate opened smoothly in front of me, and with the Seelie king's anger surging behind me, I ran through.

It felt strange to be on this side of the gate again. The world here wasn't solid and alive like I'd gotten so used to.

This place was awkward, cold, and terribly fragile. I didn't like it. Any of it. There was a light up ahead, but it was thin and wavering. I could barely see it, let alone touch it. Maybe if I got closer? I moved forward. The harsh edges of the world scraped against my feelings. Someone had burned this place down a long time ago, and it still remembered the flames. It carried the pain of them in its ashes and the resentment of them in its sluggish heart.

Then I saw her; the thin, frail woman I'd seen in the reflections of my silver chamber. She was Margaret LeRoux. She had another name too. I'd think of it in a minute. It was hard to think now that I didn't have the Seelie king and my uncle to help me. I could see the woman had done something interesting, though. She set one of the rickety, ugly tables on its feet and laid something on top of it. It was small and round with a single glowing candle set in it. With the light shining, it was almost pretty. It sure smelled good; sweet and rich. That smell was almost as good as seeing Mama again.

I stopped. Mama. This was Mama in front of me. And it really was good to see her.

"Hello, honey," said Mama.

"Hello," I said.

"How have you been?" Her voice made a shell for her feelings, like this house made a shell for the gate underneath.

I frowned. I wasn't sure whether I should answer the question, or the feelings underneath. They were so different from each other. "Home," I told her. "I've been home. With Papa."

"Yes, I know. I . . . They treated you all right? Your father said he was looking after you."

"It's home." My words were thick and sluggish from being stuffed too full of confusion. How had my father said anything to her? He had been in his chamber, always.

"Of course. How silly of me." Mama was trying to keep her voice light, but it was too thin. The emotion underneath would crack it open any second now. "Well. Now that we're here, you can have your birthday cake."

"My cake?" I looked at the candle, and the cake again. Mama had baked it. She'd borrowed the sugar, and gotten the flour on credit. I remembered that. She'd baked it in the lopsided oven in the tiny kitchen in Jack's old apartment.

Anger flashed against my back. They were coming. For me. I could see them in my head. My father was chasing after the Seelie king, grabbing at the king with his magic, throwing out his power to topple the trees onto the path, anything he could do to slow the king down and block the king's anger, which was swelling and burning so bright it was hard to see the little candle in front of me. My uncle was hanging back, watching them both. Why wasn't my uncle moving to help his king? My thoughts swung back and forth and I shivered. I shouldn't have come here. I should have stayed home, where I couldn't be confused.

"Do you like the cake, Callie?" Mama asked. "Jack helped with the frosting."

He did? I had no idea he could do something like that. But then, Jack could do pretty much anything he wanted. I remembered that too. I looked around. Jack should be here to see this. Mama had never missed making me a birthday cake. Not once, even when we were back in Dust Bowl Kansas.

Dust Bowl, someone was saying. My uncle, or maybe the Seelie king. It was hard to tell at this distance. They seemed to have gotten farther away, even though they were rushing toward the gate. *Dust. It's the dust! That's the name!*

"Go on, Callie." Mama smiled. "Make a wish and blow out the candle."

The cake was the first pretty thing I'd seen since I crossed to the human world. Its sugar flowers all had that particular, flickering light that we didn't have at home, but that seemed to be embedded in all the things humans took care with. It smelled sweet and sad. It was so beautiful, I didn't want to let it go. I wanted this forever. But the king was almost here. Papa couldn't hold him. Papa was sprawled in the Bone Forest and the forest was turning him over with its roots, pushing him down into the dirt. That was bad. I turned away from the cake. I should do something about Papa, to ease his fear. The king wanted him buried in the Bone Forest. How could that be bad if my king wanted it? But Papa didn't want it. He hurt and I didn't want him to hurt.

"What's the matter, Callie?" Mama asked. "Don't you want your cake?"

"No, I do. I just . . . I don't know what to do."

"You do, Callie. It's your birthday. You blow out the candle, and you make a wish."

That was right. That was what we did every year when she made me my cake. I'd wished and blown out the candles when I was so small I had to stand on a chair to reach them. I'd blown out the candles when Mama had had to argue for ten cents more worth of flour from the general store, and now, when she had to walk through the strange city streets to get the butter.

"I . . . I don't know."

"Calliope," said Mama. "Go ahead. Make a wish. Blow the candle out."

We've got you! You're mine! But those voices were even fainter now. The last of the Unseelie country was being pulled away from me, as if it were a quilt being dragged off my shoulders. My father was doing it. He was reaching out even while he was being shoved into the dirt to smother. Despite the distance, I could still feel the blistering heat of the king's anger. I could feel it knotting around me. I had to get away. The king would hurt me because he'd know the last of my names in another heartbeat. That name. That last name, the one I didn't know. It was the cause of all the trouble. That name was making the king mad. He'd hurt Mama and everybody else here. Because there were other people here. I could feel them now. I didn't want to be pulled back into that anger. I didn't want to be pulled down and smothered. I didn't want to be trapped.

I wish, I thought. *I wish I knew my name.*

I blew the candle out.

27

Trouble All Around

Dust. Red, brown, black, and gray. It roared around me, as if my breath had raised a storm big enough to fill the world. I couldn't see. I couldn't even stand, because there was nothing to support me against the rush of wind.

Three shadows waited in the middle of that dust storm. One was an Indian man, maybe Apache, with a battered black hat and eyes full of stars. Not starlight, like the Unseelie carried, but the stars themselves. There was a wrinkled, earth-brown woman with her white cloak wrapped tight around her and a knowing, toothless grin. Next to her stood a deep black giant of a Negro man in the spotless jacket and shiny-billed cap worn by the Pullman porters.

Told you, Dust Girl, said the Indian man. *That last wish was gonna be the hardest. But nobody listens to old Baya.*

Callie LeRoux, the Dust Girl. The porter sighed and

shook his head. *Now, you know I got a schedule to keep. You be more careful where you leave your names next time.*

The old woman just shook her head and planted three of her knobby hands on her hips. *Well, Dust Girl? You done got your name back. Now what you gonna do wit it?*

I was the Dust Girl. That was the last name, and maybe my first name as well. I'd grown up in the dust. I'd made my way through it as best I could. I'd breathed it in and almost died of it, but not quite. Neither the Seelies nor the Unseelies had been able to guess at that name, because that kind of fight and near-miss trouble had nothing to do with them. Dust Girl came from my own life, the one where I'd learned who I was and what I could do for myself. Calliope Margaret LeRoux deMinuit. Prophecy Girl, Bad Luck Girl, Dust Girl. I was all that, and just maybe a little bit more.

Well, Dust Girl? You done got your name back. Now what you gonna do wit it?

First thing I was gonna do was open my eyes. Then I was gonna get up off this floor.

I was covered in soot and had ashes in my mouth, and none of it mattered. Because Mama was there. She was grabbing hold of me and hugging me hard and we were both laughing about it. I remembered now. This had been the real plan. Papa and I had gone to the Unseelie country as a distraction. We'd been buying time so the Halfers could get ready to attack. Papa had known I wouldn't be able to keep the plan a secret once we got to the fairy lands, so he'd taken the real plan from my mind and left the other in its place. As soon as the attack was ready, Mama had come to get me out.

I knew all of this in a single heartbeat. In the next I knew something else.

"You are going to pay for this, Callie LeRoux deMinuit." The Seelie king stood smack-dab in the middle of the gate I'd left open behind me. But Ivy's skin that he wore wasn't looking so good right now. Ivy was streaked with mud and she wasn't standing up straight. Papa must have fought hard.

The king in Ivy's broken body lurched forward. "You will get down on your knees, Prophecy Girl, Bad Luck Girl, *Dust Girl.*"

The command hit hard enough to rock me back, but nothing worse. A sort of grin spread across my face, and this time I was the one who showed all my teeth.

"Get outta my way," I said to him as I stepped in front of Mama. I had bigger things to worry about than the Seelie king slinging wishes around in front of my gate. Papa was still back in the other country, sinking fast and struggling for breath. I knew what it was like to be smothered alive. I was not leaving my papa to that. "Or I'll *make* you get outta the way."

The Seelie king made Ivy grin, but even that was lopsided. "Really, Callie? Now. What's the saying I'm looking for?" He tapped Ivy's chin with one crooked finger. "Oh, yes! You and what army?"

Mama gave a little tittering laugh, and slapped her hand over her mouth.

"Oh, I do beg your pardon," she murmured.

"You have something to add, Margaret?" said Ivy, short and sharp. "Because when you were my guest before, you were not nearly so cheerful, or so talkative."

If he thought he was going to frighten my mother with that, he was badly mistaken. Mama just put two fingers to her mouth and whistled hard. I admit, I stared. When had she learned how to do that? And why was she doing it now?

I didn't have to wonder for long. Jack pushed himself away from the wall behind the burnt-out threshold. Of course Jack was there. Jack was always right where I needed him to be. I about melted with relief and pure, bright joy at the sight of him. He wasn't alone either. One by one, the Lincoln Park Halfers stepped out of the shadows. They came down off the shelves, and out of the ashes. Dan Ryan was right up front, next to splintery Calumet, and Jack. Jack had a couple of handles sticking out over his shoulders from something strapped to his back. The Halfers all carried packs of some kind at their sides or over their shoulders, and they all had steel or iron of some kind in their hands: shovels, picks, axes, crowbars beat up from construction jobs, and sledge-hammers still stained from their work at the stockyards. I wondered how much the Halfers paid for those.

"She said you should get outta the way." Jack let the crowbar he carried swing loose at his side. For a second he sounded just like his brother Ben. "Are you moving, or are we moving you?"

The Seelie king made Ivy laugh, and clapped her limp hands. "Oh, you are all so cute! You really think . . ."

I didn't see who threw the brick, but it whistled straight past the king's head, ruffling those dirty golden curls. The king whipped around, fury rising like the dust, but the Halfers and Jack had already charged, hollering at the tops of their lungs.

Ivy's voice screamed and I felt the summons rippling out through the open gate. By the time Calumet got close enough to swing his hammer at Ivy's head, there was a guardian stone in the way. The goblin leapt up, grabbed Calumet's arm, and bore down on him. Other guards poured through the gate; the stones and sticks and all the other soldiers of the Unseelie kind, shouting their own heartrending war cries. They carried obsidian spears and bronze swords. Metal and stone clashed and ground together until the old house shook from the force of the fighting and the noise. Glowing Dearborn waded through the chaos, grabbing up every Unseelie he could reach and tossing them aside, raising the stench of hot metal and burning skin. Jack shoved his crowbar into the solar plexus of an Unseelie guard twice his height and when the guard doubled over, he slammed it across the back of his head for good measure. Calumet was shouting orders. Dan Ryan had his sack open, letting out a flood of rats, and calling to the stones to get in the sack, get in the sack, get in the sack!

But fear followed fast behind the Unseelies. It blew like a hurricane wind between the Halfers. It was cold, desperate, and paralyzing. It poured over us, slowing the Halfers and making them stagger so they could be cut down more easily. The iron, magic, and anger they carried couldn't keep it all at bay and the Halfers began to stumble back. The Seelie king laughed and made Ivy wave twinkle fingers at me.

"Callie!" Mama snatched up a bar someone had dropped and slammed it across the jaw of the nearest stone.

I grabbed Mama's arm and dragged her to the edge of the fighting. "Papa's still in there!" I bawled in her ear.

She nodded, and reached into her pocket and pulled out the shining crystal wish he'd left with her. She dashed it to the floor in a shower of sparks and magic. We waited. And we waited. And around us the Halfers and the Unseelies screamed and clashed and fought and fell. And Papa didn't come. The wish that was supposed to summon him didn't. Mama blanched white, and I was having a tough time breathing.

"Callie!" someone was screaming. "Need some help here!"

I hauled my nerve and head together. Then I hauled on my magic too, gathering up the anger and the fear being smeared across my friends. I balled that feeling up, turned it around, and opened it out over the Halfers, as if it were a great umbrella to keep off the storm of the Seelie king's magic. I was instantly battered and beaten by that same magic and the orders it carried. I wanted to back away. I wanted to kneel down. I wanted to obey. But not as much as I wanted to stand there and hold the line for Jack and the Halfers. Not even close.

"We gotta go, Margaret!" A burly Halfer covered in soot and hair grabbed Mama by the arm and started hustling her toward the door to the human world. Our eyes met. She was trying to tell me she wasn't running. She had a job to do. I knew that. She was going for supplies and reinforcements and to help get the wounded out. That was the plan.

"Find him!" she shouted to me. "Promise me, Callie!"

"I will!" I called back. "Promise!"

I whipped around to face the battle again. One of the Unseelie soldiers reared up out of nowhere, his sword stabbing straight for my stomach. Jack was there, maybe from the same patch of nowhere, swinging his crowbar at the soldier's knees. The soldier screamed and fell, and a brass-and-glass Halfer hauled him away.

I stared at Jack. He grinned at me. "We gotta get the Halfers through the gate!" he shouted.

"Right!" I spun around and faced the gate, where the Seelie king was still standing. Ivy's face wasn't smiling anymore. He was making her clench her fists, and stare over the mob. I felt him straining with every ounce of will to try to knot together enough magic to pull the Halfers down, to force them to lay down their weapons and submit. Some did begin to walk toward him, but others pulled them back.

Except Dearborn. Shining bright orange in the darkness, Dearborn stumbled forward wide-eyed. No one could touch him without burning themselves. The Unseelie guards laughed and dodged out of his way. Dearborn staggered up to the king and the king stretched out Ivy's hands and his own magic.

Dearborn grabbed Ivy's slender, broken body up around the waist and tossed her aside. The king screamed and snarled and shoved Ivy upright. Dearborn and Calumet shouted and the Halfers who still could move turned to charge the king. The king snarled and lashed out with magic and searing hate. For one horrible moment, I saw the Halfers the way he did. Misshapen monsters, all of them. They did not understand the gift of their magic. They did not understand they existed to bow down before the purity and the beauty of their superiors. Aberrations, freaks, animals, food. He was going to drain us dead and dry for what we'd done. All of us.

My stomach lurched and I fought to close my magic senses against the hate. It wasn't easy, because I had to reach out as well. Jack was wishing and I needed to grant that wish. Holding the shield over the Halfers against the worst of the king's fear was hard enough. To try to hold it while I was trying to shape magic of my own took everything I had. I groped for Jack's wish and twisted it hard. The effort might have knocked me flat, except Jack was there, like always, to hold me up.

For one second, the Halfer army was in front of us, beating back the fairies. Then they weren't. The Unseelies were swinging at nothing, and staring around themselves in confusion as the hammers and crowbars and shovels clattered to the floor. I doubled over with my hands on my knees, trying to catch my breath. The Halfers were on the other side of the gate, just like Jack wished them to be. They were in the Unseelie country, all of them, and I was trying not to be sick.

Jack grinned, tipped the king a two-fingered salute, grabbed my hand, and bolted for the gate. I found my stride and raced ahead of him, leaping over the threshold, and pulling him through behind me.

The Unseelie country folded around me, but it was different this time. I didn't mistake the feelings roaring through my blood for welcome. This land wanted to claim me. It wanted to drown me. It wanted to use me because I was strong and it needed that strength. I grit my teeth and shoved the land's smothering presence back as hard as I could. I wasn't going to be able to keep this up forever, especially if I had to keep wishing for other things on top of it. But for now, I could think and I could see for myself.

Beside me, Jack was getting his first look at the Unseelie country. He was staring around himself, blinking hard in the starlight and twilight.

"You okay?" I panted.

"I think so, yeah." He shifted his weight carefully, like he wasn't sure the ground under him would stay steady.

The noise of a fight exploded up ahead, but I almost didn't notice. Now that we were through the gate, I could feel Papa out there, fighting in the dirt. His fear shivered through my bones. I had to find him. Now, before the forces that held him carried him clean away. Jack noticed, though. His face went grim, and he reached over his shoulder. I finally saw what he had strapped to his back. He'd lost the crowbar, but he'd brought an old, splintery baseball bat. Actually, he'd brought two. He handed the second to me.

"Just in case," he said.

We took off running, or, we tried to. I was used to Jack being light on his feet, but that was in the human world. Here, he lurched and staggered as he ran, like he was dragging some invisible weight. He clenched his jaw and kept slogging forward. I clamped my teeth together so I wouldn't scream at him to hurry.

We reached the boundary wall, and ran right into the battle. Calumet was shouting something and his magic rippled out, rocking the ground under the remaining squadron of guardian stones. Halfers ringed the stones, grabbed them up, heaved them aside. The goblins screamed and flailed and bounced back, but they had to fight their way through Calumet's wishing, and Dearborn's, and three or four others'. The Halfers weren't anything like as strong as the full-blood fairies, but they were used to working together, and together they could be just strong enough. They slowed the stones down, so the other Halfers could run through the gaps into the Bone Forest. I felt the hate pouring out of the Halfers. I felt how they hated their empty hands and the Bone Forest and the rest of this world for all that had been done to them and theirs. They wanted to take it apart. They'd tear it down to get to their own.

"No! Stop!" I shouted, but not one of them heard me. "They'll kill it, Jack! They'll kill the Unseelie country!" Why should I care? I didn't know. But this world was part of me, like my names and my family, whether I wanted it or not. It was all alive, and the wrong that had been done to the Halfers had not been the choice of the trees or the stones or the gardeners. They didn't deserve to die.

"Just hold on, Callie." Jack squeezed my hand and held hard. "They'll stick to the plan."

The Halfers spread out into the Bone Forest. Most of them ran forward, but some stopped near us. I saw Cedar digging its long toes into the soil and untying a sack from around his neck. The others snatched the sacks off their backs or off their belts and yanked them open. A new smell rose up on all sides, as familiar as sunrise. It was the rich smell of fried dough.

Doughnuts. Griddle cakes. Johnnycake. The Chicago Halfers pulled them all out of their sacks, and scattered them on the ground. They speared them on tree branches. They crumbled them up and tossed them into the wind.

My jaw flapped open. They were feeding the Unseelie country. All of it. Those cakes had been made with magic mixed in. The Halfers carried wishes made solid, all the way from the human world, and now they were being scattered all around. There were wishes for the Unseelies to be free, to be fed, to be strong and awake.

Jack reached out and gently pushed my jaw shut. "You'll catch flies," he said with a grin.

It was ridiculous. It was crazy as a whole colony of bed-bugs. We could not possibly have planned to conquer the Unseelie country with *doughnuts*. But things were starting to happen. The trees bent their twigs around the doughnuts, and the doughnuts vanished. The cakes that had been broken on the ground sank into the soil. Birds and butterflies and flowers floated down to catch the crumbs on the breeze.

"Mama," I breathed. "I knew you could do it."

The Unseelies moved. As they filled up on the sweet food that had been made with care and wishes, they opened their eyes, and pulled their roots from the ground. The ones who had shapes like birds and insects and butterflies spread their wings and fluttered down. All the Unseelies that made up that forest moved toward the Halfers.

"Wake up," the Halfers wished. "Wake up and meet your friends!"

"Who are you?" the Unseelies asked. "What are you doing here? What is this?"

Some of the Halfers got themselves into a loose ring around the Unseelies, and others shouted orders and waved signals, and still others loped on ahead. Then I saw what was really happening. The Unseelies that were being herded aside by the Halfers weren't rising up to join the battle, even though the Seelie king's summons still tumbled through the air. They were being taken out of the fight, and the way ahead was being cleared.

"Your mouth's open again, Callie," said Jack. "Where's your father?"

That snapped my attention back where it belonged. Papa was close, or he should have been. The trees were moving around us, wading after the Halfers. Some of them were taking up the offerings, but some of them waded off to fight. They planted themselves right in front of me and Jack and snatched at us with their branches. We ducked when we could, and slammed our bats onto those branches when we couldn't. I wished and ordered and shoved back with all the magic I could get my mind around, and we blundered ahead through the ferns and the moss. I had a picture in my head of a clearing where the edge of the wood used to be. My wish to find my father pulled me along like a lifeline, until we came to a place where the dirt and pale, rotting leaves had been churned up around a shallow hole, like somebody'd dug into a grave with their bare hands. Or maybe out of it. It didn't really matter which, because it was empty now.

I cussed a bright blue streak and dropped to my knees, driving my fingers into the dirt, scrabbling with my Unseelie senses for memories. I tried desperately to grab hold of them without losing myself to the drowning pull of the land around me.

"What's wrong?" demanded Jack.

"Papa! He was here! I can't see him!" I didn't know if that made any sense to Jack, but I didn't have the words to explain. As long as I held myself apart from the Unseelie country, I couldn't use its eyes. I couldn't see what was beyond my immediate surroundings. I could only feel it, distantly, uncertainly. I knew Papa had been here. This grave had been meant for him. He'd fought and called out, and raged. He'd called to me, but I'd been too slow.

I froze in place, my hands buried in the living warmth of Unseelie earth. I felt something underneath me. Something soft and cold.

"Callie, talk to me!" Jack stood over me, his bat in both hands, trying to watch in all directions at once.

My hands were shaking. They'd gone numb. I brushed carefully at the soil. I felt the shape of a head, then a forehead. A cheek. This was a person under my hands, and they were cold. Cold and dead. I was choking on my breath. I couldn't see.

"God Almighty," whispered Jack. I squeezed my eyes shut.

"It's Ivy," he said.

My eyes flew open and I stared. It was Ivy, or Ivy's body, anyway. Still and dead, and laid out straight in the grave that had been dug for my father.

"B-but . . . ," I stammered. "But the king was in her! What happened?" I cast my thoughts around frantically, looking for memories, but there was nothing. The king was nowhere. I scrambled to my feet again. I didn't for a second believe the Seelie king was really dead. But if he wasn't inside Ivy, where was he? What was he hiding inside now?

Before Jack could answer, there was another shout out of the shifting, struggling forest. Dan Ryan broke through the ragged line of the trees, a flock of rats scattering around him.

"Where's Touhy?" he shouted as he pelted up to us. "You're supposed to be finding the prisoners!"

"Where're the Halfers?" demanded Jack, but Dan Ryan just glanced over his shoulder, his eyes wide with anger and fear. Nobody else broke out of the forest, and the trees were starting to close ranks.

Uh-oh.

I faced the Emerald Fields. The Ebony Road was undulating and switching back and forth so like a snake, I was sure it would rear up at us any second. No going that way. The Seelie king was out there somewhere, hiding beneath the surface like a land mine. But there was still a war going on around us, and we had to get to the palace. The palace was the heart of the Unseelie country. From there we could find the prisoners, and Papa and my uncle. My uncle was out here somewhere too, and I was ready to bet my last nickel that if we found him, we'd find the king. Where else would the Seelie king have gone? If he retreated to his own country, he knew I could shut him out for good. There was nowhere left for him except inside the skin of his best friend.

Jack tugged on my arm, and pointed at the sky. I jerked my head up to see what else was coming. But it wasn't a warning. It was a reminder.

"Hold on!" I grabbed Jack with one hand and Dan Ryan with the other, and I jumped up into the air, and flew.

And dang, those boys were heavy.

28

Them That's Not Shall Lose

From up here I could see the boiling white cliffs of the Seelie country where they'd rolled up to the border of the Unseelie. I felt the waves of laughter bubbling out of them and it rocked me as badly as any wind in the human world could. The Seelie land saw the war. It saw the Halfers tearing up the Unseelies, weakening them, breaking them. It laughed and it cheered because its king cheered. Wherever he'd hidden himself, the Seelie king saw the Unseelie country being broken, and he was celebrating. Understanding landed heavily in my mind and I knew why the Seelie king ran and hid. He didn't care who won this fight. He just had to wait, to let the Unseelies and the Halfers chew each other up. Then he'd come out and take what was left. My stomach twisted up and my flight faltered.

"Watch it!" screamed Dan Ryan, digging into my arm with his pointy fingers.

"Quit squirming!" shouted Jack. "You *want* her to drop us?"

"Shut up, both of you!" I bawled back.

We had to get out of here. All of us. We had to get the prisoners and pull back, before we did any more damage to the Unseelies. Before the Seelie king could come out and destroy us all.

I jackknifed my body like I was diving into the deep end of a pool, and headed for the ground.

I didn't land us in the palace. I swooped over the broken dome and hit the ground beside the Kitchen Garden a lot harder than I meant to. I'd never used so much magic up so fast and my bones were burning with hunger and strain.

"In there," I gasped and pointed. Dan Ryan ran ahead. Jack got his arm around me and pulled me forward into the fractured daylight of the busted-down greenhouse.

"Touhy!" Dan Ryan was shouting. He had his hands on the paper vine she'd been turned into. He was trying to wish, but the Unseelie magic that twisted her up was fighting back hard. He hadn't even seen Ashland, where she lay in the mushroom bed. All his mind was on Touhy, and his horror ran right through me.

"Get her back!" he snarled at me. "Do it!"

"Well, don't just stand there, you idiot," snapped Jack to Ryan. "She's gotta have something to work with. Wish!"

He did. Dan Ryan wished harder and clearer than I'd ever felt, and I caught it. "Tola!" I called out Touhy's real name. I pictured her and Ashland like they'd been in Halferville, when we'd squared off in Touhy's tree house. I saw them in their own shapes, tough and certain, and ready for a fight. I wrapped my wish all around those memories. "You're free, Tola! Berta, you too! Ashland and Touhy, I wish you free!"

The Unseelie land had its orders. These creatures were to be held and their strength was to be made into food for the kings. But I was the heir to the Midnight Throne and I wielded the true names. I could not be ignored.

Slowly, the garden magic crumbled. The mushrooms fell away from Ashland first. She shook herself hard, and Jack ran over to help her up out of the earth. The magic around Touhy gave way more slowly, but it did give. The paper vine collapsed and unwound, rustling and crackling, until the scrap-paper girl stood in front of us again. Touhy's face flipped and unfolded into a question mark, until she got a good look at me. Then she screamed, and charged.

She had her hands around my throat before I knew what was happening, and she had a grip like a python. I couldn't breathe. I was seeing stars. She yelled at me, cursing hot, hard, and crazy.

"Touhy, stop it!" yelled Dan Ryan. "Touhy! Cut it out! She's on our side! Touhy! *Listen to me!*"

He yanked on Touhy and Jack yanked on me, and between the two of them, they got us apart. I fell gasping against Jack. Dan Ryan grabbed hold of both Touhy's hands. They stared at each other, wild-eyed and frightened. I felt Dan

Ryan remembering Touhy being the one who trusted and believed, the one he counted on. I felt how much he loved her, which explained why he'd been so mad when he thought she'd turned on him.

Slowly, Touhy blinked. Tears shone in her green eyes, and she and Dan Ryan wrapped their arms around each other.

I turned away, giving them this one second. Jack and I shared our own second of surprise, and of wishing there was time to talk.

But there wasn't, and there wouldn't ever be if we kept standing around here.

"Jack, watch the door," I said. "Ashland, are you okay?" The sparrow woman brushed the last crumbs of dirt and mushrooms off herself and nodded. She didn't look okay. She looked thin and shaky and I knew just how she felt.

There was still one more thing I had to do here. I walked up to the cherry tree. It was closed tight around the man inside, but he was still alive.

"Feodor Alexi Alexeovich!" I called. "I wish you free!"

Dan Ryan and Touhy both swung around. I might not be able to see everything here like I had before, but I could tell the tree had been feeding off Feodor for a very long time. I knew just standing there that this trap was a favorite of my uncle's, and it was not going to let go for anything as tiny as a cake crumb or an enemy's weak little wish. It was an old, malicious creature. It was the head of this whole garden, and it would. Not. Let. Go.

Dan Ryan said something. I didn't understand the words, but I knew what it meant.

"Father?" he whispered. "Father, it's me."

The tree shuddered. Cherries shriveled and rained to the ground. The branch that had grown around the sword peeled back and the sword began to struggle, swinging and slicing. Dan Ryan shouted and all of them, Ryan, Ashland, and Touhy, ran to the tree, grabbing at the shredding bark. Jack and I jumped in too, digging our fingers into tree bark and yanking it back like it was a banana peel, until at last Feodor Alexi stumbled out.

"Father!" Dan Ryan threw himself into the soldier's arms. Feodor shouted back and wrapped the Halfer boy into a tight embrace, lifting him right off the ground.

"My son," said Feodor Alexi over and over. "Oh, my son!"

Jack was wiping at his cheeks. Mine were pretty wet too. Ashland just lifted her beak-nose and turned this way and that, listening to the distant sounds of the war.

"We need to get out of here," she announced.

Feodor put Dan Ryan down and picked up his rusted sword. Touhy unfolded herself to her full size and crowded close to Ashland. Jack just gripped his bat and looked at me. Everybody was looking, waiting for me to tell them what to do. I didn't want this. I could feel the hatred beating down from overhead and the mockery welling up from the Seelie country and its hidden king. I didn't want to have to be in charge. I wanted to run away and hide. But the time for that was long gone, if it had ever existed. They needed me. Papa needed me.

"Ashland, do you think you can get the other Halfers free?" Ashland looked across the beds of earth that stretched out on all sides.

"I will," she said.

"I'll help." Touhy looked shaky and fragile, but her voice was as strong as ever. I was ready to believe she and Ashland between them could do anything.

"Me too," chimed in Dan Ryan. Hate burned in him hot enough to melt steel.

"No," I said. "We're gonna need you, and that sack."

"Then you will have us." The old soldier laid his hand on Dan Ryan's shoulder. Dan Ryan looked like he wanted to protest, but he didn't.

"This way," I said, and headed for the palace.

It was quiet inside the broken palace, but it was not still. A cold wind whipped through it, as if there was a storm on the way. The trapped light in the marble's veins flickered wildly. We passed the door to my chamber, stepping around the pool of melted silver that had spread onto the floor. We passed my father's chamber, covering our faces with sleeves and hands to keep from breathing in the golden fog that swirled out of the shattered doorway. Jack shifted his grip on his bat. Dan Ryan and his father were so close behind us they were practically stepping on our heels. Feodor had his sword at the ready, and he kept cocking his head this way and that, watching the stones, trees, and ferns around us, waiting for them to make a wrong move.

But the trees and the ferns just chuckled and bowed elaborately as we passed. I wanted to wish at them to shut them up, but I didn't have any strength to spare. Something bad was waiting for us in the Throne Room and it knew we were coming. I could tell, not because I could feel who it was, but because they had left the doors wide open.

Jack and I glanced at each other. Jack jerked his chin at Dan Ryan and Feodor, and they moved even closer together behind us. Together, we walked through the open, broken doors and into the Throne Room.

29

He's a Bad Man

The first thing I saw was my father on his knees. My uncle had strapped his broken mask over Papa's face and tied it in place with the silver ribbons, and now he had both hands spread across Papa's scalp, as if he was holding him in place. Papa's head was thrown back and his mouth was open in a soundless scream. He was fighting. I couldn't see what he saw, but I felt it crawling across his skin and driving itself into his eyes. Madness. Pain and madness, being driven into him by his brother. It played out in front of his eyes, which were covered by the Seelie king's mask.

Shake turned his blind, ruined face toward me.

Lightning rippled and flashed overhead. Tendrils of dark fog curled through the doors. When I last saw him, my uncle still had one good eye. That was gone now. The left half of his face was a mass of scars, and those scars had sealed his eyelid shut, like something had bitten a chunk right out of him. His right eye was milk white and shining and rolled constantly underneath the other, sagging eyelid.

"Your father's close to breaking, Callie." Shake grinned. His teeth were all broken or missing and it hurt just to look at him. His voice was slurred. He was spending too much strength keeping Papa on his knees. He didn't have any magic left to make his voice beautiful. Not even with the king inside him. "I thought I'd show him what sort of nightmares our new king has at his command. I owe him so many, after all." He tilted his head, listening.

But he was wrong. Papa wasn't breaking. He was holding tight, leading on Shake and the king inside him. Papa was fooling Uncle Shake. He'd been fooling Shake and the Seelie king since we got here, so he could stay close to me, and send messages out to Jack, Mama, and the Halfers about what was happening. Now Papa was keeping Shake and his king busy while the Halfers took hold of the Unseelie lands.

A voice whispered behind me, so faint it was little nothing more than a thought.

"Engine, engine number nine . . ."

"Let him go!" I shouted to my uncle and the king inside his skin. I stepped out front of the others. I let myself get angry and I let that anger grow big. Big enough to block out Dan Ryan's whisper and the stirring of his words. Jack was right at my shoulder. He knew what I was doing, I was sure of it.

"Let my father go, or so help me, you'll never see daylight again." I thought about every single trick my uncle had ever played on me. I thought about all the ways he'd tried to trick me to death. I thought about how this whole war, with all its blood and disaster, was his fault. I bundled that all up and threw it at him.

In answer, my uncle laughed. "I can't see daylight now! But no fear! I'll have your eyes when you're done with them!" He grabbed Papa's hair and hauled his head farther back. "Or maybe I'll just take my brother's sight and leave him to crawl blind at my feet!"

"And if that train should jump the track . . . ," whispered Ryan.

"Lorcan deMinuit!" I shouted. "Uncle Shake, Seelie king, get in the sack!"

And he did. He never even saw it coming.

Quick as a flash, Dan Ryan twisted the burlap bag shut while Feodor leaned a knee against it to stop its squirming. Dan Ryan pulled off the rope he wore as a belt and he and Jack knotted it tight around the sack's mouth.

"That's gonna be trouble later," muttered Jack.

"We'll worry about it when later gets here," said Dan Ryan.

Jack and I ran over to Papa. Jack held Papa tight to keep him still while I struggled with sore fingers and tired magic to unknot the ribbons. The mask fell away and Papa sagged backward. I staggered under his weight, but I caught him. His face was a mass of dark lines where the mask had dug in and I could feel the pain still winding through him. But he blinked open his shining eyes, and he saw me.

"Papa, are you okay?" I choked.

"Yeah, yeah." He covered my hand with his. "But we need to get out of here."

"I know, I know, I just . . ." I turned to the thrones. Some tremor or other had shaken my grandparents. My grandmother had fallen forward, and both her hands dragged on the ground. Grandfather had slumped across her, his arm thrown crookedly around her shoulders. "We can't leave them like this."

For a moment, I thought Papa was going to argue. I know Dan Ryan wanted to, but he moved closer to his own father, grim-faced and forcing himself to keep quiet. It's entirely possible the look Jack shot him had something to do with that.

"Whatever you're going to do, *Your Highnesses,*" sneered Dan Ryan, "do it fast."

Papa nodded and we faced the thrones and my flopped-over grandparents. He put his hand on my shoulder and I felt his magic wrapping around mine. We were both exhausted and way too weak, but together, we might just be able to call out loud enough for them to hear.

"Faelen deMinuit, Twilight Lord, King of the Midnight Throne," called Papa. Grandfather stirred, sluggishly. His fingers wriggled. His arm slid off of Grandmother's shoulders. Papa clenched his fists. "Luigsech deMinuit, Midnight's Consort, Twilight's Queen, Daughter of the Ebony Road and the Bone Forest." Grandmother's head shook back and forth. She tried to lift her shoulders. And tried again. I wished, and I wished. "Come home!" shouted Papa. "Come home, my father! Come home, my mother!"

It wasn't a physical fight, like freeing Feodor had been. It was simple and natural, like waking up in the morning. My grandparents stirred, and they sat up and opened their eyes and looked around them.

My grandfather climbed slowly to his feet, trembling like an old man. The light shone in his fairy eyes as he looked down at my father. Next to him, my grandmother sat up straight and tall on her throne. For a moment, confusion and fear flickered through her. Then she smiled and slowly, she reached out shaking hands to me. I glanced at Papa. He nodded. Together we walked forward. Papa took his father's hand and bowed his head. Slowly, half hoping, half afraid, I let my grandmother put her strong arms around me and pull me close.

"Help him," she whispered in my ear.

Papa screamed. I whirled around. My grandfather shrieked, loud and harsh and terrible. He lifted my father up in his arms.

"No!" Grandmother dove forward, trying to get her arms around her husband, trying to get her son free. Her magic lashed out, but too late, too late. Grandfather reached out with a flicker of will and laughed her name, and she crumpled to the ground.

Because I'd gotten it wrong. It wasn't my grandfather who stood there. I could see it as he turned his eyes to me. This was the Seelie king.

30

Wish I May, Wish I Might

I didn't think. I didn't have time. I looked through my grandfather's eyes. I looked down into the white and the dark and
the emptiness to the Seelie king underneath. I gathered up
my power, and I *reached.*

The Seelie king felt me coming, and he turned around,
and he ran. I cussed with every inch of myself, and I threw
myself after him.

I'd reached inside a person once before. Jack, one time
when he'd been almost killed. That had been bad. This was
worse. This was warm and squishy and stinking and wrong.
It was a long way too. Farther than I'd ever reached before. I
couldn't care about that. I had to reach farther yet. The king
had gotten through from somewhere. There was some kind
of door, some kind of gate for him to run back to in here. I
had to find it and shut it tight.

At last I felt it. It was very small and very strong and very old. But it was a gate and I was who I was. Its edges were worn smooth and almost butter soft. I found them anyway. I found the lock. I twisted it open, and I was through, and into the Seelie country.

And the Seelie country was filled with dust.

I stood alone, staring and staring some more. White shining dust swirled around me. It grated against my skin. I could taste it in my mouth, and it burned in my throat and lungs. This was why the white cliffs shifted so wildly on the borders of my grandfather's kingdom. I should have recognized it. It was like the billows of a dust storm, right before it rolled down across the countryside.

"You killed it," I said, and I coughed and spat. The Seelie dust tasted like cold copper. "You used all the magic in it, and the country dried up and died." This was why I'd never seen any Seelie soldiers in the palace, or anywhere else. All the fairies had been Unseelies, traitors and friends of my uncle. That was why they wore his masks. It wasn't just to show their loyalty; it was so they could hide from my grandparents.

Very good, Callie LeRoux, said the Seelie king. His voice was plain and bland, beyond feeling or weight. He had no shape of his own. That was why he could fit himself anywhere. He'd even used up his own body, trying to feed his hunger. *No one has ever come to meet me in my own palace.*

Well, you haven't exactly put out the welcome mat, have you? I put my hand over my mouth to try to stop the dust, but it wormed its way in. I coughed, and coughed again.

So, why did you come? It was a dreadful risk.

*No choice. If I didn't, you'd be running out the back door.
You're good at that.*

Coming from you, that's a true compliment. The king
laughed, a flat, hollow sound. *Well, Callie. Now that you are
here, what do you propose to do?*

He was waiting for me to attack. He was figuring on one
last pitched battle, which he'd win. He'd devoured a whole
world, and was looking to down another. He was stronger
and hungrier than I'd ever be. He was just waiting for me to
make the first move. That was his game. He set people up
and knocked them down. The despair as they fell fed his
greed like nothing else could.

Well, Callie? said the king.

I reached out with my power. But not to the king. I
reached back the way I'd come. To the gate. I found the lock.
I twisted it shut.

NO!

The king screamed and roared past me, shaking the
edges of his dead kingdom. The dead wind blew cold, forcing the dust into my eyes and throat. But there was nothing
to break open, nothing to knock down. He was too late. The
gate was already gone.

See her now, three roads to choose, I said. *Where she goes,
where she stays, where she stands, there shall the gates be
closed.*

The Seelie king raged; he screamed. His fury battered
me, and it hurt. It hurt a lot. But I'd been hurt before.

Open the gate! he ordered. *Callie LeRoux deMinuit, Prophecy Girl, Bad Luck Girl, Dust Girl, OPEN THIS GATE!*

That all you got? I really missed not having arms to fold, then something occurred to me. *What's your name, anyway? Or did you eat that up too?*

I'd meant it as a kind of joke, but as soon as I shaped the thought, I knew it was true. That was why he had no shape, no heart, nothing but emptiness. *You've got no power left, have you? You used it all up. You've only got what you devour, other people's power, other people's lives, and you've eaten everything here.*

I will make you suffer for eternity!

So do it. I put a shrug into my thoughts. *Make a meal outta me, like you do everything else you get near, but you'll still be stuck here, and you're going to starve to death because you've got no gate to drag the power through anymore.*

The king surged forward. He grabbed hold of me and started to squeeze. I closed myself up, and I tried not to be scared. He squeezed harder. It hurt. It hurt. But it'd be over soon. This was it. This was the end.

Open the gate! The king's order beat against me. *Open it! Open it!*

I was really going to die this time.

Open it! Open it! Open it!

Hunger. I'd taken myself to the end of the world and there was nothing here but hunger. After all the fighting and the schemes and the glamour and deception, there was only the king's hunger and it was going to kill me dead.

Open!

But it was okay. I'd seen what was out that way, and it wasn't so bad. I'd seen worse. I'd miss my parents. And Jack. I'd always miss Jack, but at least he'd be alive, and he'd be free. The Halfers, the Seelies, the Unseelies, Mama and Papa, and Jack, they'd all be free if I just held on.

Openopenopenopen!

You know what the funny part is? I said back. *None of this had to happen. If you'd just left us alone, I never would have come after you. I never would have known anything about you!*

OPEN!

No.

Then he whispered. *Then curse you, Callie LeRoux . . . wish you . . . wish you . . .*

And there was nothing. I was alone. The king was dead. He'd burned himself up, and there wasn't even a single extra grain left. The wind fell away, and the dust dropped like snow around me, piling into dead white dunes under a dead white sky.

I pulled my thoughts together. Victory was a strangely quiet, tiny thing. I was so tired. I was hungry too. That wasn't surprising, or it shouldn't have been. I was a fairy too, after all. I needed magic just like the rest of them. I turned. Even when I'd closed a gate, I could feel its seams. I could get my power into that and open it again.

But this time there was nothing. The king had cut it off from me, or me off from it. That was what his last wish, his last curse had been. He'd burned himself trying to trap me in here to die of fear and starvation in this dead dust country, all that remained of a fairy kingdom.

"Don't be afraid," I told myself. My voice was thin and small. I coughed. "They'll find you." Mama, Papa, and Jack. They'd always find me. I just had to be patient.

I sat down on the crest of the dune. Each movement kicked up a little of the sparkling dust. I coughed. It hurt, a terribly familiar pain I thought I'd left behind. The dust couldn't get me, but I was going to get hungry soon, for food and for magic. Thirsty too. And there was nothing here. Nothing but me.

They'll find me. They will. It'll be okay. I just have to wait.

There was no time. No motion except my beating heart. There was no sound except my coughing and the grinding of grains of dust when I shifted my weight.

It'll be okay, I told myself. It hadn't been that long yet. They'd find me. I wasn't that hungry yet. I wasn't that thirsty. It hadn't been that long. It'd be all right.

I'd won. We'd won. That was what mattered. Not the endless, still white dust. Not the silence pressing against my ears and my mind. It hadn't been that long yet. It hadn't been. I was only shaking because I was scared. I wasn't getting weak. Not yet. I had plenty in me yet. They'd find me. They'd find me. They wouldn't leave me alone. Mama, Papa, and Jack, they'd know I had to be somewhere. They wouldn't give up. They wouldn't turn away. They couldn't possibly think I was already dead.

I wasn't going to end up in the dust. It wasn't going to end like that. It couldn't. This wasn't why I was named the Dust Girl. I wasn't going to think about how the prophecy talked about the gates closing, but never about them opening. I'd made my stand here, and the gates had closed. But that wasn't the end. It couldn't be. My family would find me. They'd come help me. They had to. They had to. Had to. Had to.

I lay down in the dust because I couldn't sit up anymore. The prophecy had come true, and this was the end. I wondered if Daddy Joe and his train would come for me here. Or if I'd just be the Dust Girl for real and forever.

Thhheeerrre shhheee isss . . . , said a voice, and my head jerked up. *I ssseeee hhheeerr. . . . Theeerrre shhheee isss!*

Papa? I couldn't talk. My throat was too dry and dust clogged.

But it wasn't Papa. And it wasn't my uncle.

It was Jack.

Of course it was.

And I reached out, and I took his hand, and Jack pulled me through, and home.

Epilogue—The Child Who's Got Her Own

Once upon a time, there was a girl named Callie LeRoux. She left her home in the Dust Bowl and traveled across three different worlds to free her parents from the evil king. On the way she found her worst enemy, her best friend, and her own name.

When the evil king had been conquered, and the worst enemy captured, and her grandfather mourned, and all was reconciled with her grandmother, Callie and her parents and her best fella, Jack, all settled down in the great city of Chicago. There, her parents claimed the bones of an old manor house and opened the Midnight Club. People said some strange things about it, but they still came there from all across the country to hear jazz and blues and eat the food and enjoy the scene. On weekends Callie worked as a hostess, or helped her mama in the kitchen, and sometimes she sang with her father's band. Her best fella, Jack, got a job as a copyboy for the *Chicago Tribune* and wrote stories for magazines like *Weird Tales* and *Black Mask* and *Thrilling Wonder Stories*. When she was old enough to go to college, Callie got her degree in restaurant management and came home to marry her best fella and open up some of the finest nightspots in all Chicago. And when the war came, Jack went to Europe as a correspondent, and Callie sat up late, listening for his broadcasts on the radio and wishing hard.

But no matter what else she did, Callie LeRoux still kept a close eye on the Midnight Club, and people still said all kinds of strange things about it. They said there was a back room where you could catch sight of a whole lot of funny-looking people coming and going. But that was Chicago for you. Nobody asked too many questions. But they said other things too. They said in the basement of the Midnight Club there was a different back room, and in that back room was an old iron safe. They said if you went and put your ear up to it, you could hear something rustling, like cloth, and somebody whispering, and somebody knocking.

Despite all the things people said, Callie and her parents and her best fella, Jack, just kept getting on with the business of living happily ever after.

Until . . .

Author's Note

I knew from the beginning Callie was going to wind up in Chicago. There were a lot of reasons why. First among them was that Chicago is right in the middle of the country and the middle of the two courts, as I always saw the Seelie court as being based more on the West Coast and the Unseelie more on the East Coast. Since Callie was always walking the line between worlds, loyalties, and identities, it made sense to have her ending come in the middle of all of these.

There's also a personal connection. My mother grew up in Chicago. My grandfather worked for the Rock Island Line (and, incidentally, tried his hand at writing). It's also where my parents met. Chicago shaped my ideas of what a major city is and could be. I don't get back as much as I'd like to, but when I do, I still have the sensation of coming home.

Another reason for finishing the story in Chicago is that Chicago was a significant end point for Americans who made the Great Migration. The city offered relative freedom for African Americans in the years between the World Wars. Chicago is one of the furnaces that forged American culture from the beauty, struggle, creativity, sweat, and blood of the people who make their journeys here, whether voluntarily or involuntarily.

Then, of course, there's the blues. There are a lot of arguments about the exact birthplace of the blues, but there's no question that they flourished in Chicago. As American music has been such an integral part of these books, I couldn't end the story without acknowledging blues. I've included one more playlist here. Some of these songs didn't emerge onto the scene until after the year when the story takes place, but because they are icons of early blues, I'm exercising a bit of artistic license in including them.

I want to thank everyone who has shared this journey with Callie and Jack. It's been a tremendous adventure, and I can't wait to see what's next.

Playlist

"Aunt Hagar's Blues," W. C. Handy and J. Tim Brymn, circa 1920

"Double Trouble," Brownie McGhee, 1941

"Easy Street Blues," Henry Thomas, *Texas Easy Street Blues,* 1928

"God Bless the Child," Billie Holiday and Arthur Herzog Jr., 1939

"Goodnight, Irene," Huddie "Leadbelly" Ledbetter, 1933

"Hellhound on My Trail," Robert Johnson, *King of the Delta Blues,* 1936

"Mama Don't Allow," traditional

"The Midnight Special," traditional, made famous by Huddie "Leadbelly" Ledbetter, 1934

"Nobody Knows You When You're Down and Out," Jimmy Cox, 1923

"Oh Daddy Blues," Bessie Smith, 1924

"Papa's on the Housetop," Leroy Carr and Scrapper Blackwell, 1934

"Reckless Blues," Jack Gee and Fred Longshaw, 1925

"Rising Sun Blues," traditional, collected by Alan Lomax, 1937

"Rock Island Line," traditional, collected by John and Alan Lomax, recorded by Leadbelly

"St. James Infirmary Blues," traditional, made famous by Louis Armstrong, 1928

"St. Louis Blues," W. C. Handy, 1914

"Stackerlee," traditional American murder ballad, lyrics first published in 1911

"Sweet Home Chicago," Robert Johnson, *King of the Delta Blues,* 1936

"Walkin' Blues," Robert Johnson, *King of the Delta Blues,* 1936

"Willow Weep for Me," Ann Ronell, 1932

About the Author

Sarah Zettel is an award-winning science fiction and fantasy author. She has written more than twenty novels and many short stories over the past nineteen years, in addition to practicing tai chi, hiking, learning yoga, marrying a rocket scientist, and raising a rapidly growing son. The American Fairy Trilogy is her first series for teens. Visit her at sarahzettel.com.